LITTLE
DIRT ROAD

BAD MEN ON WHIDBEY ISLAND

TED MULCAHEY

OTHER TITLES
BY TED MULCAHEY

Bearied Treasure

Teed Up for Terror

ONE

"Kevin, Jenne, wow! What are you two doing here?"

Robbie Burns had surprised the O'Malleys while they sat at the bar, killing time, waiting for their room to be made up.

"Robbie, hey! What a stunner seeing you." Although slightly less than enthusiastic, Kevin's tone seemed to escape Burns's awareness.

"The US sales division brought all the leading dealerships here for a meeting. I've never been here before, but man, this inn is spectacular. How about you two?"

Even though the O'Malleys had stayed at the lodge a few times in the past, Kevin was reluctant to get into anything other than a cool hello with this fellow, despite their being casual acquaintances from their membership at the same golf club. "We're here for a few days to relax and visit a few wineries. Hope you have fun. We're just heading over to reception to pick up our room keys. Maybe we'll see you later."

The two interior designers quickly made for the exit and set out for the quaint bungalow that housed the reception area. "Kinda gave Robbie the bum's rush, eh, Kev?"

"Yeah, well, we're here to unwind, and the less I have to deal with that asshole, the more relaxed I'm going to be."

"Just because we stopped working for him on that barn out in Carnation doesn't mean he's a bad guy." Jenne was slightly less critical of the man.

"I'm not saying he's bad or mean. I just think he's a pompous ass, very enamored with himself, and I'd rather not be around him." On the other hand, Kevin was less inclined to be subtle about these things.

They strode up to the reception table, where Aaron was looking expectantly at them. They knew it was Aaron because his name tag said so. The lodge included forty or so separate bungalows, each a duplex, spread over a magnificent valley with sumptuous views of the entire valley.

"Mr. and Mrs. O'Malley, your room is ready for you now. Would you like two keys?"

"Aaron, can I ask you a question about another guest? It's not that I'm prying, I just don't like the guy, and I don't want our cottage to be anywhere near his. I understand you have privacy rules, but we're here to relax, and he's not very relaxing to be around."

The lodge hadn't gotten to be exclusive without being attentive to their guests. The staff was trained to serve above all else.

"I understand, sir. What's the guest's name?"

"It's Burns—Robbie Burns."

Aaron looked up from his screen with a pleased smile and said, "Not to worry, Mr. O'Malley. He and his associates are at the far end of the property. You're in the clear."

With Aaron's assurance that all would be well, they hopped a shuttle to their Napa-style cabin, their home for three nights.

The drive to the wine country was always relaxing. Seven hours to Ashland, OR, to spend the night and break up the drive, and then only four hours to the epicenter of winemaking in the US.

The O'Malleys had been looking forward to four days of decompressing at the famous and very expensive Meadowlark Lodge in Rutherford. It had been a bizarre year.

Their Bellevue, Washington-based interior design firm had more business than they could handle now. Their unwanted entanglement in a white separatist terrorist attack at Kelsey Creek Country Club had been at the forefront of the national news for the last twelve months, the resulting unsolicited publicity a windfall to their practice.

After arriving at a pristine cottage on the hillside overlooking the valley, they unloaded their things, then sat on the deck and inhaled the fragrant lavender-filled air.

"Finally," Jenne commented. "It feels great just to sit and listen to absolutely nothing."

"I'm pretty sure there's a golf tournament on. We could see who's in the lead." Kevin was a big fan of the sport and rarely missed an opportunity to indulge himself with some prime Golf Channel viewing.

"You turn that thing on, and you'll be having sex with yourself the next three nights." Jenne—pronounced "Jenny"—was less enthusiastic about the game and was enjoying the "quiet time."

"Okay, well, you put it that way, then hell, I don't need no stinkin' TV." Kevin only needed to be told once about the penalty for interrupting their silence. Three days in this beautiful place without frolicking in the sheets would be a waste.

After a half-hour of basking in the autumn sun on a cloudless October afternoon, Jenne was ready to take a leisurely stroll up to the main lodge for the daily wine tasting.

While the lodge was world-famous for its hospitality, its owner was renowned for his cult wines, offered at enormous prices. The regular tastings were excellent producers from Napa Valley and were accompanied by appetizers.

As the couple entered the lodge's foyer, they were greeted by George Harmon, the owner. He felt it was his duty to occasionally show up at these social gatherings to welcome the guests.

"Mr. and Mrs. O'Malley, welcome back, and thanks for revisiting us." Kevin had to hand it to the man—he knew his business. They had been there two years ago, so it must have taken some effort on the owner's part to research the current crop of visitors.

"Thanks, George. We love coming here. It's got to be the most beautiful place in this part of the country." That Jenne, Kevin thought. She knows how to suck up to a potential client.

"I agree," chimed in Kevin. "You also do a wonderful job with your staff. They always make us feel welcome." If Jenne could suck up, then Kevin wouldn't be far behind. Much of the O'Malleys' work was in the hospitality sector, and they were always on the lookout for marketing opportunities.

Kevin caught the immediate eye roll from his wife and took his cue to dial back the schmooze level.

Kevin, in his mid-fifties, and Jenne, five years younger, had been married for less than five years. Strangely, it felt both old and new at the same time. They were together almost constantly because of their design firm, but he never tired of it.

Her stylish auburn hair framed a beautiful olive-complexioned face, only enhanced by her wide-set hazel eyes. Avid hiking and a dedicated workout routine kept her physique in better shape than women ten years her junior. Her brilliant mind, paired with an overwhelming intellectual curiosity, frequently made Kevin wonder what she saw in him. *Yes,* Kevin concluded, *I'm a fortunate man.*

"So, what do the two of you have planned for the next few days?" Even though Harmon's question seemed superficial, his apparent sincerity was appreciated.

"We'll visit a few wineries, do a little hiking, and kick back. We might even play nine on your executive course." Kevin had toured the little nine-hole course here at the lodge the last time they'd visited, and although small in scale, it was still a hoot to play.

"If you don't already have appointments, perhaps our concierge can set up a few things for you. There are several small family-owned producers nearby that make fabulous wine. Most people haven't heard of them because they're boutique places, smaller than a few thousand cases. Most of their production is sold to upscale restaurants, but you can still purchase from many of them."

"Geez, George, that would be terrific. Who should we talk to?" Jenne was never shy about leading the way.

"I'll take care of everything. We'll even have our car and driver shuttle you around to ensure you can enjoy yourselves without any concerns about directions or driving after tasting."

Kevin wasn't sure why Harmon was being so solicitous, but he sure as hell wasn't going to look a gift horse in the mouth. "That's very kind of you, George. We appreciate it."

After they'd confirmed the following day's schedule with the concierge, they headed back to their cottage. Rather than eat at the restaurant, Jenne suggested room service and a nice Oakville cabernet to celebrate their first night.

Kevin was secretly hoping that the festivities would continue in the bedroom, but he knew better than to suggest dessert just yet. He thought that these things always seemed to work out better if *he* didn't do the planning.

The lodge was sandwiched between two steep hillsides, making for a cozy, quiet retreat from the hustle and bustle of the tech world humming on the coast. On this clear, moonless evening, with the temperature dipping into the forties, the climb up the gentle slope to their cabin was refreshing.

Illuminated by pools of subtle garden lighting, the footpath meandered through sweet-smelling pines, lavender, and clumps of feather grass. Rounding the last turn just short of their rooms, they looked up at the darkened porch leading to their door. The only other cottages they could see had their porch lights on.

"Looks like our light is burned out. Not something you usually see at this place with all their attention to detail." Kevin wasn't overly concerned, given the security of the resort.

"Kev, it looks like the door isn't closed all the way. I'm pretty sure I closed and locked it when we left."

"Maybe housekeeping left it that way when they did their turndown service." Kevin's suggestion sounded more hopeful than reassuring. The Meadowlark did not make mistakes like that.

"Stay here for a minute and let me take a look first." Jenne didn't chime in with a sarcastic feminist line this time—she waited slightly nervous. Kevin stepped up to the porch, reached inside to find the light switch, and flipped it on. Immediately, the landing was brightly lit. "I guess the light works. It just wasn't turned on."

"You'd think housekeeping would know better." Jenne was happy to write it off as a mistake, perhaps a new employee on the staff.

"Yeah, maybe. Hold on a sec until I get the lights on in here." Kevin flicked the rest of the toggle switches up as he stepped inside, bathing the simply but elegantly designed interior in soft, efficient lighting.

The cottage was comprised of a foyer-like living room area with a wood-burning fireplace connected to a bedroom furnished with a king-sized bed, complete with Frette linens. Carrera marble and white subway tiles were the finishes of choice in the spa-like adjacent bath.

Usually, Kevin would have relaxed at the sheer comfort of the place. Unfortunately, the sight of Robbie Burns's limp body lying at the foot of the turned-down bed and the deep red bloodstains on the lavish linens were going to curtail the planned activities he had counted on for the evening.

TWO

It was past midnight by the time the O'Malleys had moved into a new cabin and settled down for the night. The kitchen had been kind enough to stay open to provide them a light dinner, and it was delivered seconds after they arrived.

"I say we forgo the lovely cab and head straight for the scotch. Whaddya say?"

"Works for me. I'm not very hungry, given, well, you know." Jenne seemed exhausted.

"Hey, at least you didn't have to see good old Robbie in that pool of blood. I wonder if they'll be able to get it out of those linens."

"So, you saw a murdered body in *our* cottage, and the first thing that pops into your head is concern for the bedding?"

"Not concern, more just musing. Those goddamn sheets are expensive, you know." Kevin loved any opportunity to inject a spark of levity regardless of the seriousness of the situation.

"Honey shut the fuck up and pour me a drink." Jenne, on the other hand, was a little more on point.

Kevin proceeded to pour them each two fingers of Dalwhinnie with one ice cube. Seated on one of the loveseats flanking the fireplace, Jenne eagerly reached for the glass.

"Okay, good news first." Kevin considered himself a glass-half full kinda guy. His wispy gray hair, ruddy Irish complexion, and deep-set inquiring hazel eyes topping a slender six-foot frame suggested he always knew more than he let on. "We were upgraded to a full-sized cottage, complete with kitchen, *and* we don't have to pay for it. All of our winery visits are comped, we have a car and driver at our disposal, *and* we get to have dinner with George Harmon at *his* place, with his exclusive wines.

I'd say we've done quite well." Kevin felt better about everything now that he had said it out loud.

"Yes, darling, and all you had to do for all that was witness a murdered body in our room. Nice going. Maybe you can do that for future trips as well." Once Jenne started with the smart-ass talk, Kevin knew it was time to get serious.

"I never really liked the guy, but . . . seeing him there in a puddle of blood wasn't something I'll soon forget. I'm glad the manager moved us over here to the other side of the property. We've gone from the hillside view to the golf course view. Things are definitely looking up." Kevin nibbled at the tray of food.

"Kev, let's forget the trivial shit and figure out what to do about tomorrow."

Kevin thought that compared to murder, wine tasting *was* trivial shit, but he was astute enough not to bring it up. "You do realize that our morning interview with the Napa County Police might alter our plans a bit?"

"Yeah, but I can't imagine it'll take too long, and then we can climb into our dedicated limo, complete with driver, and be on our way."

Once again, Jenne's ability to compartmentalize her priorities astonished him. First, she was on him for worrying about the bloody sheets; now, she was focused on tomorrow's wine tasting—just an amazing woman.

"Makes sense to me, Jenne. Let's call it a night." They threw back the scotch.

"What, no sex?" Yes, she *was* amazing.

Next morning brought another sunny day, with the temperature in the sixties. The O'Malleys were seated comfortably in the bar area of the lower lounge, the wood-burning fireplace serving to negate the morning chill. The management had convinced the police to interview them on-site and provided the venue—now closed to the public— to be sure not to inconvenience the O'Malleys.

Coffee in hand, French pastries on the coffee table, and the smell of crackling applewood logs, it was the perfect setup for a discussion about last night's gruesome murder.

"Mr. O'Malley, Mrs. O'Malley, I'm Sergeant Fred Decker of the Napa County Sheriff's Office. We'll be doing the investigation, at least for now. I'm here to get your description of what happened last night." The investigator looked to be in his mid-thirties, with a ruddy complexion, mousey brown hair, and possibly a donut addiction.

Before he answered, Kevin, made a note of the caveats in the sergeant's opening statement. The "at least for now" part hinted at some other agency getting involved, and the "your description" portion left him feeling somewhat disingenuous.

Putting aside his concerns, he figured the best approach was to just get this over with. "There's not too much I can offer, Sergeant. We noticed our porch light was out and could see by the garden lights that our door was slightly open. I reached inside, turned on the porch light, and then the interior lights. I told Jenne to wait on the porch until I looked inside, where I saw Robbie Burns lying in a pool of blood. That's about it."

"And you, Mrs. O'Malley?"

"I really can't add much. As Kevin said, I was waiting on the porch."

"Mr. O'Malley, why did you tell your wife to wait on the porch?"

Kevin thought it was self-explanatory but put aside his annoyance to answer. "Mostly because of the open door. It just didn't feel right. Sorta gave me the creeps."

The sergeant made a few notes, looked up, and asked, "Did you touch anything in the room?"

"Of course we did. It was *our* room. Did you think maybe we wore gloves while we were in there?" Kevin's Irish temper was never far away, confirmation that he suffered fools poorly. A look of frustration in his wife's direction caused her to glare at him, perhaps a suggestion that he tone down the sarcasm.

While the investigator's face reddened a bit, Kevin attempted to recover. "Sorry, Sergeant. We didn't get much sleep, and we're a bit upset at this whole turn of events. When I saw the body, I just turned and left. We only touched things in the room previously—the light switch. I touched the light switch, that's all.

"Mostly, I saw a puddle of blood. And a man's legs sticking out from the other side of the bed. Then when I leaned over, I could see it was Robbie Burns. It was a quick glance, and I just saw the top of his head and his eyes. They were wide open, but that was enough. I left in a hurry."

Decker seemed to regroup as well. "Sure, I can see how this is upsetting. I don't think there's anything else, but if something comes up, can I reach you here?"

Jenne seemed to think it was best if she responded. "We'll be here for two more nights, Sergeant Decker, then we're headed back to Washington. We'll leave our cell phone numbers if you want to get in touch again. Will that work?"

"Certainly," he replied as he stood to take his leave. "Thank you for your help."

After the door closed, Kevin noted her look of disapproval was still firmly in place.

"Sorry, Hon. I know he's just doing his job. We came here to relax, and we don't seem to be doing much of that."

Her smile finally broke through the mask. "No worries, Kev. Let's see if we can make that happen."

The Oakville Cross Road, connecting Route 29 to the Silverado trail, was littered with some of the most revered wineries in the world. After stops at Turnbull, Pahlmeyer, and Saddleback wineries, the O'Malleys were exhausted. The previous evening's events, along with the morning's interview with Sergeant Decker, had left their energy levels wanting. Visiting three of the top Oakville wineries on top of everything else had guaranteed them a substantial mid-afternoon siesta.

"Thank goodness George provided us with a driver. There's no way either of us could manage the drive back to the resort." Jenne's eyes were already at half-mast.

"No argument here. Do you think we'll be in decent shape for dinner tonight at Harmon's place?" Kevin seemed to be second-guessing their plans.

"You *are* aware that he'll be serving a vertical from his private cab collection? There are three 100-pointers in there." Jenne's frequent perusal of the *Wine Spectator* had served her well.

"Okay, okay, I hadn't considered that. Let's get to the cabin and catch a couple of hours sleep. That should help us pull it together."

The dinner was exceptional, the wine superb, and the home defined understated luxury. However, it proved to be impossible to avoid some discussion about the murder of Robbie Burns.

"So, George, did the police figure anything out yet?" Kevin figured that waiting until the first course was sufficient time.

"If they have, they haven't told me. I can't tell you how much this has upset my staff. We pride ourselves on our hospitality and our security. The front desk said you knew Mr. Burns. Did you know him well?"

"I knew him because we were members at the same golf club, and we've done some work for him. He owned several auto dealerships, and his reputation was, shall we say, less than stellar. I think his sales numbers were always great, but he and his employees were known as 'hard sell' people. I gather that getting the sale was more important than keeping the customer. He took over the dealerships about three years ago when their sales were lousy, so he looks like a star to the three manufacturers he represents."

"Do you have any idea what he was doing in your cottage?" George appeared to be wondering what Kevin was thinking as well.

"I don't. We did some design work for him last year, but that was about it. He was so difficult to work with that we finally suggested finding another firm. We think he was pissed off about that, and until yesterday, he'd been very cool toward us. In fact, I was a little surprised that he came up to say hi when we were in the bar."

"How did he get shot without anyone hearing it?" Jenne asked no one in particular.

"The only thing I know for certain is that he *wasn't* shot."

"What? How do you know that, George?" Jenne was fully engaged now.

"Just before the investigator left the property this morning, I overheard him talking to someone at the coroner's office. Something about his throat being sliced from behind. The sergeant was telling whoever was on the other end that as big and strong as Burns was, he was surprised that anyone could manage to kill him that way."

Their main course, all but forgotten, Kevin picked up the thread. "Robbie used to play ball for the Mariners. He was up and down from triple-A ball to the main club for a few years before being their catcher for an entire season. Man, he could really hit, but his defense was terrible. Once, he hit the pitcher in the head when he tried to throw out a guy at second.

"Apparently, he spent all his time in the weight room and not on perfecting his craft. The guy had some serious muscles. When he retired from baseball, his father gave him a bunch of money to buy the dealerships. With his name recognition in the Seattle area, he was able to get the sales up with a barrage of TV advertising. I think if folks got to know him, not just his public face, they'd be less likely to buy cars from him."

"Okay, gentlemen, what do you say to tabling this depressing conversation and getting back to what we're here for—eating this incredible food and drinking?" Jenne grabbed her glass and offered a toast to the resort owner as a way of steering things in another direction.

THREE

"Make sure you remind Bill about Saturday night," Jenne shouted as Kevin left the studio.

"Didn't you and Shelly talk about it?"

"Yes, but you know how sometimes Bill's work takes his full attention. Probably best you remind him."

"Got it. Will do." Kevin thought back to the previous year's events as he left the office.

Through an extensive series of events, Kelsey Creek Country Club had been the site of a potentially brutal terrorist attack. Bill Owens, the chief of detectives at the Bellevue Police Department, along with the SAIC of the Seattle branch of the FBI, had helped prevent a terrible disaster.

Because Kevin and Jenne always seemed to be around when things went awry, they had crossed paths with Owens and had become good friends. Shelly, a former client and an unfortunate victim of the events had ended up meeting the detective and finally marrying him. The two women were best friends and frequently got together socially.

"I'm supposed to remind you of our dinner on Saturday." Kevin made sure to get his assignment out of the way as he and Bill pulled up chairs to grab soup and a sandwich at Kelsey Creek.

"I'm aware, Kev. Shelly reminded me as I left the house this morning. Do all of you think I'm senile?"

"Well, you *are* old and not very alert—mentally, that is." Kevin could get away with the insults since the reality was exactly the opposite. Owens was in his mid-forties, with plenty of muscle applied to a six-foot-three frame. The product of an African American mother and a Native American father, his short-cropped gray-brown hair accentuated a receding hairline, drawing attention to a pair of chocolate-brown, inquisitive eyes.

When needed, his imposing presence could easily intimidate. More often, his soulful looks made him look sympathetic to suspects and witnesses, serving both parties with more civility and success than the former.

"So, Bill, I'm sure you've heard about Robbie Burns's murder. You've also probably heard that he was found in our cabin. Have you been asked to participate in the case?"

"You know, Kevin, you *are* a shit magnet. Even when you go on vacation, trouble seems to find you. Yes, I've heard, and yes, I'm involved in the case, and *no*, I'm not telling you anything."

Owens delivered the message with a measure of seriousness, but Kevin knew his friend would eventually relent and fill him in. "You *are* aware, Bill, that we did some design work for Burns last year, at least for a couple of months. Maybe I can help you with things."

The detective cracked a smile and replied, "Just what I need, a goddamn interior designer trying to help solve a murder. If you hadn't been so instrumental in stopping that attack last year, I wouldn't even be talking to you."

"If I hadn't been around, you most likely wouldn't even be here. This is the thanks I get. You've wounded me something terrible." Kevin couldn't help himself. He was famous for twisting the knife just a little.

"Okay, asshole, here's what we've got." Owens relented. "Burns, the owner of four local auto dealerships, was found with his throat sliced open in *your* hotel room."

"Um, it's a lodge, not a hotel. And yes, this I already know."

"You wanna hear this or not? Please shut the fuck up while I'm talking."

"Yes, dear, I'm sorry. Please proceed."

Owens, with a glare at his friend, continued. "The Audi, Porsche, Ford, and Toyota dealerships he owned were initially purchased with a loan from his father and were all performing at record sales numbers.

"Last year, he was investigated by the attorney general for inappropriate sales practices. A former employee spilled the beans on one of his techniques. He used to bug whichever car the prospective customers took for a test drive. The salesperson would use two cell phones. One would be hidden in the console or in the back. It was connected on an open line to the other phone, the one kept by the salesperson. He'd tell them to take a test drive by themselves and then listen in to their conversations.

"After he knew how much they wanted to spend, it was easy to close the deal. The guy was a star. It was amateurish, and eventually, he was found out, but not until he'd made salesman of the month four months in a row. The guilty peddler said Burns encouraged his people to pull shit like that.

"Standing up on the conference table and screaming at his employees was a favorite tactic. It seemed fear was his first choice in motivating his people. He was not well-liked."

"I didn't know him very well, but I'd heard some of these stories. When we were working with him, putting aside his total lack of design sense, he'd insist on some detail that would be counterproductive to what he was supposedly attempting to achieve. It was frustrating enough that we told him he'd be happier with another firm. He did not take it well."

Owens nodded as though he understood and continued. "Makes sense. I found out that the inventory in all four dealerships was paid for, not 'floor planned' with the manufacturers as most dealers do. He had plenty of money, it seems."

"Did it come from family?"

"Probably some of it. He'd been killing it the last several years, though, and I think most of it was as a result of that."

"How come you have so much information on him? He was only murdered a few days ago."

He resumed his commentary with a smile that indicated the detective knew more than he was letting on. "Rob Burns came to see me about a week ago. It must have been the day before he went to Napa. He told me that he thought some people were after him and asked if there was any way for us to investigate.

"I told him that unless there was a crime, there wasn't much we could do. He wasn't particularly forthcoming, so I did some research just in case. That's how I know all this stuff. You *do* know, Kevin, that I *am* a detective?"

"Yes, Bill, and a damn fine one," Kevin replied, still with a hint of sarcasm. He fully respected his friend and was always amazed at how thorough and prepared he was.

"So, I guess maybe he was correct, and someone *was* after him?"

"It looks that way. I'll be busy with this for a while, I'm afraid."

"I'm guessing no golf for you Wednesday, but we'll see you Saturday for dinner, right?"

"Correct. See you Saturday."

FOUR

"Kev, Sergeant Decker called just after you left for lunch. He said it wasn't urgent but wanted you to call him when you got back," Ilene, O'Malley and Associates' incredibly capable office manager, informed him as he came through the door.

Their studio was in an old fire station on Main Street in Bellevue. It was one of the few remaining historic buildings yet to be razed in sacrifice for the "gentrification" of the wealthy Seattle suburb. The O'Malleys had been offered five times what they had paid for the small building. Still, they were reluctant to see the place cast aside in furtherance of the bland multistory mixed-use atrocities favored by overly aggressive developers.

Ilene had been with them since shortly after they'd formed their interior design company and was a good chunk of the soul of the firm.

"He didn't say what it was about?"

"Kevin, I think you know what it's about." Her curly red hair dipped in his direction as she gave him a knowing look.

Kevin knew better than to trade barbs with her; she would eat him alive. He sat down in his work area and called the Napa sheriff's office.

"Sergeant Decker, I was told you wanted to speak with me."

"Thanks for calling, Mr. O'Malley. We found a note under the bed when we made our third pass through the crime scene—that would be your previous room. Burns must have had it in his hand when he was attacked. We think the murderer must have inadvertently kicked it underneath while he was slitting his throat."

For a moment, Kevin's visualization of the gruesome event caused his recent lunch to do flip-flops. Recovering quickly, even as Ilene showed some concern, he asked the expected question. "Okay, Sergeant, and what was in the note?"

Decker answered without any rancor. "It said, 'I need to talk to you; please give me a call when you get back.' It was signed 'Rob Burns.' Do you have any idea why he wanted to speak with you?"

"None whatsoever." Kevin was flabbergasted. Other than their fleeting encounter in the bar, he hadn't talked to the man for over eight months.

"Except for a brief hello in the bar last week, we hadn't spoken since we'd stopped working for him. I can't imagine what he wanted to talk about." He searched his memory but could retrieve nothing that might serve as a reason for any conversation with Burns.

"Well, if you do remember anything or come across something that might help, please call me, or better yet, tell Bill Owens of the Bellevue Police. He's working on it at your end."

Kevin couldn't help but smile at the thought of his friend finding out that his interior designer buddy was once again smack in the middle of a shitstorm. "I'll make sure to do that, Sergeant. I certainly will."

The following Saturday evening was typical for late October in Woodinville—overcast skies and drizzle. Shelly and Bill Owens had timed the twenty-five-minute trek from West Bellevue perfectly and missed most of the traffic. Their new Range Rover bounced along the half-mile gravel road that served as the driveway to the O'Malleys' A-frame cabin sitting on the banks of Bear Creek.

Shelly had come into some money, hence the new car, due to her divorce from her now-deceased husband, and Bill, married to her for less than a year, was still slightly uncomfortable with the trappings of wealth.

As they crossed the tiny bridge that led up to the cabin, the familiar barking of Emma, the O'Malleys' German Shepherd, pierced the gloomy dusk. "Gotta tell ya. If I was a robber, I sure as shit wouldn't be coming to this place." Shelly was well known for her colorful language.

Her husband smiled and concurred. "No argument. I've personally seen that dog in action. I know she's a sweetie, but if someone messes with either Jenne or Kevin, they're in for a rough time." As they pulled up to the back porch, the O'Malleys were standing there to greet them. There was no sneaking up on *this* house.

After hugs all around, the four friends proceeded inside to sit by the fire and share a bottle of Mumm's.

Jenne and Shelly were the best of friends. They had gone from designer-client acquaintances to victims of serious crimes in the past two years. Shelly was perky, cute, and spontaneous, with very few unspoken thoughts. Jenne was thoughtful yet bold and direct, which served her well when communicating with the many contractors she encountered during the construction phase of their projects.

They seemed more like sisters than just friends between visits to Nordstrom's and rounds of golf together. It was fortunate that Kevin and Bill also liked each other.

While the women discussed the local political issues, Kevin took the opportunity to tee up a soft one for his friend. "I hear the sheriff's office in Napa found some kind of note at the crime scene."

The deep sigh and the look of annoyance from Owens were expected. "I know you've spoken with the Napa sheriff's department, and *I* know that *you* know they found a note. I also know that you know what it said. What I'd like to know is *why* did Burns want to talk to you?"

"I'll tell you the same thing I told Decker. I have no idea. I hadn't seen the guy since we stopped doing the design work on his barn out in Carnation. Though, I'm pretty sure he was pissed that we told him to find another firm, but that's about it."

"Kevin, there's gotta be some reason he wanted to see you. No idea?"

"None."

"Just curious, why hire an interior design firm to do work on a barn?"

"It wasn't just any barn. They were going to use it to raise Arabian horses. When we started with them, he'd already sunk a couple of million into the place. Incredibly luxurious stalls and tack room with a loft that had to be over six thousand square feet. They had solid oak flooring and his-and-hers bunk rooms with adjoining shower rooms.

"We had to revisit every color and specification. The deal-breaker was when he wanted to put a clawfoot tub in the women's shower room. He insisted it *looked* good. We suggested a shower made more sense, you know, to hose off all the sweat and horse shit, but he insisted. He was always late, and the place was way the hell out there, so we finally said fuck it and told him we'd had enough. He stiffed us on our last bill."

"Sounds like a charmer. Did you go after him for the money?"

"Nah, it wasn't enough for us to waste our time. We were just happy to be done with him. It's why we were surprised when he was so friendly to us in the bar down there in Napa."

Owens paused for a moment while he considered these revelations. "It does seem a little odd. All we know is that he wanted to talk to you badly enough to go to your cabin and then leave a note when you weren't there."

"Yup. I promise if I suddenly think of something, you'll be the first to know."

Abruptly, the earsplitting sound of a concerned German Shepherd pierced the air.

"Emma, Emma! Easy, girl; calm down." Jenne's efforts at quieting the animal were useless. Once she caught a scent or heard anything that wasn't normal, it was considered a threat to her pack.

"Kevin, will you see what's got her upset?"

He rushed out onto the deck overlooking the creek. The half-mile two-track that served as the driveway to the O'Malley home wound through 200-year-old cedars, firs, and cottonwoods. It had a large turn-around area just before the little bridge. Because their residence was deep in the woods, the gravel road's only vehicles belonged to UPS or FedEx or invited guests.

Once or twice a year, someone curious might drive down the driveway. However, they always ended up turning around rather than negotiating the wooden bridge. This was the case now. A late-model pickup stopped before the bridge, idled for a minute, negotiated a three-point turn, and spun gravel in retreat. It was too dark to see either the driver or the vehicle's make.

Back inside, it was obvious that whatever threat Emma had sensed was no longer present. "Must've been someone either lost or nosy. They sure as hell left in a hurry."

"What kind of car was it?" Bill asked in his officer-on-duty voice.

"Oh, just an old pickup."

"I'm always a little concerned when someone comes down that road. After that thing with those white separatists, I still get nervous." Jenne was referring to an altercation she had had the previous year when Emma had inflicted serious damage on a racist jewel thief brandishing a gun.

Shelly screwed up her perky Meg Ryan face and offered her two cents. "That fucker got what he deserved. I hope the bastard rots in prison."

"I'm sure it was nothing. Let's throw that salmon on the grill and get serious about this dinner." Kevin's change of subject was met with sighs of relief all around.

FIVE

Wednesday afternoon at the Golf Club was considered "Men's Day." It went back to the old days when doctors and dentists usually took that afternoon off. These professionals, mostly men at the time, were among the more highly compensated of society. Naturally, they were members of private country clubs and, also naturally, they couldn't have women on the course to *annoy* them.

Of course, those were the *very* old days before the wealthy Gen X and Gen Y tech youngsters mucked up the scene. Now, most of the "private" clubs were family affairs, and anyone could play at any time. Still, perhaps as a nod to the old-timers who had started the club, Wednesday afternoons were *mostly* for the men, and Thursday mornings were *mostly* for the women.

On this late October afternoon, the skies were brilliant enough to be considered peacock blue. The sun's acute angle in the Northwest delivered the soft golden hues that brought back memories of first loves and the smells of college textbooks mixed with piles of raked and decaying leaves. An eclectic mix, but Kevin O'Malley was an eclectic person.

He walked up the hill from the eighteenth green with the rest of his foursome when he heard his name being called from the practice putting green. A glance over offered no help as to the source of the hail.

"Kevin, Kevin, over here." In the lower corner of the green, a short, stocky fellow in red plaid knee-length shorts was beckoning him.

O'Malley did not recognize the outlandishly garbed golfer who apparently knew *him*.

"Kevin, my name is Tom Mahoney. I'm the general manager for the Robbie Burns Automotive Group. I've been with Rob ever since his first dealership. I guess I should say *had* been. It's just awful what happened.

I heard you were the one who found the body. It must have been terrible. Not sure what I would've done."

Kevin wasn't sure where this guy was going with his nervous conversation and preferred to be back in the bar with the rest of his friends.

"Nice to meet you, Tom. Sorry for the death of your boss." He could think of nothing else to say and turned to walk over to the clubhouse.

"No, wait. I'm sorry, I've been a wreck ever since the murder. I really need to talk to you. Some weird shit has been going on at the Ford store."

"Thing is, Tom, you should be talking to the police, not me."

"No, that won't work. You have a reputation around here as someone who's always in the middle of things, and I know Robbie wanted to talk with you."

Kevin's interest was piqued since only the cops knew about the note. "How do you know that?"

"He told me that when he returned from Napa, he wanted to get together with you. He said he wanted to discuss something about his barn."

Kevin thought this was becoming curiouser and curiouser. "I thought you said something about the Ford store?"

"I did, but it's all tied in together. Please, can we have lunch or something tomorrow?"

The thought of breaking bread with this man was not enticing. "Tell you what. If it's *that* important, I'll meet you for coffee at the Starbucks across from Nordstrom's at ten tomorrow. Will that work?"

"Yes, yes, that would be great. Thank you."

Kevin tipped his cap and dashed to join his buddies.

SIX

The following morning, Kevin entered the cacophony that most large Starbucks venues sported. The grinding of beans, the hissing of steamed milk—all seven different kinds—the rustling of newspapers—a few were still in print—and the murmurs of business folks and homemakers alike permeated the place.

The sounds bounced off the concrete floor and the glass storefront while the smell of just-roasted beans hung heavy in the air—just another day in Coffeeland, USA. Kevin spotted Mahoney at a small two-top in the corner. The car guy was wearing khakis and an Izod golf shirt. Evidently, his dedication to the game was endless.

Kevin looked in his direction and held up a finger to let him know that he would be getting his latte first before joining him. Always better to caffeine up before any meeting, he thought. He had no clue where this was going.

"Thanks so much for meeting with me, Kevin. I've been on edge for a while now and then the murder. God, I don't know what to do." Kevin had barely pulled his chair out before Mahoney started on.

"How about you slow down for a minute, take a breath, and let's start at the beginning? We'll see where we end up. Make sense?"

Mahoney did slow down, and he did take a very deep breath. "Okay, thank you. First, I need to tell you a few things about Robbie Burns and how he ran his dealerships. Then I'll tell you about the unusual stuff."

Kevin wasn't certain how involved he cared to get, but he *was* here, and he thought he might as well listen to the guy. "Go ahead, Tom, tell me stuff."

"I'm sure since you did some work for him, you know that he wasn't the easiest guy in the world to get along with. I'm still there because I was a 'yes' man and just did what I was told. Once, when I first took the job, I disagreed with him, and he came down on me like a ton of bricks. Told me he'd can my ass if I ever disagreed with him again.

"I'm not real proud of that, but he paid me very well, and I liked and got along great with the rest of the sales staff and employees. You could say I was the buffer between the annoying prick and the rest of the employees. We had over two hundred people on the payroll between the four dealerships.

"Not only that, I've got three kids, two of them in college, and a wife who lives at Nordstrom's. It was best for all concerned to bite my tongue and keep things running smoothly. Now that he's dead, I'm not sure what's gonna happen. I think the widow is talking about things with the lawyers. Meantime, we'll just keep moving along."

Kevin was losing interest in the narrative and was looking longingly at the exit. Fortunately, Mahoney seemed aware enough to notice and got to the meat of things.

"I'm sorry to drag this out, but I thought you'd want to know how things were, you know, for perspective."

"Enough with the perspective, Tom. Tell me why I'm here."

"Okay. Robbie was always looking for ways to make as much money on a deal as possible. When there were incentives by the manufacturers, like trips or luggage or something, he would keep them and not pass them on to the customers. I'm sure you've heard of the microphones in the sales offices.

"One time, after one of the hurricanes flooded the South, he bought hundreds of cars that had been in the floods for pennies on the dollar. He sold them without disclosing they had been underwater and made a ton. He was obsessed with making money. I guess all that time in the minors without being up in the 'big show' bothered him. He figured this was his big chance to cash in."

"So, he was greedy and took shortcuts, *and* he was deceitful and unscrupulous. You do know, Tom, that the number of folks who operate like that form a pretty sizable club?"

"Yes, I do. But how many members of that club ship cars into the US from Mexico with fentanyl stuffed in their tires?"

If Kevin's mind had started to wander, it immediately corrected course. "What did you say?"

"A couple of weeks ago, we got a dozen cars in from the Ford factory in Mexico. Somewhere between when they left the factory and when they got here, someone stuffed a dozen small bags of drugs into one of the tires. It's not hard to figure out that it had to have been done before they got to the border in San Diego."

"And you know this how?"

"I know this because one of the new Escapes came in with a slow leak in the front left tire. I was in the service bay when the tech pulled the tire off to repair it. It was full of small plastic bundles of the stuff."

"How did you know what it was?"

"When I first saw it, I was pretty sure it was drugs. I took the bags and went to Robbie's office to let him know what had happened. What bothered me was that he looked less surprised than he did worried. He took the bags and told me not to worry or think about it that he'd get it to the authorities.

"Last week, as I was walking by his closed door, I heard him shouting at someone on the phone. I didn't hear much, but I did hear the word fentanyl. After the call, he came into my office and told me that he'd taken care of things and not to give it a second thought. That was a few days before *Napa*."

"This is all interesting, Tom, but like, I said, you should be talking to the cops or the FBI, not me."

Mahoney kept talking as if Kevin hadn't spoken. "I began wondering if this was some random thing or had it happened before. I asked Jerry, the mechanic who pulled the tire off if he'd ever seen anything like it. He said he hadn't, but there had been some scuttlebutt surrounding one of the kids who had quit a few months ago.

"It seems this guy was directed to receive all the new Escapes when they first arrived. He was just a detailer. I'd never met him since he just reported to the manager at the Ford store. I guess he was kind of a loner, but Jerry said he seemed to know Robbie *really* well. Said he'd seen them talking several times."

"Tom, once again, what the fuck has this got to do with me?"

"I'm getting there. Give me just another minute. I started to wonder about things, so I talked to the manager and got the guy's contact information. His name is Oscar Salazar, and he lives up in Stanwood."

"He lives in Stanwood, and he worked in Bellevue?"

"Don't ask me. I guess things are cheaper up there. Anyway, I looked the guy up, and he agreed to talk to me. He told me that for the last two years, he was the only one Robbie would let detail the new Escapes that came through San Diego.

"He also told me that he was directed personally by Robbie to inspect the front left tire of every Platinum version of the vehicle. He said once every couple of months he'd find one with something inside, and whenever that was the case, he'd pull the tire off and retrieve what was in there."

Kevin, although still very impatient, was mentally engaged by the narrative. "Why did this guy even do it? He must have known it was drugs."

"It seems his dad came into the country illegally, and Burns suggested he could make trouble for him if the kid told anybody anything. He told me he felt uncomfortable about the whole thing, so he quit and got a job in Mount Vernon. He was stunned to hear of Burns's murder, but he did say it didn't surprise him."

"Why not?"

"He told me that whoever Burns was getting the stuff from would be a 'very bad person'—his words. Seems as though the kid knew of others in that sort of business."

"Again, Tom, why am I here? Why do I care?"

"You care because the drugs are being kept in Burns's Arabian horse barn. Robbie bragged to everyone that he had this hotshot design firm working for him when you were doing the design. He was pissed when you quit."

Kevin was just beginning to see the light at the end of the tunnel. "How could you possibly know that's where the drugs are?"

"Because the kid told me. Said he brought them out there one time; it was way out east in Carnation Valley. Met him in the barn. Salazar said Burns left him for a few minutes after giving the bags to him. Supposedly he went up in the loft, then returned without them."

"Maybe he just put them somewhere temporarily."

"Maybe, but it seems like that would be a good place to hide them. As far as I know, nobody's been working there since the construction stopped, and I guess it'll stay that way until the wife figures out what she's going to do. Anyway . . . *that's* why I wanted to talk to you. You can do whatever you want with this information. I just thought that since you worked on the barn *and* you're pals with the head detective at BPD, you could pass it on."

Kevin was reluctant to be the conduit for this evidence, but he could see why Mahoney had wanted to fill him in. He had to agree with his detective buddy, though; he did seem to be a shit magnet.

"I'll pass it on, Tom, but I'm certain Owens will want to talk to both you and Salazar, and probably sooner rather than later."

SEVEN

Albert Herrera was a nasty fucker. It wasn't his fault, though; life had dealt him a rough hand. He was an average-looking man of average height. Regardless of the weather, he *always* wore long sleeves. At 5' 10", weighing in at 185 pounds, he rarely garnered a second look from members of the opposite sex or, for that matter, the same sex. His brownish-gray hair, cut short and brushed to one side, further served to render him innocuous. Upon closer inspection, his closely set, piercing brown eyes and hawk-like beak did suggest some inner turmoil that might occasionally migrate to the surface; however, he did his best to keep those flames on simmer.

Given up for adoption even before being birthed by a fifteen-year-old child, herself raised under unfortunate circumstances, his early years were difficult. An inexperienced doula delivered Albert with a quick pull rather than a gentle tug, resulting in a fracture of the newborn's right ankle. This grievous injury went unnoticed save for the incessant crying of the little guy.

He was born in San Ysidro, just north of the Mexican border. His parents were hoping his arrival would be the antidote to a failing marriage, but, alas, that was not to be. The constant crying led to a trip to whatever passed for "child protective services" at the time after just two weeks. He was shuffled from one foster home to another from that point on.

It wasn't until his fourth home when he was still only a toddler and unable to walk that a diligent social worker noticed the abnormal-looking right ankle. That it might be the root of the boy's endless crying was suggested. Because it had taken almost two years to notice, the resulting corrective surgeries were many, and the recovery time seemed an eternity to a boy so young.

To say Albert was wheelchair-bound as a youngster would not be the whole story. His foster homes were lower-income families, and because of the young boy's growth spurts, the only wheelchairs supplied were second-and third-hand models. The bearings on the wheels of these torture devices were rarely if ever, lubricated. For Albert to move only a few feet in his first machine required almost superhuman effort. To get across the room required several months of effort.

As he grew, the size of the chairs increased, but apparently, the level of maintenance on the buggers did not. His efforts at just getting from room to room resulted in overdeveloped forearms, biceps, triceps, and shoulders, although no one said anything since the development was gradual.

It wasn't until the first grade, when he was finally able to walk, that other kids noticed his unusual physical development. That was when the bullying commenced. For several months, Albert tolerated the name-calling and snickers of the other kids. His attempt to silence them by covering up the now immense muscle development of his upper append-ages only served to encourage the little pricks.

One day, as he bent to pick up a dropped pencil, he was shoved from behind by a particularly vicious classmate. The boy was big for his age, assisted by being held back for two years and the ringleader of the bullies. As Albert started forward, falling toward the wall, he lashed behind him with his powerful and incredibly strong right arm. The surprised youngster was thrown into the adjacent wall, smacking it loudly and slumping against it in a semi-conscious state.

The school expelled him for a week, which annoyed his foster parents. Upon returning, Albert found he was no longer bullied and no longer the subject of name-calling. His decision to wear long sleeves seemed to quieten the stares, so he made certain to keep his arms covered if he was in a public space.

Although not the butt of any further derision, Albert found he was rarely included in any groups or games. He became a loner. Nothing seemed to change as he progressed from grammar school to high school. He felt different; he *was* different. His incredible strength did not go unnoticed by the football and wrestling coaches, but he would have none of it. Years in the foster home system provided enough team activity for one life.

He found that continued weight training and running provided him with some semblance of peace. The strength in his arms increased if that were possible. Running helped him develop stamina but, at the same time, visually accentuated his massive arms, further committing him to a life in long-sleeved shirts and sweatshirts.

His remaining years in high school were spent just getting by. He was an intelligent kid and a quick learner, so hours spent studying weren't necessary. His antisocial tendencies were further reinforced by several attempts to interact with members of the opposite sex. If he somehow managed a date with a girl, it was one and done. It could have been his unevolved personality, but he attributed it to his freakish physical presentation. He finally gave up trying.

Upon graduation, he joined the Navy and spent his final two years aboard the SS *Kitty Hawk* as an airplane mechanic. His ship was based in San Diego, so he was comfortable with his surroundings. His crewmates tolerated him, but they too were fixated on his unusual physicality. Although a loner, or maybe because of it, he overreacted on several occasions when he felt eyes assessing his inordinately muscular arms.

After several altercations with the offenders, he ended up in the brig, while the unfortunate gawkers ended up in hospital beds. He received a general discharge due to his scuffles and found the document an impediment to finding employment as a civilian.

When numerous weeks of searching for gainful employment in the environs of San Diego produced nothing, he finally said *fuck it* and crossed the border into Tijuana. Because he had been raised a hop from Mexico, he had managed to learn enough Spanish over the years to get by effortlessly. His hours on deck at sea in the sun had weathered his skin sufficiently for him to easily pass for a native Mexican.

Finding work in the poorer country wasn't foremost in his mind. It was more an effort to clear his head and assess his future plans. The 1981 Triumph that he had purchased from a crewmate was perfect for weaving through traffic in the vast city. He felt bad for breaking the guy's leg and thought that by relieving him of his motorcycle—the one he could no longer ride—the gods might forgive his burst of anger and the resulting bodily harm he had caused.

Three days of visiting local markets and watering holes for no apparent reason other than postponing some possible future inspiration resulted in Albert holing up in a shithole hotel in El Centro.

At forty bucks a night, he figured he could spend a few days while waiting for some divine intervention. He was told at the front desk to step into Johnnie's across the street if he wanted a decent meal, which was where he now found himself.

The building looked tired and dirty on the outside and worse once he entered the place. The twenty-foot-long wooden bar smelled of thirty years of stale beer and cigarette smoke and was offset on the opposite side of the room by a half dozen Formica-topped tables that might have been wiped down a week ago.

Albert took a seat at the bar, thinking that at least *it* might have received a quick once-over with a sour bar rag. He joined three other patrons, two of whom were nodding off, probably the result of spending the entire afternoon soaking up the booze.

The third guy was a big man with a red face and closely cropped hair. His short-sleeved polo shirt, tight around prominent biceps, advertised his dedication to the gym. His untucked shirt appeared to cover a sidearm, bulging on his left hip.

A dark-skinned, wrinkled woman of indeterminate age, but certainly north of sixty, stood behind the bar. She nodded in his direction. The stump of a Parodi cigar in the corner of her mouth contributed mightily to the aroma and atmosphere of the place.

The woman's name was Juanita, but everyone knew her as Johnnie. She owned the place and had for over thirty years. The small kitchen in the back offered only one item per day, and the scratching on the child's blackboard leaning on the back bar announced that it was enchiladas today.

The sales of beer, booze, and food in no way supported the continued existence of Johnnie's. That was what the back room was for. Several "businessmen" used it for their meetings two or three times a week. They were well behaved and polite to Johnnie, and they paid her very well. They did not purchase any food or drink, only her discretion. She counted on their continued patronage for her existence.

Albert knew none of this yet, but he did hear the occasional chuckle or murmur from the back room. He ordered the enchiladas and a bottle of Negro Modello. Johnnie produced the beer and shuffled back to the kitchen without even a nod of acknowledgment. He hoped she'd be back with some food; he was famished.

In her absence, Albert noticed the big guy glancing between his watch and the door to the back room regularly. The drink in front of him appeared as though it hadn't been touched. *Something's going on here*, he thought. *Not my problem, though.*

Halfway through his beer, he heard plates and silverware rattling in the kitchen area. *Damn, I hope that's dinner coming. I'm starving.* From behind the ratty curtain that separated the kitchen from the bar, Johnnie appeared a steaming pile of chicken enchiladas, beans, and rice on its way. Albert could feel his mouth watering, even in this poor excuse for a restaurant.

At the same time as the plate was placed in front of him, the door to the back room opened. Three men, two with cigars following a nattily attired diminutive fellow with acne-scarred cheeks, walked briskly toward the front entrance.

The big guy jumped off his stool, pulled out a lethal-looking pistol, and turned to the three. "Hold it, Navarro. My boss says he's tired of paying you. He can't afford it anymore."

"He should have thought about that when I loaned him the money."

"He also says this is payback for what you did to his brother."

The apparent Mr. Navarro looked more resigned than afraid. And Albert was mildly pissed off. He was starving, and this dipshit was interfering with his dining. Swiftly, he shoved himself away from the footrail with his left foot. He encircled the big guy's neck with his powerful left arm while simultaneously twisting the gun from the would-be attacker's right hand. Continued pressure on his windpipe resulted in an unconscious slump to the slick concrete floor.

Albert stood up, straightened out his long-sleeved sweatshirt, and turned to the three men. "I've no idea what's going on here, but I'm fucking hungry. If a couple of you would remove this guy, I'll get back to my dinner."

With a look and a nod from Navarro, the two cigar smokers managed to drag the unconscious gunman from the establishment. Albert turned to begin the assault on Johnnie's culinary creation while the shortish man approached him from behind.

"I don't know who you are, but I like the way you handle yourself. Would you consider working for me?"

Without even turning, Albert responded, "No offense, but I don't know who you are either, and I'm starving. If you don't mind, I'd just like to be left alone to finish my dinner."

Navarro didn't persist but instead tried a different approach. He reached into a tailored sport coat and pulled out a roll of Benjamins. "Take this," he said as he placed the money on the bar. "If you have a change of heart, give me a call. Here's my card with my personal cell number on it. Call anytime." With that, he turned and walked out the door.

Albert put the roll of cash in his pocket and finished his dinner. It was, surprisingly, excellent. Johnnie hadn't moved since the attempted assault; the two other patrons had fallen asleep, heads on the filthy bar.

With the Parodi still intact, she turned to Herrera. "Do you know who that man is?"

"Nope"

"That's Hugo Navarro. He is from this neighborhood."

"Good to know."

"He is a businessman with many employees and much money. He treats everyone kindly and supports all the local businesses. He is the reason I am still here."

"I'm very happy for you, Johnnie. I suspect his 'business' somehow rhymes with 'bugs,' but I don't give a shit. I'm leaving now. Here's a little extra for you."

"You should not disrespect Mr. Navarro."

"I mean no disrespect. I haven't yet decided what I'm going to do for employment. Maybe I'll call him—maybe I won't. Good night." Albert abruptly turned and vacated the premises.

That was three years ago.

EIGHT

Bill Owens was incredibly fond of both Jenne and Kevin O'Malley, but he had to admit that they always seemed to be smack in the middle of the mayhem du jour. The Burns' homicide was no exception. After his interviews with Tom Mahoney and the lot kid, Salazar, he was afraid that there was no avoiding having the O'Malleys in the middle of this one too.

Friday afternoons in the summer were some of the busiest days on the links. Today, though, on the final day in October with overcast skies and temperatures in the mid-fifties, the course was wide open.

Kevin and Bill frequently played during the offseason in the Northwest. As only a twosome, they could easily play in under three hours, and it was an opportunity to share stories, jokes, concerns, and future prognostications. It was also a perfect time for ridicule and mockery, albeit with affection. Often, when a single or another twosome would join up, the newcomers would never have believed the two were close friends, such were the barbs and sarcastic remarks. It was only after the completion of such games that the new acquaintances would finally grasp the warmth and fondness Kevin and Bill had for each other.

This afternoon it was just the two of them. Owens waited only until after the first tee shot hit the fairway to begin his assault on O'Malley's involvement in the Robbie Burns murder investigation.

"It's just impossible for you to keep your nose out of things, isn't it?" Bill attempted to look like the stereotypical hard-boiled detective some thought he was. It seemed, though, that Kevin was having none of it.

With an innocent glance across the fairway, he announced, "Are you accusing me of interfering with police business? Come now, Detective, you should know better than to accuse your good buddy of getting involved. Besides, Mahoney came to me with his story. What would you have had me do, just blow it off?"

34

Owens gave up on playing bad cop. "Shit, Kevin, you're always involved in stuff when you shouldn't be. I gotta admit, though, this time it seems unavoidable."

"Glad you finally see it my way. Any ideas about this thing? You get any help from the cops down in Napa?"

"Other than the coroner's report, they have bubkes. They reported that his throat was sliced open, probably from behind and most likely by a right-handed person. Whoever it was had to be incredibly strong. That Burns was a big muscular guy."

"So basically, it's up to you to figure things out?"

"Seems that way. They're certain it wasn't a robbery or a crime of opportunity, so the default is someone who had a beef with the guy. They think whoever did it followed him to your room, and when his back was turned, he did the deed. They also think the answers are here and not there. I'm inclined to agree with them."

"So, has that steel-trap mind of yours come up with any suspicions?"

Bill knew he was being baited, but he enjoyed the conflict. "What I think is this: Robbie Burns was either screwing his supplier or screwing his distributor, and they were pissed. These guys don't fuck around, and they're not overly concerned about who they kill.

"We've got our computer guys pulling all the information off his cell, and they're backtracing his calls. Someone had to know he went to Napa. Hopefully, we'll come up with something. We're scheduled to interview the wife first of the week. We thought it prudent to give her a little time."

"Do you think she's involved in any way?"

"We just don't know. Word is she's a nice person, lots of friends. She's got two kids from a previous marriage. Burns had a reputation for screwing around when he was away from home, so we think his home life maybe wasn't the best."

"When we were working on the barn, we only met her once. Robbie was calling all the shots. So much so that we figured she wanted no part in the project. We got the feeling that Burns was doing it just so some of the glitterati would pay attention to him. Guy was a peach."

As the two friends continued play, the conversation shifted to more mundane issues. The Seahawks, the Mariners, and the PGA tour were favorite topics and the eventual drift to politics. Kevin was left of center by a couple of clicks, while Bill tended toward more libertarian views.

While they agreed on many issues, there was also ample fodder for dissent. The one subject both had extreme opinions on was the Trumpster. Both were vowing to move to another country if that douchebag got elected again. Most people they knew in the Northwest were of the same point of view.

The two friends completed the round and, after a beer in the bar, agreed to touch base after Owens had interviewed Mrs. Burns on the coming Monday.

NINE

Elizabeth Burns, Liz to her friends, was still in shock, resting in the denial phase. She knew she had to snap out of it and cope with her husband's death. Even though he was unfaithful, it was still going to be difficult.

She was attracted to him initially because he was a well-known professional athlete. If not great or even good, he was famous within the local community, and she was smitten with this adulation.

Looking back to those days, it was understandable, maybe even inevitable. She had just divorced her high school sweetheart after a predictably downward-spiraling marriage. Her self-image had taken a beating, and the prospect of dating a famous ballplayer was enticing. She basked in the glory of his fame for six months before tying the knot with him. She had two young boys to provide for, after all, and they too were starstruck.

At first, she enjoyed the nods and stares of those who thought how marvelous it was to be famous. There were always autograph seekers and flirtatious glances from other women. Little leaguers and their dads looked on in misplaced adoration.

Liz sometimes missed the obvious, but a few years in, even she realized she had probably taken strike two in her second plate appearance at the marriage game. The good news was that Robbie was away at sales meetings, trips, and conventions much of the time. The bad news was his tendency to screw any woman that blinked in his direction.

It was just part of his DNA.

He was a good provider, even if he did fuck around. Liz had a personal shopper at Nordstrom's and a private trainer at the Bellevue Club. Her two boys, now sixteen and eighteen, were enrolled at the Lakeside School, whose past graduates included Paul Allen and Bill Gates. In her mid-forties, she was an attractive woman and sported the usual plastic surgery enhancements. Liz had made peace with her lot in life and had settled for a near loveless and celibate existence.

Robbie's recent fetish for the Arabian horse crowd was just the latest attempt at rubbing elbows with the rich and famous. He thought he could hold receptions in his new fancy barn and endear himself to those with much more money than he would ever have. That he had never been near a horse in his life seemed to make little difference. Liz chuckled at a comment by a friend: "The man's a horse's ass all by himself. He doesn't need horses, Arabian or otherwise."

Still, the murder of her husband had left her stunned. The sheer mountain of things that needed to be done was daunting. Robbie had taken care of all the financial and legal stuff, and now it was up to her. She didn't know much about the car business, and she didn't know anything about any of the legal issues. She needed help.

She wasn't looking forward to meeting with the detective this morning, but she understood he had a job to do.

Bill Owens arrived promptly at ten a.m. on Monday. Julie Houser accompanied him, a newbie on the detective squad—always a good idea to have someone else with you when interviewing a member of the opposite sex. Julie had relocated to the Seattle area from Southern California and was still getting used to many days without Old Sol visiting.

Bill directed the questioning, with his junior partner taking notes and looking exceedingly interested. The conversation centered mainly around Robbie's friends and acquaintances. Liz shared the few folks she knew and even some whose names she had heard mentioned. Owens learned quickly that her knowledge of his business activities was limited. No, she knew of nobody who wished him harm, and yes, if she thought of anything, she'd make sure to call.

Owens asked if she had had much to do with the barn project, and she said, "Very little."

"Would you mind if we took a look in there?"

"Be my guest. Just be careful; it's still under construction. When those designers stopped working for him, the contractor had to leave to work on another project. Robbie was pissed and never did get around to hiring another firm. He had some guys in to do some drywall, but other than that, it's just been sitting there for almost a year."

"We'll be careful, and we'll just take off when we're done looking around. Thanks for your help, and we're sorry for your loss."

As they departed the 5,000-square-foot ranch home, a bright red Mercedes convertible chirped to a stop alongside the blue Crown Vic that belonged to the detectives. The attractive woman driving flashed a beaming grin at Owens as she jumped out of the vehicle.

The detective did a double-take, then stopped in his tracks while on his way to the barn. "Julie, why don't you go on ahead, and I'll meet you at the barn in a sec? I need a word with this person."

Julie was a rookie, but even she had heard the stories of the BPD's foiling of a mass murder by a white separatist group the previous year. It was national news, after all. She had also seen the woman before and knew why her partner wanted a word with her. It was because she was his wife.

"Shelly, what in the world are you doing here?"

"You *are* aware that I still have a few clients from my house cleaning days, correct?" Before Shelly's previous marriage, she had been the proprietor of a successful house cleaning company. Even though she had dissolved the company, she'd held on to a select few clients, mostly because it gave her some semblance of independence but also because she enjoyed the work, and the remaining clients were also good friends.

Perhaps it was because she and Bill Owens had been married less than a year or maybe because she'd never thought it was necessary to inform her husband just who her clients were. In any case, to say Owens was surprised was an understatement.

"Robbie Burns's wife is one of your clients?"

"Yup."

"How come you didn't tell me?"

"Well, I guess because maybe it never occurred to me. I wasn't aware you were coming out here to interview Liz but had I known, I would certainly have informed you." Shelly and Bill were soulmates, but that still didn't preclude a little smugness on occasion.

Appearing somewhat sheepish, Bill had to admit that it was difficult to fault his wife's reasoning. "Well, hon, when you put it like that, it makes sense." Bill also knew that it was best to stay in her good graces. Her pixie-like appearance and sunny disposition disguised a will of steel, and a level of persistence few could match.

"Okay, well, good luck in there. She seems overwhelmed at what she's facing. Not so much the loss, more the realization that she needs a crash course on how to run her home and *his* businesses. Julie and I have to check out the barn, and then we'll head back to the station."

"I'll see if I can help. How about you pick up some halibut at the grocery, and I'll make it the way you like it?"

Owens caught up with his rookie partner just before entering the enormous building. "So, Bill, that cutie in the sports car, could that have been your wife?" Julie offered the question accompanied by pursed lips and a quizzical tilt of her head.

Bill had been told she was a bit of a smart-ass, but if that was offset by a clever mind, then he was okay with it. "Yes, Julie," he began in a resigned tone, "that was Shelly. Liz Burns is one of her three clients. She spends a great deal of time now with a couple of charitable organizations, but she still makes time to clean for three of her customers because they're her good friends."

Houser appeared to sense the depth of her boss's feelings and went in another direction. "Hey, boss, look at the size of this place. Damn, you could hold a Seahawks game in here."

As it turned out, she was almost correct. The sixteen-stall facility sported an 80 x 200 indoor arena, wash stalls, grooming stalls, a laundry room, a grain room, a kitchen, bathrooms, and small apartments. The loft overlooked the arena while also offering a 3,000-square-foot lounge for entertaining clients and friends. The structure would eat up the better part of three million dollars when completed.

At this time, the structure was completely framed-in, sided, and roofed, and the interior construction was well underway, or at least it had been. Since the O'Malleys had declined to continue working with Burns, all construction had ceased. The interior spaces were framed, and drywall hung, but that was all. No casework, painting, or finish work had been completed. Without well-documented finish drawings, it was difficult for any contractor to complete the project.

Had Burns paid the original architects up front to do the plans instead of piecemealing them along the way, then it would have been much more straightforward to complete the structure. The permit set of drawings only went so far when it came to the actual construction of the building. The man was genuinely penny-wise and pound-foolish.

"According to the information given to us by Salazar, the kid who worked for Burns, he'd meet his boss out here and give him the drugs. The kid was scared to death we were going to arrest him for getting involved. I told him we understood that he was forced to do it since Burns threatened to turn his dad over to ICE. We're pretty sure he told us everything, and I believed him when he said he didn't know anything more."

"You think he hid the stuff somewhere in this place?"

"It's possible, but I can't even begin to know where to look. Salazar said they met in the loft. When Burns took the drugs and left him alone, he said it was only for a few minutes, so it must be somewhere up here in the loft."

"Yeah, either that or he just put them in here temporarily and moved them later. They could be anywhere." Julie appeared to be doing her best to think like a drug supplier.

Owens seemed to be having similar thoughts, then he decided, "Let's look around for a few minutes. Maybe we'll get lucky. Since I'm almost certain we won't, we'll have to come back with the drug dogs. Maybe they'll find something. I'm gonna have a conversation with O'Malley as well. Maybe he knows of some secret place in here. He *did* work on the place."

"Boss, how is finding the drugs going to help us solve this killing?"

"It probably won't, but if we do find them and make it public, then at least we won't need to worry about some drug outfit coming here from Mexico and murdering other folks."

"Hey, maybe if we find the drugs, there will be a little note in the bag that says who supplied them, ya think?"

"Julie, shut up and start looking." Owens could see how sharp she was. Obviously, she had a mouth on her as well.

After a half-hour of searching with nothing but rat turds to show for it, they called it quits. "We'll bring the dogs out here tomorrow. In the meantime, I'm gonna have a chat with my buddy, O'Malley. Maybe he'll have some ideas on where in this cavernous building someone might hide a stash of fentanyl."

TEN

Shelly Owens was a wealthy woman. With a house worth millions located in the affluent town of Medina and a conservative stock portfolio of over seven million, she felt her future was secure. The source of this affluence was the liquidation of the real estate holdings of her previous husband, now deceased. That he was a crook and an attempted murderer were details better left in the past.

She had met Bill the previous year when he'd played a pivotal role in foiling the terrorist attack. They were very much in love, sharing mutual respect, and each gave their spouse as much independence as the other required. She had owned a well-respected house cleaning company years ago, and it had since been sold to several of her employees.

The one caveat was that she kept her original three clients, who had since become good friends. Truth was, she would have done the work for nothing. It was her form of therapy, and it provided a subconscious sense of independence that was hers alone.

Liz Burns had been her first client. Shelly knew about the wandering eyes of Robbie and felt terrible for his wife. After her second weekly visit to the Burns home, she was invited to sit and have coffee with Liz. It was then she learned of the sadness in her marriage.

Shelly could identify with her client since she, too, had made an unfortunate choice in her first attempt at marital bliss. Robbie Burns may have been unfaithful and of questionable integrity in his business dealings, but hell, at least he hadn't tried to murder his wife. That first cup of coffee led to many future ones, and their shared commiserations became the foundation of their friendship.

Though she was aware of Liz's shortcomings, Shelly accepted that these were a small part of the complex mosaic that formed the complete person. They established a solid friendship, they liked each other, and if either needed help, the other would be there.

"How are you holding up, Liz? I'm sorry you have to deal with all this crap. What can I do to help?"

"Thanks, Shelly. I appreciate you coming by. It's true that Robbie and I didn't have the best of marriages, but at least he took care of things financially. According to the lawyers, he hadn't updated his will since we married. As it stands now, everything—the dealerships, including all the real estate, as well as everything at the ranch here—transfers to me."

"That's good, isn't it?"

"Well, it simplifies things, but I don't know anything about running car dealerships, never mind all the household finances and that stupid goddamn half-finished horse barn out there."

Shelly had run her own business, albeit a significantly smaller one. She possessed a disciplined mind and had admirable organizational skills. "First things first, Liz. Did Robbie have a second in command? Someone in charge of all the dealerships?"

"Yes. That would be Tom Mahoney. He's been with the company since the beginning. I've only met him a few times at company outings and parties. He must be capable, or Robbie wouldn't have kept him around."

"Okay, set up a meeting with him. You and I will sit down with him and discuss what happens with the dealerships going forward, at least in the short term.

"You'll need to keep things running smoothly until you figure out what you'd like to do. Maybe you'll want to keep things as they are, or maybe you'll want to sell the whole organization to one of those national groups. There are several out there, and they're always looking to expand. Next, you'll have to hire a house manager."

"What's that?"

"Someone to take care of the boys, the bills, the appointments, and the construction if or when you finish the barn. You're gonna be busy, and you won't have time for that shit. Your boys are gonna need you too."

"Where do I find someone like that?"

"I'll find you someone. One of my other clients is moving to the desert permanently, and hers will be available. She's a great gal—knows her stuff."

"I can't thank you enough, Shelly. The way you approach things makes it seem almost doable."

"It is, Liz, don't worry. We'll get through it together."

ELEVEN

Hugo Navarro had met Burns in a chance encounter when they were both at a gathering at the Coral and Marina Hotel in Ensenada, Mexico. It was the final event of the annual Newport to Ensenada Yacht Race. The affair was taken seriously by many of the contestants, but most treated the 125-mile race as a weeklong party.

Burns had a dealer buddy in Newport Beach who entered a yacht in the race. He promised Burns there would be ample poontang available, which was all the car dealer needed to hear.

Navarro wasn't a sailor; in fact, he eschewed the water. Growing up in Mexico City was not a place kids learned to swim. He was a drug supplier, among other things, and he figured there would be plenty of rich Americans at the end-of-race celebration. Though he preferred to keep away from public gatherings, the opportunity to expand his market further into the States was too much to pass up.

He didn't care about recreational cocaine users or even heroin users. Those folks were handled by mules much further down the line. Hugo Navarro preferred to remain above the fray.

At first, Robbie viewed Navarro as just a connection for his cocaine purchases. Even after his return to the Northwest, he kept the communication lines to Navarro open. Cocaine for personal use grew into Burns supplying the stuff to his friends and, in turn, their friends. Robbie's idea was to stuff the product into new cars coming into the country—an idea he possibly saw in the movies.

Hugo eventually suggested that Robbie would like to try importing a more lucrative product since he was doing a couple hundred thousand a month hawking cocaine. Navarro had recently taken over a competitor with a heroin and fentanyl distribution network in place in the Seattle-

Tacoma metropolis. All Burns needed to do was import the stuff and distribute it to the dozen or so peddlers already in place.

That was twelve months ago. It wasn't that Burns needed the money—he was already wealthy. Importing the drugs had an air of danger that stirred some primitive thrill in the ex-ballplayer. The element of control he felt over the lives of the wretched humans that were hooked on the stuff was disgusting but real, nonetheless.

Since it had been his idea to smuggle the stuff in via his new vehicles, he felt a sense of superiority over Navarro. Burns considered him only as a drug supplier and a thug. And thought *he* was the brains of the deal.

Why Burns withheld payment on the last shipment was unclear, even to him. More power over someone, perhaps; maybe leverage for some future product. He'd been so used to browbeating his sales team that it was second nature to extend the treatment to his drug supplier. He mistakenly figured the Mexican would recognize he was dealing with a man of superior intellect.

TWELVE

Albert Herrera was tired. He was tired of driving, *really* tired of these huge fucking trees, and really, really tired of the goddamn rain and clouds. It had been only a week since he had left California, yet it seemed like months ago.

When Hugo Navarro had told him to get his ass up to Seattle to retrieve his unpaid-for product, he'd thought it might be nice to see Washington State since he had never been there. Well, he had now seen the place and longed for the sun and warm temperatures of Southern California.

The Napa detour had been unplanned. While on the road, he'd called the offices of Burns Automotive Group to make sure his prey would be available, only to find the guy had left for a conference in Napa Valley. Fortunately, it was but a short detour to the Meadowlark in Rutherford.

After three years of being Navarro's right-hand man, Albert had learned a thing or two. He had always been a loner and had often gotten into scuffles. His average build and non-threatening appearance—in his long-sleeved sweatshirts—often resulted in folks underestimating his physicality.

While he had seriously injured people in the past, he had never really killed anyone until he entered the business. The drug business was comprised of many rival enterprises, and very few of these responded to quiet conversation or negotiated deals. It seemed slicing a throat open here, and there was a necessary part of the process.

Albert was taught the proper technique during his first week on the job. It wasn't something the navy was in the habit of teaching unless you were a seal. His overdeveloped upper limbs made things easier. There

47

was no need to be concerned about leverage points or optimum angles of attack. He simply encircled his target's head with his left arm, making sure the poor fucker's eyes were snug in the crook of his arm. It was a simple procedure to take the four-inch blade in his right hand and slash his victim's throat from left to right.

His instructor happened to be Hector Ramirez, Navarro's bodyguard. After giving the new guy instructions, he let him practice on a couple of CPR dummies. He seemed to get the hang of it, even if his moves were a little on the crude side. Hector should have been proud of his teaching skills. Unfortunately, the would-be future murder instructor was the victim of his pupil. Navarro had discovered Ramirez skimming product on the side and told Albert to make an example of the man, which he did. Hector's last thoughts were those of a proud man, though. He had taught his craft well.

Albert had never been far from Navarro's guidance from that second week of his employment. He had graduated from bodyguard to procurement to sales and then to management. He had lost track of the number of men he'd killed along the way. Now, however, he had people working for him to provide those skills. It was only on special operations that Hugo wanted Albert to take care of things personally. Robbie Burns was a special case.

Herrera was frustrated. His boss was generous and gave him considerable freedom to carry out his assignments. If there was anything he had learned over the last several years, though, it was that Hugo Navarro never let any slight, no matter how small, go unpunished.

That Navarro had sent Albert to personally retrieve the drugs *and* dispense with Burns spoke massively of the man's commitment to righting any perceived wrong.

When he had arrived at Meadowlark Lodge, he'd simply told the gate attendant he was part of the auto dealer's group and asked him to direct him to where they were holding their meetings.

Navarro had supplied him with photos of Burns, so it was a simple matter to ID the man and shadow him until nightfall.

He followed him as he left his bungalow but was surprised at his route. Instead of joining the rest of the dealers for cocktails, he traversed the entire property, ending up at one of the Hillside Cottages. Herrera watched as Burns approached the simple yet beautifully designed accommodation.

As he stepped onto the porch, he noticed the housekeeping staff had arrived for the turndown service. Burns reached into the tray on the top of the cart used to provide supplies for the rooms and retreated into the shadows of the nearby landscape.

Herrera was confused by the man's actions. He was a patient man, though, so he waited.

As soon as the staff vacated the cabin, Burns stepped from his place of concealment up to the porch, opened the door with his stolen key, and entered the building.

Still unsure of precisely what was going down, Albert knew an opportunity when he saw one. He quickly but quietly negotiated the entry only seconds after Burns. He caught up with him just after Robbie had switched the bedroom lights on.

Encircling his quarry's head with his far superior strength, he held his knife just under Burns's right eye, deftly piercing the skin, drawing a considerable amount of blood.

"Mr. Navarro sends his regards. He would like you to return the product we sent to you several months ago. Don't say anything. Just nod if you understand what I'm saying."

A quick shake of his head conveyed Robbie's acquiescence.

"Where are they? You can talk now, but don't move. I wouldn't want this thing to go any deeper."

"They are at my ranch, in the barn. I'll need to get them for you."

"Maybe. What are you doing here, in this cabin?"

"These people did some work for me on the barn. I needed to touch base with them."

That the auto dealer had had to hire a *designer* to build a goddamn barn spoke volumes about this asshole.

Albert was a man of action, not conversation. He was already tired of this guy. "Tell me where they are, and I'll let you live."

"There's a hidden space in the barn, and it's a very big barn. I'll have to get them."

"So why talk to *this* guy?"

"They were the designers. He doesn't know I put them there, but they drew up the plans, and there's something quirky about it. I need to confirm something with him."

"Okay, well, thanks and goodbye." Albert quickly removed his knife from under the man's eye and promptly sliced his throat from ear to ear. He thought back to his instructor and how proud he would have been as he did so. He'd managed to avoid almost all of the spurting blood.

He'd already been in the state too long for his liking. Last night he had tracked down the O'Malleys to what looked like an A-frame cabin about a half-mile deep in the woods. He had stopped at a wooden bridge that led to the property after hearing dogs and seeing cars. Herrera had attempted to get in touch with his boss, but the cell service in the area was sketchy at best.

Navarro was pleased by the local news reports that Burns was no longer among the living and was looking forward to getting a full report from Albert.

Since he had scaled back his drug distribution in favor of more mainstream investments, he had moved to San Diego. The weather was spectacular, and his 10,000-square-foot ranch house offered every comfort money could buy.

"Boss, I tried to get you last night. Looks like Burns hired some barn designer who probably knows where your stuff is. I'm pretty sure he doesn't know about the drugs, but according to Burns, there's some secret hiding place that the guy designed into the barn. What should I do?"

"Shit. Sometimes I hate this business. There are always loose ends." The phone was quiet for so long that Albert thought his boss had hung up.

"Boss?"

"Albert, get back here. I have other things for you to attend to. If those drugs are well hidden, they're probably safe for a while. If we start accosting people, we'll most likely draw too much attention. We'll let the Burns thing settle down for a while. We can figure out how to get the fentanyl later."

Albert didn't need to be told twice. He couldn't wait to leave the place. *How can anyone stand to live in this fucking rain forest?*

THIRTEEN

Several months passed with only marginal headway on the murder of Robbie Burns. Bill Owens was a persistent, talented investigator, but even *he* was frustrated at the lack of progress.

The Napa sheriff's office had been helpful at first, but local cases eventually nudged out the murder of a Washington car dealer. There was plenty of homegrown crime for Fred Decker to deal with.

Owens had been out to the Arabian horse barn twice more, with the drug-sniffing dogs, to no avail. Regardless of his darker side, Burns was still a well-known member of the business community, and the lack of headway on the case was causing grumblings among the higher-ups in the Bellevue Police Department.

Still, there was very little evidence from which to deduce.

The O'Malleys, meanwhile, had negotiated to sell their firm to their employees. Finally, wearying of the dark and rainy days of the Seattle winters, they decided to relocate to St. George, UT, where the weather and the geography were glorious.

They would certainly miss their friends, especially Bill and Shelly, but they reasoned there would be plenty of house guests from folks looking for a brief respite from the dreary winters of the Northwest. Kevin and Jenne knew a few Seattle transplants in the area, so it wasn't without *some* familiarity that they embarked on this new phase.

While they kept in touch with family and those close to them from Washington State, most of the next eighteen months were filled with golf, hiking, pickleball, and meeting new buddies.

There was the occasional infrequent consultation on interiors. Then, a brief relationship with a group trying to put a bid package together for a new resort was enough of a reminder of why they'd retired to cause them to commit never again to be tempted. The lead guy seemed decent enough, but the level of detail required them to put in way too much *work*. Besides, it competed for hiking and golfing hours.

After a year of fun in the sun, the O'Malleys had to admit they missed the trappings of their former lives, even if it meant returning to the dark, wet, gloomy days of winter in the Northwest.

"Kevin, it's not like there aren't *some* nice days in Seattle." Jenne verbalized what they were both feeling.

"I'm aware. Hell, half the year, it is spectacular. It's the other half that depresses me."

"I know, I know. But I miss the restaurants and the folks at Kelsey Creek. I especially miss Shelly and Bill, and did I say Nordstrom's?"

"You did not. But I agree with everything you said, except maybe Nordstrom's."

"I say we head back home to the shit weather and the good friends. We can always come back here for a few weeks when the winter depression sets in. We good?"

Kevin looked over at his wife and mentally congratulated himself again on being fortunate enough to have stumbled across such a terrific partner., friend, and soulmate.

Their return to the Seattle area was all that they thought it would be, except for the explosion in real estate prices and the dearth of product on the market. The pandemic seemed to have stirred some primal urge in people to spend ungodly amounts of money on homes and properties that would typically have stayed listed for months. As it was, as soon as anything remotely livable became available, it was gobbled up, usually at well over the listing price.

Their home search eventually led them to where they had lived some twenty years earlier—an island in the middle of Puget Sound.

FOURTEEN

It was the last boat for the evening. The ferry left Mukilteo at 11:30 for the twenty-minute trip to Clinton on Whidbey Island. Since it was a weeknight, the traffic was negligible. Also, the weather was shitty.

It was November fifteenth, forty degrees, and raining. The queue in the holding lot consisted of twenty-two cars and four pickups. Kevin's ride was the fifteenth in line. The day's activities and the dinner and wine had left him drowsy, and he dozed through the ten minutes while he was waiting.

He jolted awake at the blast of the horn—the pickup directly behind him kindly waking him with a reminder that it was loading time. 11:20. Kevin turned over his engine and caught up to the taillights ahead of him.

The Washington State Ferry employee, clad in her dayglow yellow reflective vest, dutifully pointed out the proper lanes for the few souls making the last trip of the night. The first dozen or so cars were directed to the cavernous central deck of the *Suquamish*, while the rest of the vehicles were funneled to the outer portion of the ferry. Kevin's four-year-old Ford Explorer ended up second from the front on the starboard side of the 360-foot vessel.

The brief crossing notwithstanding, he reclined his seat and once again dozed off, only fleetingly recalling the two three-putts on the final holes that had cost him fifty bucks. The fluorescent overhead lights did little to dissuade him from nodding off.

THUNK.

"What the fu—?" He jumped, instantly awake, heart racing, at the sound of the slap on his window.

"Open up, asshole. We need to talk."

Kevin was not a stupid man. The large red-faced fellow with a shaved head and intermittent facial hair suggested a less-than-pleasant encounter. The tears tattooed on the man's face further cemented his lightning-quick appraisal of the situation.

"What do you want? What do we need to talk about?" Kevin shouted through the closed window. No way was he opening the door or lowering the window. The big guy had evidently come from the pickup behind him since no one was now in the truck. The driver in front of him was zonked out as well.

With an even redder complexion now, the man slammed a meat slab of a hand against the windshield. "I said open up! If you don't, I'll follow you all over Whidbey. It *is* an island, you know; there's no place to hide."

Whidbey *was* an island, but it was a big one, and there were plenty of places to hide. Unfortunately, they were all in the forested areas, and the thought held little appeal for Kevin O'Malley.

"Why don't you give me some idea of what you want, and then I'll see what I can do?"

"I've been parked alongside that holding area for two weeks, waiting for you to show up. My brother says to bring you to see him."

Kevin cracked the window half an inch only because he was tired of yelling. "Why were you waiting to find me, and who the fuck is your *brother*? And what does he want with me?"

"I was looking for a dark green Explorer with Utah license plates. That's you."

Now that his confronter spoke at a somewhat lower volume, he appeared marginally less threatening. Still, having a conversation with this colorful character and speaking loudly enough to be heard above the 6,000-horsepower diesel was a challenge.

"You *are* aware that there may be more than one green Ford with Utah plates out there?"

"Don't think so. Not goin' to Whidbey Island."

"Who's your brother, where is he, and why does he want to see me?"

"He lives off of Goss Lake Road, just north of Melody. He said it had something to do with that Snow Canyon project you were involved with down in St. George."

"What's your name?" And how did this guy know about Snow Canyon?

The big guy seemed taken aback that someone wanted to know his name. "It's Francis." He said this in barely a whisper.

"Francis?"

"Yeah. Wanna make something of it?" His surliness ratcheted up along with his voice.

"Nah, just wasn't sure if I heard you. Tell you what, Francis, I don't mind talking to your brother. In fact, it's not too far off the route I take to my house. It's very late, and I'm tired. I have to go back to Seattle tomorrow so I can stop by his place on the way to the ferry. Will that work for you?"

"How do I know you'll show up? Maybe you won't."

"Francis," Kevin had to catch himself and not come across as if he were talking to a child. "If I don't show up, you can park down by the Clinton terminal and wait for me to come by again. Remember? Unless I want to drive three hours through Anacortes, I have to take the ferry."

The logic of Kevin's approach seemed to seep into the brain of Francis. "Well, you'd better make sure you do, or I'll be looking for you."

Kevin had a thought. "Why didn't your brother come and talk to me himself?"

"He can't leave his house. He's stuck in a wheelchair, and he's what they call an *agoraphobe*."

Kevin was pretty sure Francis meant agoraphobe, yet he was impressed the man came as close as he did to getting it right. It was all he could do not to correct him. Now his curiosity was getting the better of him—an agoraphobe in a wheelchair on Whidbey Island. *Go figure.*

"Tell him I'll be by in the morning, around ten-ish. Tell him I'm looking forward to seeing him."

Kevin watched Francis in his side mirror as he ambled back to his black Ram pickup. He felt the boat nudge into the dock as the *Suquamish* arrived at Clinton on Whidbey Island. The final trip of the night.

FIFTEEN

The O'Malleys had lived on Whidbey Island for only six months. The slim pickings for real estate in the Queen City was their original reason for moving there, but now they enjoyed the pastoral insouciance of the island. They appreciated the slower pace of things, especially compared to the frenetic tempo of life in the Seattle area. Since becoming the home of Amazon, Microsoft, Starbucks, and a host of spinoffs, the cost of real estate had accelerated faster than in any city in the country, with the traffic to match. The pandemic had only exacerbated things.

Whidbey Island was not without its quirkiness in both customs and inhabitants, yet the tolerance level was a welcome change, especially during the current political climate.

Jenne was dozing soundly on the sofa when Kevin entered their waterfront bungalow. Even the noisy crunching and snapping of the gravel drive did little to disturb her sleep. Rather than wake her, he covered her with the quilt from the back of the sofa, turned off the lamp, and tiredly went up the stairs to hit the sack and contemplate what his morning meeting with the *agraphobe* would bring.

It was finally light enough to see by eight a.m. on Thursday morning. The constant rain this time of year combined with the exceedingly short photoperiod made for a very quick morning. Over his breakfast of oatmeal and fruit, Kevin relayed the strange events of the previous evening to his wife.

"You'd think there might be other ways to talk to you. Like maybe a phone call or something."

"Maybe he didn't have my number."

"So he sent his brother to accost you? How does that make any sense? What is the agoraphobe's name? Are you seriously going to see him?"

"I don't know—that's four questions at once. I don't think I can remember all of them. How about I just tell you what I think? The guy knows *me*, and he knows we live on the island, so if I don't visit his brother, I'm sure Francis will find me again. He's a scary-looking guy, but he didn't come across as threatening after we talked for a bit. I'll just stop by the place on my way to the ferry. It shouldn't take very long."

"Go ahead, be a smart-ass. Do whatever you want. If you get murdered, I'll be widowed, all alone, on an island. What will become of me?"

Kevin could always count on his wife to lighten things up. Her unique sense of humor and irreverent approach to life's challenges were the first things that had attracted him to her.

"If it makes you feel better, you can track me on the Life360 app and see when I leave the guy's house. If I'm there longer than fifteen minutes, you can call me—tell me there's an emergency or something. Will that assuage your concerns?"

"Yes, dear, that will most certainly assuage me. Maybe we could do some assuaging tonight too. Ya think?"

"What I think is, you're getting your verbs mixed up."

"So, you don't think we could manage to do some assuaging tonight?"

Kevin knew when to throw in the towel. "Yes, Jenne, of course, we can, and I'm looking forward to it." He hugged her as he headed off into the rain, promising a call as soon as he left his curious appointment.

Goss Lake Road runs east to west on South Whidbey Island for about two miles, ending at East Harbor to the west and Lone Lake Road to the east. It's surprisingly hilly in places, especially where it wraps over the north end of Goss Lake.

Kevin turned left off East Harbor and climbed the hill to Melody Road. There were few residences in the wooded area, and none could be seen from the road. He took the first gravel drive north of the tiny street. Proceeding slowly through the tall firs, he came upon a clearing with a sprawling log ranch home in the center. There were two smaller outbuildings behind it, while parked in the driveway was a black Ram pickup. Francis's. It had to be.

The wheelchair ramp leading to the side door suggested that Francis's brother occasionally left the confines of his home. Situated to the side of the front door, the Ring doorbell announced his arrival. The door opened before he had a chance to use the device.

"You're Kevin O'Malley."

"Correct, and you are …?"

"My name is Jake Early. You've met my brother, Francis."

"I have, and while we're on the subject, why send him after me? What's the matter with a phone call?"

"I'm sorry about that. I didn't have your number, and I asked Francis if he could locate you and contact me. Sometimes he uses a two-by-four instead of a polite introduction. Francis is my little brother. I've been looking out for him since the seventies. I was injured in Vietnam, and when I returned, Francis did his best to care for me. He's the only family I have, and there were some complications when he was born. He's always been a little socially challenged."

Early had to be in his late sixties, but he looked much younger. He had short gray hair in a brush cut and piercing cobalt blue eyes. For an agoraphobe, his face appeared weathered, suggesting he spent a good deal of time outdoors. His well-built physique confirmed many hours spent in the weight room.

"Once I finally recovered from my injuries, I built this place up here on the island. Francis helped during the construction and then managed to get himself involved in some drug nastiness. He spent five years on McNeil Island before they closed that place down. Did you know that it was the last of the island prisons in the country? Anyway, that place didn't help him any. When he got out, he came here to live with me. Now I watch out for him as best I can."

"I'm curious why you wanted to chat with me, but I've got to ask, why the reluctance to leave this place? Francis said you were an agoraphobe."

With a self-deprecating smile, Jake replied, "Francis always had a little trouble with that word. I'm not sure I can explain it. After he came to live with me, I started spending more and more time here. Sure, I've got a wheelchair-accessible van and even had my license for a while. I started working out—I've got a well-outfitted gym here—and spent less and less time away from the house. I gave up any hope of finding a love interest—no way I could perform in that area anyway.

"We have a garden out back that provides most of our veggies and herbs in season, and I spend hours a day out there. We've even paved the areas in between the rows, so my chair moves easily."

"Don't you miss seeing other people, going places? Hell, you live on this beautiful island and never go to the shore?"

"Look, I'm not saying it makes any sense. It's just that I have no interest in other folks. I watch sports on TV—love the Seahawks and Mariners, by the way—and with streaming now, there are a million channels. Francis goes to the market and shops for me, and I stay here. Now I'm sorta fearful of leaving the place."

Kevin couldn't hope to wade through the cause of or contributing factors to the man's anxiety, so he finally asked the million-dollar question. "Jake, what the fuck do you want with me?"

"You lived in St. George for a few years, right?"

"Yes. We thought we'd try it out, see how it was to live in the sunshine for a bit."

"While you were there, did you do any work for the Snow Canyon Spa?"

"We did. Why?"

"Did you work with a guy named Peter Hall?"

"We did. I met him at the golf course. He said he needed some help on the specifications for the interior furnishings."

"Peter and I have some history. I may be a closet case, but I spend a great deal of time on the internet. I'm able to support myself and my brother through investments." Jake glanced down to where his legs should have been and then continued.

"My settlement with the army was decent at the time, and my pension helps keep us in food and drink. No way, though, would it have paid for this place and helped me support Francis. While I was recovering, I started reading up on investment vehicles. I learned about the stock and bond markets, REITs, hard money lending, and IPOs.

"For a while, I made some money in the markets and then started investing in limited partnerships. Most were formed to fund resort projects throughout the country. That's how I got involved with Hall.

"About five years ago, I came across a solicitation for the first round of funding for a small resort in Santa Fe. It turned out to be Hall's group,

CP Ltd. I kicked in 20K just to see if there was anything there. The project was sold before the first shovel hit the ground, and I doubled my money. Since then, up until a year or so ago, I've done very well investing with Peter's outfit."

Just then, the Dubliners began singing "Dublin in the Rare Old Times," Jenne's ringtone. "Jake, please excuse me for a moment. Yeah, hon, what is it?"

"You *know* what it is. You told me to call in fifteen minutes if you hadn't left. I'm calling to give you an out. The app says you're still there."

"Yes, Jenne, I'll remember to pick that up on my way home."

"So, you're still talking with that guy?"

"Sure thing, dear. I'll get that as well."

"Okay, sporty, you're on your own. Don't say I wasn't here for you. Be careful and call me when you leave that place."

"Okay, babe. See you when I get back."

Kevin turned to see a smirking Jake Early. "That your rescue call?"

He knew it was useless to deny it; Kevin's Irish features had already turned scarlet, giving him away. "Well, Jake, you never know. You could have been a serial killer or one of those QAnon guys."

"Yes, I suppose I could have. Anyway, would you like to leave, or should I continue?"

Kevin was ambivalent about where he fit into this saga, but he was interested enough to hear more. "Please go on, Jake, but maybe get to the part where I fit in sooner rather than later—I have a ferry to catch."

"Fair enough. When the Snow Canyon project offering came up, I put two million into it. This was just the first phase for the land procurement. Turns out I was ten percent of the funding. That was two years ago. Hall assured me that things were proceeding nicely, and the acquisition went smoothly.

"The pandemic slowed things down a little, but that was to be expected. The succeeding rounds of funding were for A&D fees and initial construction costs. I put up another three million. I had no concerns back then, especially since I had done so well with Hall in previous ventures. Peter kept me posted on the progress, even told me some of the big boys—Marriott and Royal Caribbean—were sniffing around.

"About a year ago, I became concerned. The job site cameras were disabled, and I got wind that there was some conflict between the local

Paiute peoples and the construction crew. It seems a portion of the hiking trails went through an ancient ceremonial site. They considered it a holy place that Hall's outfit was desecrating. I heard all this second-hand from one of the other investors.

"As soon as I did, I tried to contact Peter, but he never returned my calls, texts, or emails. Now, I'm pretty well off, but losing five million would undoubtedly put a dent in my portfolio. I'm very concerned and just a bit pissed off.

"I spoke with the AG in Utah, and she said she had received two other complaints. She's put a BOLO out for Hall, but so far, nothing. It's like he's disappeared."

"Uh, Jake … why am I here?"

"Sorry, Kevin. When I think about it, I get carried away. I wanted to see you to ask a few questions and see if I could figure out what happened to Hall and my money. My discussions with one of the other investors led me to believe you had provided services for the project, so I wanted to see if you had been paid and what your impressions of Hall were."

"You do know—I know I've brought this up before—that a simple phone call would have been far preferable to sending Francis after me. What were you thinking?"

"Yeah, I know, I know. I'm sorry, but I'd drunk just a little too much cabernet, and I mentioned to Francis that I'd very much like to talk to you. He may seem a little slow—well, he actually is a little slow, but only socially—except sometimes he takes me literally and runs with it. Also, he spends eight hours a day on his computer. And he heard me talking to James, the other investor, about you. Next thing I know, he's Googled you, found out about your company, and eventually tracked you down. He's sort of protective of me."

"So, all this cloak and dagger stuff was just to see what I thought of Peter Hall?"

"Well, um, yeah."

Kevin thought it best just to turn around and walk away from Early, but he rather liked his demeanor, and what could it hurt to tell him what little he knew of CP Ltd.?

"I told you we only had a small contract for the initial furnishings specifications for the Snow Canyon project. About eighteen months ago, we met with Peter and several of his associates. We agreed to come up with a preliminary list of furnishings and a budget to finalizing the funding for the project. All told, we only had a month's worth of time in the thing. I think we ended up billing about twelve or fifteen grand for our services."

"Did you get paid? What were your impressions of Peter and his people?"

"Well, we got paid promptly. Peter seemed a bit scarce like he had other things on his mind. His associates absolutely deferred to him; they may as well not have been there. When we presented the furnishings package, it was just to Peter. No one else was present."

"Was that unusual?"

"A little, but that sometimes happens when developers are just trying to pull funding numbers together."

"Well, shit." Jake looked somewhat defeated as if he'd been expecting a tale more sinister.

Kevin felt a smidgen of sympathy for the guy. Here he was, a recluse confined to a wheelchair. Sure, he had money, but that couldn't restore his health or overcome his phobia. "All I can tell you, Jake, is that Hall was a little quirky for sure. In this business, though, we've come across many folks that proved to be far more peculiar. I'm sorry I can't shed any more light on this thing."

Kevin's empathetic offering seemed to jerk Early away from his musings. "Thanks, Kevin. You're a stand-up guy for even agreeing to see me. I'll continue to research this outfit—with Francis's help, of course. If I have any more questions, can I call you?"

"Of course. Hell, we're neighbors now. I know *you* are a little socially challenged, but I'd love to bring Jenne by sometime. I think you'd enjoy her."

Jake's feigned annoyance gave way to a wide grin. "I'd very much enjoy that. Perhaps sometime down the road."

SIXTEEN

The Last Chance Casino was just as the name implied. Its location, several blocks west of the Vegas Strip, made it the only casino in the small industrial area on the other side of I-15. Under the current zoning requirements, its placement would not be allowed. It owed its exception to its longevity. It was built long before the Bellagio fountains, even before Steve Wynn got involved with the Frontier Hotel.

Built by Sean and Liam Murphy shortly after the downfall of prohibition, it soon became a significant competitor to the Golden Gate Hotel, the very first casino in Las Vegas. During the thirties and early forties, the Murphy brothers, formerly of County Cork, were able to charm and bullshit their way to the most successful establishment in town. The Irishmen were born promoters and supposedly excellent money managers, which was especially peculiar for this Irish family.

In 1945 they sold the place and took their "winnings" to begin a new adventure. At the behest of their wives, both of whom everyone knew were the brains behind the brothers' success, they searched for a quieter venue at which to spend their later years. Sarah, Sean's wife, suggested to Emily, Liam's mate, that perhaps a nice grape farm in the lovely Northern California town of Oakville could be an attractive place for the extended family.

The Last Chance was sold to the Ortega Brothers, Hector, and Roberto. The brothers grew up in Santa Isabel, a small town to the west of Mexicali, and were already living on the streets in their early teens. They were industrious boys and quickly learned how to steal without getting caught.

They were keen observers of human nature, and they soon developed an uncanny ability to appear innocent and sympathetic even while hoodwinking "customers" into purchasing their purloined goods.

Driven by the lure of riches from the States, the Ortegas slipped across the border with a commandeered package of marijuana. Although Calexico was simply a small agricultural community, there were enough folks willing to take a spin on the wild side for the brothers to ply their goods. Soon the weekly visits by the duo were eagerly anticipated by their customers.

When the Marijuana Tax Act of 1937 criminalized the drug, it changed everything for Hector and Roberto. Weed went from an easily available commodity to something illegal to bring into the US. In other words, the stuff quadrupled in demand, likewise in price.

Supply could have become a problem had the brothers not quickly reacted to events. With a small nest egg from their questionable enterprises, they were able to purchase two acres of land just north of Santa Isabel and just south of the US–Mexico border. In two dilapidated greenhouse structures, they began their pot-growing operation.

With excellent quality control, ample weed supply, and increased value thanks to the United States government, their profits increased exponentially. By the time they were in their twenties, their cannabis trade had spread from the Southwest to the West Coast of the States, and their operations employed over a hundred people.

Because they were among the first large drug suppliers, they became targets for rival smugglers aiming to move in on an ever-increasing customer base. The Ortegas were not exceptionally violent folks, but their hands were forced after losing a few of their "sales force" in El Paso.

Hector knew a guy who "knew" a guy, and so began the brothers' enforcement division. Whenever one of their own was attacked or killed, retribution was swift and bloody. The more vile the execution, the more effective it was on the competition. Word on the street was, "do not fuck with the Ortegas."

One day, after a particularly violent episode, the brothers sat down for a leisurely lunch in the sleepy town of Dana Point, just north of San Clemente in Southern California. This area of the country was their most profitable, and they enjoyed the spectacular weather and beautiful beaches here.

"Roberto, I think I'm tired of this business."

"I have to admit, when we started, it was exciting and challenging. These days, though, it seems we're always looking over our shoulders. Always some new assholes trying to steal our customers."

"What would you say if we could take our money, invest it in a new venture, and just leave all this messy shit to the vultures?" The look of concern on his brother's face led Hector to follow up quickly. "Don't worry. I've thought about this for some time. This new business will allow us to keep our long-time employees, we can make at least as much money, and best of all, it's legal."

"You sound like you've been using some of our product, Hector. We're smugglers—what else can we do?"

"No. We're businessmen and salesmen. We run a large company with many employees. Sure, it's illegal and unpleasant at times, but we've made a lot of money at it. The new business would require us to move permanently to the US, and there would be very little travel."

"Sounds like you've done some work on this." Roberto wanted to hear more.

"There's a small place in Nevada called Las Vegas. For some reason, gambling is legal there. Lotta folks from LA come over to spend money. Prostitution is legal there too. A couple of Irishmen are selling their casino, and I thought we could make them an offer."

"So, you're saying prostitution and gambling are legal in this town? How can this be?"

"It seems as though after the Depression and the mines petered out, there was no income for the state. The legislature voted to legalize gambling to get tax money to supplement their coffers. It's the only place in the country that allows gambling. There are only a few casinos there now, but they expect more coming. The Last Chance is killing it. I've already seen their books."

Roberto appeared somewhat miffed at being out of the loop. "So, you did all this on your own? We're partners, you know."

"Of course we are. I didn't think it made sense to talk about this if it wasn't gonna go anywhere. When you went on ahead to California, I took a side trip to Vegas to meet with the Irish guys. It seems as though their wives are the brains behind things. The books are tidy, and their profits are impressive. I told them we'd get back to them before the end of the week."

"Well, I guess that makes some sense. What do you think?"

"I think it's a chance to get in on the ground floor of something that's gonna do nothing but grow. Plus, I hate all this messy, bloody shit.

Also, being in Mexico when all our customers are in the States sucks. We'd have to apply for visas and all, but if we owned the casino, that would just be a formality."

"You make a good case, Hector. Maybe it's time we settled down and looked ahead instead of looking over our shoulders."

And so, as World War II was ending, the Ortega brothers began their careers as casino owners and operators.

SEVENTEEN

The population of Las Vegas continued to expand, as did the number of casinos. At the same time the Last Chance continued to attract patrons, newer and bigger casinos were built. Early on, the Golden Nugget shared the majority of nightclub goers with the Ortegas.

With time, more visitors meant more places. The Desert Inn, the Horseshoe, the Holiday, and then the MGM, Caesar's, Steve Wynn's places, and a host of others still could not satisfy the demand.

When the early 2000s arrived, Hector and Roberto were in their seventies and were still seen roaming the aisles of slots and the hotel's corridors. Their sons had taken over the day-to-day operations of the place and had modestly upgraded the facilities when needed. They had neither the flair nor the dedication of their fathers, but they seemed to understand that if they fucked things up, at least while their fathers were alive, there would be hell to pay.

Robert Ortega and his cousin Benny were the beneficiaries of their fathers' hard work and dedication by the time 2014 rolled around. For the past half dozen years, they had sucked the life out of the Last Chance.

Its formerly pristine casino and well-appointed hotel now resembled a third-world enterprise. Money originally budgeted for improvements and upgrades was now destined for the two D's: drugs and debauchery. Instead of well-heeled patrons from LA and across the country, the only frequenters of the establishment were drug suppliers, hookers, and thugs.

The Last Chance had fallen into such a state of disrepair that the situation even managed to penetrate the muddled minds of its owners. After a particularly exhausting week of booze, drugs, and sex, Robert felt the time was right to have a chat with his cousin.

"This place looks like shit, Benny."

"Yeah, I guess maybe it does."

"Maybe that's why nobody stays here anymore. For a while there, I thought it might be because of all the new places."

"Yeah, that's what it is." Benny had never been considered a source of evolutionary thinking. He'd always deferred to Robert's leadership when it came to most, if not all, decisions. It wasn't always the best way to go, but he didn't seem to care one way or the other.

"No, that's not *what it is*. *What it is* is, we need to fix up this fucking place." It wasn't that Robert cared at all about their fathers' legacy. It was much more the realization that their money machine would evaporate unless there were some changes.

"We're gonna have to remodel. We need to make the casino bigger and glitzier. The hotel needs a complete redo. It'll take us a year or so, but I think we gotta do it. All our old customers are camping out at the new places. We need to show them that we can compete with the big boys."

"Uh, Robert, we're, uh … we're gonna need some money to do this thing you're talkin' about. Didn't you tell me we took out a mortgage on the place?"

"We did. We're going to have to come up with private money to do this."

"Private money? Where do we get that?"

"Investors. We get it from investors. There was a guy in here last month. Said he was looking for a place to invest some money. He said he could get as much as we needed, and we only had to pay him ten percent."

"That seems a little high, doesn't it? We're paying, what, six percent on our mortgage, right?"

If Robert was surprised that Benny knew their mortgage rate, he didn't let on. Every once in a while, his cousin surprised him. "You're right, Benny, we are. That's because it's with a conventional bank. The guy I'm talkin' to has a pile of money, and he just wants to park it somewhere, as long as he makes ten percent on it. He's able to charge that much *because* he's willing to lend it to us. We're maxed out with the banks, and we can't get any more from them."

Robert had been having conversations with the fellow for several weeks. He seemed to think if he had all his ducks in a row *before* he broached the subject with Benny, selling him on it would be far easier.

"So, how much do you think we'll need to borrow?"

"I figure we'll need at least fifteen or twenty million to polish this turd enough to compete with the other guys." Robert figured he'd pad it a couple million as compensation for having to do the legwork on the deal—sort of a finder's fee. Since Benny was always half in the bag, he'd probably never notice anyway.

Eighteen

Peter Hall was tired. The money he'd taken from the Snow Canyon partnership was plenty for the rest of his life but hiding out in another country was exhausting. Going "underground" in Vancouver had been a mistake. The place was fucking cold and wet. He had figured it would be easier to blend into this metropolitan area of two and a half million people than to hide out in the States.

The smaller investors he couldn't care less about. That Navarro character, though, was cause for serious concern and putting an international border between the two of them seemed a prudent option.

He'd been here on a trip once with his brother Bobby and their parents, but that was years ago. His mom had thought it would be good for them to reconnect with his much older brother, who had moved here years ago to avoid the draft. Peter didn't know him and wanted nothing to do with him. If it hadn't been for his mother's insistence, he would gladly have skipped the journey.

He supposed there were plenty of other cities from which to choose. Maybe, though, just the presence of a sibling, albeit an estranged one, had tipped the scales.

If only those goddamn Indians hadn't been such a pain in the ass. He had heard something about the property, including numerous petroglyphs, but he'd figured that would only enhance the hiking experience for the spa guests. How could he have known it was where they worshiped the sun or whatever they did there? Shit, it was hundreds of years ago. Who would even care about that anymore?

Well, the elders on reservation *did*. And the fuckers didn't bring it up until after the second round of financing for the development when over thirty million was invested.

He would have felt much better if most of the money hadn't come from Navarro. When he'd run into the guy in that third-rate casino in Vegas, his gut had told him to move along, but his more mercenary tendencies had won over.

Hall's development group was small—only five people. CP Ltd. had incorporated in early 2009, just after the shit hit the fan on the mortgage crisis. He had graduated with a business degree from the University of Utah in 1990 and bounced around several commercial real estate firms, managing a comfortable income.

As the youngest of three boys, whose parents were older than most, he had a great deal of freedom. Throughout college, his efforts to hang out with the kids of well-to-do parents resulted in more student loans than necessary. He lived in a constant state of debt, which carried forward into adulthood.

He took more chances than necessary when it came to life choices, especially investing. Successful early on, rather than taking a conservative approach to his earnings, he poured all of it into banking and mortgage stocks. Even as the end of 2007 approached, Hall was convinced things would turn around. Alas, he was mistaken.

The next three years were difficult. He managed to keep his real estate license but could only eke out a living doing part-time gigs at home improvement stores.

While it was true that he was enamored with riches, it was also true that Peter Hall was not without brains or talent. He rightly assumed that what goes down must come up, and he began planning for the end of the Great Recession.

He had come across like-minded real estate operatives during the downturn and suggested that they form a company to prepare for the rebound in the economy. Hall made sure that the members he recruited came either from well-heeled families or at least from families with connections.

His first project was a small twenty-room inn located in Oro Valley, just north of Tucson. With the stampede of wealthy snowbirds in the winter, the area was widely recognized as an up-and-coming vacation spot. The modest offering of syndication was gobbled up during the first week, primarily by family members of those who formed CP Ltd.

The project was so successful—it was sold shortly after breaking ground—that several more followed. Each was more impressive than the last. It wasn't long before Hall's partnership no longer needed promoting. Those with plenty of disposable income saw an opportunity for remarkable returns and sought out the developer.

The first hint of difficulty occurred when Hall put together an exclusive spa and tasting room in Napa Valley. The total cost was pegged at twenty-five million dollars. Naturally, the offering was quickly sold out, and the construction process began.

Napa was a different animal from all of Hall's previous ventures, and the national outfits took a pass on the purchase. It seemed that affluent oenophiles owned almost all the valley establishments, and each had its own personality. The cookie-cutter approach that most large resort chains adopted did not translate well to the wine country.

As good as Hall was at packaging investment vehicles, he was less so at managing the construction of them. The Oakville Inn and Spa, as it was called, began hemorrhaging money. Mismanagement, delays, and cost overruns resulted in an increase of twenty percent by the time of its completion.

The twenty to forty percent returns that the subscribers were used to did not materialize, and disappointment was widespread. CP was forced to sell the completed project at a loss, making matters worse.

NINETEEN

The Snow Canyon Spa had been under development during the final construction phase at the Napa project, but confidence in Hall's outfit was on the decline. Jake Early, an investor in a few of the previous very profitable endeavors, had passed on the Oakville deal and agreed to jump in on the St. George project.

Unfortunately, without the majority of funds provided by his incestuous benefactors, he needed to go elsewhere to complete the subscription.

After he finally got out from under the costly Napa Valley project, Peter focused his energies on making the Snow Canyon Spa his crowning achievement. He pegged the development to come in at thirty-five million when all was said and done.

He figured if he could scrape away four or five million out of the deal, he'd be able to call it quits and find some quiet place to retire. Problem was, he needed to come up with a large chunk of change pretty damn quick.

During the early stages of the Snow Canyon deal, Hall needed to be on-site in St. George. He took out a six-month lease on a casita at the inn at Entrada, from where he could manage the spa development.

While St. George is a charming town, there were some drawbacks for a single guy looking to have a few drinks and occasionally get laid. Being a wholesome family community where the vast majority of residents were church-going LDS disciples, the small Southwest Utah town did not lend itself to nightlife and social activities for single adults.

Fortunately, everything that St. George did not offer was readily available a scant two hours south in the significantly larger town of Las Vegas. Sin City, where whatever happens there, stays there.

This was where the slightly overweight, prematurely balding real estate developer in his early fifties, a Paul Giamatti doppelganger, found himself several nights a week. He eschewed the big showy casinos where the rich and snotty played while they made every effort to be seen. No, Hall preferred to keep a low profile, especially after his Napa Valley debacle. His Vegas hangout was a newly if poorly, remodeled joint off the strip called the Last Chance.

The owners, a couple of guys named Ortega, were friendly enough, although they always seemed a little stoned. He became friendly with the croupiers and occasionally took comfort with the courtesans, of whom there were always a goodly number. To the staff and the hookers, he was just another customer to be fleeced, but he knew this. He was a real estate developer, after all.

Hall was still woefully shy of the money needed to completely fund the Snow Canyon Spa. He had spent the day in 110 degrees watching a Caterpillar D8 shove dusty red dirt around the parking area for the new project. It was easy to get lost in the minutia of the day-to-day activities even *if* the surrounding vistas were some of the most spectacular in the States.

He'd made the two-hour journey to Las Vegas and was sitting at the horseshoe-shaped bar wondering how the fuck he was going to come up with the fifteen million he needed to finish the job. Tired and slightly inebriated, the three vodka martinis had provided their desired effect. He barely noticed the smallish Hispanic-looking fellow nursing a Modelo Negra directly across from him.

"Mr. Hall, how are you this evening? Very glad you could make it tonight. Is there anything I can get for you? Perhaps a private dance, a massage?" Robert Ortega knew that Peter Hall was a frequent visitor. The casino owner wasn't overwhelmingly intelligent; however, when it came to making his customers feel wanted, he was a pro. He had retained enough of his father's teachings, though, to have some awareness of what was called for when he came across a patron who appeared down on his luck.

"Not tonight, Robert. I think I'll just sit here and play the poker slots."

"You seem unhappy. Is there something I can do for you?"

"I don't think so. We've just got some funding issues on the spa we're developing up in St. George. I just need to figure out how to come up with fifteen million dollars, hah! You don't happen to have that lying around, do you?" Hall's sarcasm was heavy as he turned back to his cocktail.

"No, Peter. *I* do not. But depending on what your tolerance is for the source of funds, I may know someone who can assist."

Hall suddenly forgot about his drink and glanced up at his host. "What are you talking about?"

"You see that little guy over there? The one with the blue sport coat and the bad skin? Maybe you should buy him another beer."

After the introductions were made, Hall went into his canned spiel on the rewards and returns of investing with CP. He replayed all the previous projects and the returns they provided. All except the Napa Valley disappointment.

Hugo Navarro sat through this presentation, feigning close attention. He had been coming to the Last Chance semi-regularly ever since loaning the cousins the money for their remodel. It was mainly to keep an eye on them, but that no longer seemed necessary. They were stoners, but they paid regularly and didn't gripe about the interest rate.

Navarro may have been a drug czar, but stupid he was not. Nor was he a pig when it came to looking for a return on his millions. He realized that aggressive but reasonable returns for his money were preferable to putting them at significant risk with dubious operatives. He was also meticulous in his research regarding where he placed his many millions.

The Last Chance may have been in the shitter when he loaned the Ortegas the money, but it was *still* a valuable piece of real estate. Since he was in first position on the loan, he wasn't worried about being paid back. If the shit hit the fan, he could always take it over and sell the place.

Hugo was always looking for places to hide his ill-gotten gains. He'd let Robert know that he would be grateful if an opportunity presented itself; perhaps even a finder's fee would be in the offing.

Robert had pointed out several wealthy patrons to Navarro during the last few months. He'd gleaned a bit about CP Ltd., mostly by listening to Hall whine about where he was going to come up with the balance of the funds to complete his St. George project. Navarro had promised ten grand if he could assist in finding other investments, and he'd mentioned Hall to the drug dealer several weeks before.

As Peter was winding up his sales pitch, Navarro interrupted. "Excuse me, Peter. Let's cut to the chase. You need fifteen million dollars, and I have it available. I know your track record, and I also know about that loser of a project you just got out from under up in Napa.

"I don't care about projected returns or your fancy graphs. I'll loan you the money; you pay me ten percent interest only, monthly, for five years, and then the balance on the sixtieth payment. How does that sound?"

"It sounds expensive. That's a million and a half a year in interest. If you invest the way we normally do things, you could get twenty percent in year two. Doesn't that make more sense?"

"Nope, not for me. I prefer a sure thing, especially after knowing how you fucked up that Oakville deal."

Peter's usually pasty complexion paled even more. It was apparent he was not used to having hat in hand.

"You'll also need to make sure my company name is in first position on the lien." Navarro had several shell companies he used for such purposes.

Navarro stopped talking. Hall was quiet too. He was mentally calculating whether it was worth doing.

"What if we sell it in year two? Can I pay off the balance then?"

"If you did, I'd lose over four million in interest. Nope, but I'll tell you what I *will* do. If you manage to turn the thing around that quickly, I'll let you pay me off early for two million."

A little color crept into Hall's chubby face. It looked as though if things went smoothly, he could still salvage several million from the deal, even after paying Navarro the five million vig. "Okay, let's get this done."

TWENTY

Very little progress had been made on the Robbie Burns murder investigation. The number of times the subject came up during the weekly visits to the links by O'Malley and Owens had diminished considerably.

When Kevin did broach the subject, his efforts were either ignored or rebuffed by his friend. "So, I guess the subject of the car dealer's murder is off the table, eh?"

"Kev, we're getting nowhere on it, and every time I think about it, I get pissed off. Forgive me if I don't want to go there."

"Does that mean if I bug you about it, you'll lose your focus and start fucking up a few shots? Cuz if it does, I'm not leaving it alone. I need the money."

"You *are* aware that you can be a colossal asshole at times, right?"

"Yes, I am aware. But if it weren't for me, you'd have no friends at all. So I guess you'll have to put up with me."

And so the constant bickering between the very close friends continued for months, each aware of the fact that the more water under the bridge, the less chance of solving the crime.

Kevin sometimes bumped into Francis Early at the Star Store. The general store in downtown Langley was the center of the universe on Whidbey Island and had been since 1919. Groceries, apparel, fresh fruits and vegetables, wine and liquor, and greeting cards were available. It was a place the locals loyally shopped and the tourists frequented.

Now that he knew Kevin was friends with his brother, Francis turned out to be an amiable sort. Once O'Malley had gotten past his rugged appearance, including the facial tattoos, he actually looked forward to seeing him.

On this particular day, as he was looking for capers in one of the extremely narrow canned food aisles, Kevin felt a presence beside him.

"Hey, Kev. Jake wondered if you and your wife would like to come by for dinner this Saturday. Can you do?"

The last time he'd spoken with Early was over four months ago, so he was mildly surprised at the offer. "I think we can make it, Francis. What's the occasion?"

Francis moved closer to O'Malley as if not to be overheard. "I'm not sure, but I think he maybe wants to work on his agraphobia."

Kevin suppressed a wry smile. Francis was still tested by the term. "Please tell him we'd love to. What time?"

"He says dinnertime, so I guess that's six-ish. He also says not to bring anything. He wants to show off his wine cellar, and he thinks he's a good cook. But what do I know? Anything's better than prison food. Hah!"

A genuine smile now from Kevin. The man had a sense of humor, after all.

Saturday arrived, along with the eighth day in a row of March drizzle. The ten-minute drive to the Early residence in the gloom that passed for early evening in the Pacific Northwest passed in relative silence. They took the winding gravel driveway off Goss Lake Road and parked in front of the log home.

Well-designed landscape lighting highlighted the abundant plantings as well as the structure itself. The misty moisture gave off a surreal ambiance.

"Yikes, Kevin, I feel like I'm in a Hansel and Gretel story. This place is something else."

"If you could see it in the daytime, you'd be impressed. Jake used some architect from the island when he built the place. She was nationally famous for her log home designs."

They made their way up the bluestone paver walkway to the massive front doors. Just before they could reach for the button, the right-hand door swung open.

"Welcome, Kevin. I'm happy you could make it. This has got to be Jenne. She's every bit as beautiful as you described her."

Kevin was impressed that Jake Early, agoraphobe, managed to both compliment his wife and credit him in the same sentence. The guy could certainly teach him a few things.

Jenne's ear-to-ear grin showed her appreciation and even earned a nod in her husband's direction. As always, Kevin was now thinking he owed Early bigly, especially if he managed to get lucky when they got home.

"Thank you, Jake. I've heard a lot about you. I must say this is an amazing place you have." Jenne at once managed to focus Kevin's mind on the present.

"Well, as I'm sure your husband told you, I get to spend a lot of time here. All of it, actually, hah." His self-deprecating nature made Jake easy to like. "Please come on in and have a seat. Let me get you both something to drink."

With his muscular upper body, Jake maneuvered smartly throughout the great room. In only a few minutes, he went from a disabled shut-in to gracious host and conversationalist.

"I wasn't sure of dietary restrictions, so I put together some tapas that should satisfy both the carnivores and the vegans. Francis should be here in just a bit as well. He's just finishing up some research on the computer."

"Jake, everything looks delicious. If it's not too nosy, though, could you give me a tour of the place before we eat?" Jenne could never pass up the chance to check out well-executed interior design, even if she wasn't the one doing it.

"Of course. Grab your wine glass, and let's go."

The journey through the 4,500-square-foot home would have only taken twenty minutes had the threesome not gotten sidetracked by the 3,000-bottle wine cellar on the lower level. With its hand-hewn tasting table and sophisticated mood lighting, it took very little arm-twisting for Jake to convince the O'Malleys to taste the selections for the evening.

They were about to head for the elevator to the upper level when Francis joined them, and introductions were made for Jenne's benefit.

"It's a pleasure to meet you, Francis. Kevin has told me a lot about you, especially your computer skills. Would you mind terribly if I called you from time to time when I run into problems? Kevin is no help at all."

Kevin was no IT guy, but he *did* know his way around a computer. He let this one go, still thinking about his romantic opportunities later in the evening.

The blush on Francis's face turned the tattooed tears purple as he immediately fell under Jenne's spell. "Thanks very much. *You* can call me anytime. I can only imagine how inept your husband might be."

Kevin did a double-take before he realized Francis, too, was sticking the knife in. He'd make it a point not to underestimate him.

The balance of the evening was delightful. The four of them interacted like old friends. That Jake was conflicted about leaving his home still made no sense to Kevin, but he'd finally written it off as something he'd never understand.

Francis, on the other hand, was very entertaining. Except for the ambush on the ferry, he seemed to have inherited his brother's self-effacing style. He made stories of his prison tenure sound like summer camp, with no end to the colorful personalities sharing McNeil with him.

His drug experience dictated a life of alcohol avoidance, but he was more than happy to keep others' glasses full.

As the evening wound down, the subject of the St. George project came up, with Jake saying he still had heard nothing from Hall and wasn't sure how to proceed.

"I'll run it by a friend of mine who's a detective and see if he has any suggestions," Kevin offered. "I'm sure it's way off his beat, but maybe he'll be able to steer you in the right direction."

"That would be helpful, Kevin. Thanks a million. Uh oh, bad choice of words, huh?"

As the O'Malleys stood to leave, they couldn't help but smile. They were both sure that this wouldn't be their last visit to Casa Early.

TWENTY-ONE

Hugo Navarro had the dreadful misfortune to have been born in Neza, home of one of the nastiest slums in the world. Neza-Chalco-Itza, located just northeast of Mexico City, housed over four million people in squalor and overwhelming poverty.

At eleven years of age, he still had no idea who his mother was or what had become of her. As far back as he could remember, his nights were spent huddled on the dirt floor of one of the unsanitary rat-infested half-stucco, half-cardboard shoe boxes that, stacked upon one another, resembled a dystopian Jenga-inspired hellhole.

Being extra small for his age was an added burden that made him easy prey for the older kids. He could never remember a time when he wasn't hungry. It seemed like whenever he managed to steal a piece of fruit or a chunk of bread—it was taken from him. He put up a semblance of resistance early on, but his underdeveloped strength only resulted in more severe beatings.

Through some freak of nature or perhaps a mutation in his genetic code, Navarro was blessed with an incredibly high IQ. At every opportunity, he'd escape the barrio to wander the less hostile streets of the nearby neighborhoods. Although still very poor, these areas represented at least a degree of civility and family structure.

He'd often hide out to observe a life that he had never known. Kids his age, dressed in uniform, were seen walking off to school as their parents bid them goodbye. The families appeared well-fed, even happy. It was something Navarro had never experienced.

After several visits to one community, he began watching one particular family's comings and goings. A boy around his age and his older sister by several years were his subjects.

Hugo could estimate the time within a few minutes even without a watch. He made a note of when they would return from school. Usually, the boy would come home by three and his sister sometimes a half-hour later.

Being raised with no parents in a disgusting slum ruled by competing gangs was unfortunate. Throughout his brief time on planet Earth, Navarro learned to steal when he could, maintain as low a profile as possible, and only pick on those younger or weaker than himself.

The boy he watched walking home from school, backpack in hand, was not younger. However, not being raised in Neza-Chalco-Itza certainly ensured he'd be weaker.

As the boy neared a driveway near his home, Navarro bolted from behind a large poinsettia bush and pounced on the kid's back, making him face-plant on the dirt sidewalk. Several punches to the side of his head made certain the youngster would not get up.

Hugo grabbed the backpack, turned, and bolted back the way he had come.

However, on this particular day, the boy's sister, Maria, had come home early. No soccer practice.

She looked up to see a filthy boy wearing torn clothing beating the shit out of her brother.

Maria was thirteen and large-boned for her age. As a center back for her team, she was feared as an enforcer. Her backpack contained a three-inch-thick *History of Mexico* text.

Hugo, purloined property in hand, finished his turn with a face-plant of his own—right between the two already well-developed breasts of Maria Gomez.

As stunned as he was, it took Navarro fully three seconds to realize the young soccer player's knee had been deposited, rather forcefully, deep into his nutsack. On his way to the ground, Maria followed up with a right-handed smash to the head with her backpack.

Never in his brief existence had Hugo experienced such pain. He lay in the fetal position while Maria stood over him, threatening more pain if he moved.

While the attacks played out, Mrs. and Mr.—or rather Officer— Gomez rushed to their injured child. Daniel was sobbing but rose to a sitting position, blood and snot streaming from his nose. Maria had yet to move as she straddled the skinny, quivering, filthy Navarro.

While Daniel's mother comforted him and started cleaning him up, Officer Gomez bent over and picked up the would-be thief by his shirt.

"You're one of those kids who live in the barrio with the gangs. Why did you attack my son?"

Navarro still could barely squeak a word out. Damn, his nuts hurt. "Yes, sir, I live in the project, but I'm not in the gangs. They beat me and steal from me."

"So, you think it's okay to attack and steal from my son?"

"No. I'm sorry. I was hungry, is all." Hugo saw no way out except for groveling. He was used to it.

A look passed between the adults. Whether it was the overwhelmingly downtrodden look he displayed or just a tiny pearl of kindness in a world full of ugliness, he never knew.

When he finally stood, Maria was still glaring, and Hugo was still very afraid. The adults steered the three children into their home.

"What's your name?" Officer Gomez demanded.

"Hugo."

"Last name?"

"I don't know."

"Okay. We'll figure that out later. Daniel, take Hugo up to the bathtub. If you're going to eat with us, you're going to have to clean up and smell a little better."

After dinner, the first full meal he could ever remember having, he was allowed to sleep in the basement of the Gomez home. He spent most of his days doing menial chores around the house in the weeks to come. While Daniel was uncertain about Hugo, he was nonetheless friendly enough. Officer Gomez had explained to his son that some children were less blessed and thus should be helped if possible.

While Navarro still did not know what to make of his situation, he was smart enough to bide his time, sensing an opportunity here somewhere.

On a Tuesday evening, after about a month or so of living with the Gomezes, Daniel's father pulled him aside. "Hugo, I appreciate that you've helped us out around the house and behaved yourself. You're a smart boy; I can see that. I have a job for you, and it may be dangerous, but I think you can handle it."

Hugo wasn't sure where this was going and was afraid to ask. He'd gotten used to three meals a day and a warm bed to sleep in at night.

"There are many gangs in your barrio. I'm sure some of them have even picked on you. The police don't care what goes on in Neza. But one of the gangs has been running drugs throughout Toluca, making us look bad. They are very young, and many people don't take them seriously. We need to find out who they are working for so we can put a stop to this."

"Why are you telling me this?"

"We think you can go back there and join them. Then you can let us know where and when they contact those who are running them."

Returning to that hellhole was the last thing Hugo wanted, and his worried look confirmed it.

"If you help us with this, we will make sure we take care of you. Whenever you can leave, you can sleep here. We will help with your studies, and we will put money in a bank account for you."

"Suppose I'm afraid to do this and don't want to?"

"Then I'm sorry, but you'll have to leave my house, and I'll have to take you to the station for assaulting my son."

As a young boy, Hugo did not have much experience in the ways of the world. However, he had been raised in the worst human conditions possible, so he knew when he was fucked.

"How would I do this?" With much disappointment yet a steely resolve, Hugo relented.

Over the next week, and with a great deal of patience, Officer Gomez explained to Hugo what he should do. He told the young boy about the gang leaders and where they hung out.

"The leaders usually meet with their suppliers on Thursday afternoon. They take their drug supply back to the barrio, divvy it up among the younger members—kids your age—and they, in turn, sell it to the guys on the street, who resell it. The kids take their money back home and give it to the leaders, who then pay the supplier, usually on Monday morning."

Hugo was a quick learner, but he was still unsure how to proceed. "How do I get to be one of the runners?"

"That will be up to you. Sometimes it takes a bold act to make the leaders take notice. You are a resourceful boy, and I have faith you can figure something out."

TWENTY-TWO

The Neza cartel was the most ruthless gang within the confines of Neza-Chalco-Itza. It was also responsible for ninety percent of the drug distribution in Central Mexico and beyond.

A cadre of a dozen teenagers ranging in age from sixteen to twenty supervised over one hundred "runners." These were children as young as eight. The younger they were, the less likely they were perceived as troublesome.

The jefe jefe, the "chief" boss, was Ronaldo Navarro. He directed his dozen gang members, who in turn managed the runners. Navarro was the only individual allowed to negotiate with the drug suppliers living outside the barrio.

Hugo had returned to the squalor that was his birthright. He was but one of the million kids who moved about anonymously through the dark and filthy alleys and debris of the notorious slum.

After several weeks of walking and observing, he was able to identify several of the jefes who were responsible for managing the runners.

Still unsure how to get hired, Hugo began paying close attention to one particular jefe that Gomez had told him about. His name was Eduardo Aguilar, and it was apparent that his runners feared him. Rather than rewarding the kids working for him, he disciplined them severely if they did not reach their quota.

Hugo had only heard about this until one Sunday when the youngsters returned to the barrio to turn in their receipts. Pedro, one of the few overweight kids, was late for the third week in a row. Hugo passed a broken-down hut that served as a meeting place for Aguilar when he heard a scream.

"Where is the rest of my money?" Aguilar punched the chubby runner in the face and began kicking him as he fell to the ground. The remaining youngsters stood by, terrified but accepting.

"Get away from me, you fat little fucker. You are not on my team anymore. We are through with you."

As Hugo huddled beside mounds of garbage and filth, he watched the poor kid limp away. A little later, the meeting disbanded, the youngsters leaving Aguilar alone in the decrepit meeting place.

Hugo was worried. He knew he'd probably not get another opportunity to get on the Neza cartel team, so he made his play.

As Aguilar vacated the hut, Hugo purposely bumped into him. A backhand across the face and a snarl smacked the small boy back into the pile of odiferous refuse. "Watch where the fuck you are going, you piece of shit."

Wiping his face, Hugo was quickly on his feet. "I may be little. I may be a piece of shit, but I can do better than the rest of those kids you have working for you."

"How do you know who I am and what I do?" Aguilar was both taken aback and curious at the balls on the kid.

"Everyone knows you are one of the favored ones in the cartel. They say your group of runners is the best and brings in the most money." As young as he was, Hugo was smart enough to blow sunshine up this guy's ass if it helped him get a job.

The truth was, Aguilar was *not* bringing in the most money and was concerned.

"How do I know if you're any good?"

"If you'll take me around the territory tomorrow, I'll memorize where to go and who to contact. Next weekend can be a trial for me. If I work out, you can hire me."

Aguilar was now a little suspicious. "How do you know where my people go on the weekends?"

Since Pedro could no longer show his face in the barrio, Hugo figured piling on wouldn't hurt any. "Pedro told me the other day. He was whining about you hitting him."

Placated, Aguilar seemed to think this made sense. "Be here tomorrow at nine. I'll take you around."

Thus Hugo became one of Aguilar's runners. His first weekend on the streets, he hustled his ass off, delivering brown bags of meth and pot, making sure he collected the proper amount. Aguilar, favorably impressed, made him a permanent member of the team.

After a month or so, Hugo was able to get away for a night to meet with Officer Gomez. The policeman appeared impressed with the youngster's success at being accepted into the gang. He listened carefully as Hugo explained the distribution network, giving the names of the major players.

After spending the night in the Gomez home, Hugo returned to Neza and prepared for his weekend of running drugs. After a wildly successful several days, he returned to the grungy hut where Aguilar would collect his receipts. As he approached the dilapidated structure, he felt a sudden stillness in the air. He entered. A dozen or so grimy boys stood in a circle around the jefe jefe, Ronaldo Navarro, who was speaking.

"Your boss is no longer with us." The kids looked at each other, not knowing what was going on. "As he was leaving yesterday, he was picked up by the police. We are not sure what will happen to him since he is still a minor, but we are also not sure what information he might give them."

Hugo felt certain his visit to Officer Gomez had something to do with this development. Still, he was surprised at the suddenness of the event.

"Until we have a better idea of what this means, we are cutting back the distribution in this territory. Only three of you will continue working. You three are the most profitable, Roberto, Mario, and Hugo, so you will keep going. You will report directly to me. The rest of you should disappear until you hear from me."

Hugo's stomach was doing cartwheels. He supposed that Aguilar talked with Navarro about his runners, but it surprised him that the head boss knew his name. He raised his hand to question the leader.

"What, Hugo?"

Shit, he acted as he knew him. "Jefe, will we continue to meet here?"

Ronaldo smiled. He had been told about this precocious youngster. "No. You three will meet with me separately at a building on the other side of the barrio. I'll give you your allotment, and you will return to me with your collections. We will keep this arrangement until we see what the police do."

Eduardo Aguilar simply disappeared. No one knew whether the police had kept him or if he'd just run away. The three boys met twice weekly with Navarro for six months and continued running drugs. Because of his enthusiasm and intelligence, Hugo quickly became a favorite of the capo.

He was treated better than the rest of the runners, given food, money, and a nicer hut to sleep in. Because of all this attention, he could not get away to meet with Gomez, and the necessity had diminished because of his better living conditions.

Despite the benevolence of Navarro, Hugo had no illusions about his underlying ruthlessness. He continued to perform his duties exemplary and became Ronaldo's right-hand man at the tender age of twelve.

On one sweltering and muggy Saturday afternoon, as Hugo hurried to complete his deliveries and collections, he heard someone yell his name. Walking briskly away from the shouting, he found himself being grabbed by the collar from behind.

"Hugo, where have you been? I haven't seen you in quite a while. Tell me what has been going on."

It was Officer Gomez. Hugo had been so wrapped up in his commitment to Navarro that he had all but forgotten his original pledge to provide information. He was now respected and admired by the members of the Neza cartel, and his close relationship with Ronaldo had earned him food, comfort, money, and no small measure of security and protection.

"Officer Gomez." With a nervous smile, he quickly formulated an acceptable response. "It has taken me some time to get in with the gang. When Aguilar disappeared, I ended up working with Ronaldo Navarro."

"We know this. We have been keeping eyes on you whenever you leave the barrio. Now that you are working directly for the jefe jefe, have you forgotten our arrangement?"

"No, sir. It has just been very difficult to get away." After seeing how quickly his former boss had been eliminated, he was no longer sure he wanted to deliver Navarro to the cops. Hugo had gotten used to his elevated position within the cartel and wanted it to continue.

Gomez's thin mustache twitched, and his eyes narrowed as if he doubted the boy's sincerity. "Tell you what, Hugo. I'll give you another week to come to us with information on where we can arrest your boss. After that, we will come looking for you."

"Yes, sir. I will meet with you at your home in one week." Gomez released Hugo's T-shirt, and the kid immediately hustled down the sidewalk.

For the next week, all Hugo could think about was how to deal with his situation. He had grown very fond of Navarro, and the feeling was mutual. The last thing he wanted now was to have anything to do with Gomez and his family. As a twelve-year-old, he had limited vision for his future. What he knew for sure was that he wanted to be with Ronaldo. The problem was breaking the news to his boss that he had turned on Aguilar.

It was Monday morning at Navarro's hut. The other two runners left after turning in their receipts, and Hugo sat nervously facing his benefactor.

"Ronaldo, I have something I need to tell you."

"Go ahead, Hugo. What's on your mind?"

Fearfully staring at the dirty floor, he began. "I think I know what happened to Aguilar."

With a slightly amused look on a face that could easily have passed for forty, the twenty-year-old capo replied, "And what do you think happened?"

"I think the police picked him up . . . I told them about him. I'm very sorry. I didn't know what else to do. Last week, I tried to steal from one of the officer's sons, and his sister kicked me in the nuts."

"So, you let a *girl* beat the shit out of you?"

"She was big and strong, and she hit me from behind." Even to himself, his excuses sounded whiny.

"Do you know what the cartel does when they find out someone ratted on them?"

"No."

"They kill them. They take a four-inch blade and slice their throat from here to here." The capo's left-to-right slicing motion across Hugo's throat with his finger caused the youngster to piss his pants.

"What do you think is going to happen to you, Hugo?"

"I don't know. I'm sorry, very sorry. I'm telling you because they want me to let them know where you are so they can pick you up. You've been very good to me, and I don't want to let them know. I want to stay with you, please. I just didn't know what to do." Hugo was close to tears.

"Eduardo is dead. The police didn't pick him up. I cut his fucking throat myself. He wasn't making his numbers, he was stealing from me, and then he even tried to go to the cops to get money to turn on me. Before I killed him, he confessed he had been talking to Gomez all along. He knew you were a plant."

Hugo looked stunned. "I thought you told us the cops picked him up."

"I did."

"But why?"

"I try to do what is most effective. If our runners think the cops may be on to us, they'll be more careful. There are times when fear is a good motivator, but not in kids so young. Gomez will do anything to get noticed by his superiors. He told Aguilar about you just as a favor, hoping for bigger fish. Like me."

"So, I didn't have anything to do with his disappearance?" Hugo was still trying to grasp the situation and was still very afraid.

"You did not. When Aguilar told me you were talking to Gomez, I made sure you were one of the three reporting to me. You're smart. Talented and productive. I kept you busy and close by, so I'd know if you tried to contact Gomez. I was hoping you'd have the balls to come to me after Gomez cornered you the other day."

"You knew?" Hugo was surprised at how wide a net Navarro cast.

"Hugo, I have many eyes on the street. Very little happens that I don't find out."

Hugo was quiet for a full minute. He could only think of one question. "Are you going to kill me?"

With a crack of a smile from Navarro, Hugo started breathing again. "Nope. Not this time. You've shown me what you're made of. But we do need to take care of someone."

"Gomez?"

"Yes, Gomez. He has become a pain in the ass, and it appears he won't give up."

Up until this point, Hugo had witnessed several violent assaults and the associated treachery that was an integral part of his line of work. The thought that he had to play a role in such things was becoming a reality.

"Let's do this, Hugo. Visit Gomez as you told him. Tell him he can find me at my 'office' on Tuesday at one in the morning. I'll make sure we have a reception for him."

TWENTY-THREE

Hugo followed Navarro's instructions. On the night in question, contrary to his mentor's directions, he positioned himself to the left of the dilapidated structure behind a pile of refuse. He made sure to arrive before midnight.

He felt it was odd that he was the first to arrive, but he assumed Navarro had things well in hand, so he dismissed the thought.

Ronaldo arrived shortly after 12:30. He sat and waited, holding a four-inch Randall Model 1. It was his favorite blade.

Officer Gomez showed up just before the appointed hour. He sauntered through the doorway confidently. "Navarro, nice to finally meet you."

Hugo crab-walked up to the side of the porous building where he could easily hear the conversation. He positioned himself just to the side of the open doorway.

"I'm sorry it had to be like this, Gomez, but you're impacting my business."

"Like what? Do you think those lieutenants you have working for you are going to show?"

A shadow of concern crossed the younger man's face. He grasped the handle of the knife tightly.

"You're a loser, Navarro. We've had two of your understudies reporting to us for months. Those two are long gone, and the others that were supposed to be here to ambush me were rounded up earlier this evening. You're fucked. Hand over the knife."

Navarro bolted to his feet while kicking his chair back. He assumed a fighting stance as he faced the cop.

Gomez exhaled a resigned sigh as he pulled his service weapon from its holster.

"Goodbye, Eduardo," Hugo heard the policeman say, and then he heard the gunshot.

Hugo was stunned and terrified. The blast left his ears ringing but not hearing. He stumbled through the doorway as Gomez bent down to survey the damage he had wrought.

Navarro's body was on its back. A ragged round hole was punched through his cheek. His lifeless eyes were still open.

Gomez stood. "What are you doing here? Get the fuck out before the rest of my team comes. I'm going to need you in the future."

Hugo's mouth hung open, and he slumped over his jefe's body as tears rolled down his face. Gomez replaced his weapon as he turned to leave the scene of the carnage.

In his dazed state, Hugo's eyes zeroed in on his friend's knife. He grabbed it quietly, stood, and with blazing speed and a blood-curdling scream, vaulted onto the back of Officer Gomez.

The cop had just started to turn at the commotion when Hugo sank the knife to its hilt into the unfortunate policeman's throat. Hugo stabbed again and again as the two of them dropped to the floor, both soaked with the man's geyser-like pulsing blood.

Hugo slumped on top of Gomez, breathing heavily. After several moments, he stood, the policeman's blood still dripping freely down his arms. Taking one last look at Ronaldo, he turned and stumbled out into the night.

He was a teenage murderer—a cop killer. At least now, though, he had a last name. It was Navarro.

Hugo Navarro went into hiding for over a dozen months. During this time, his revenge on the police grew to legendary status among the former cartel members and runners, now mostly disbanded.

One or two of the remaining gang who had worked under Ronaldo attempted to reconstruct the drug enterprise but were unsuccessful.

Occasionally there were whispered sightings of the young killer, all contributing to his growing cult-like status.

Hugo sent word to the remaining two cartel supervisors on his thirteenth birthday. He also contacted three more senior runners, all of whom he knew and trusted. There was to be a meeting at Ronaldo's previous "office."

His elevated status within the barrio was such that the five young men attending the gathering immediately deferred to the smallish but intense Hugo.

An organizational plan, complete with bylaws, rules, compensation, and penalties, was presented. They were going back into the distribution business, but this time, all the players knew the policies and the consequences for coloring outside the lines.

Even at such a young age, his managerial skills garnered respect from those reporting to him. There were occasional bumps in the road, but the severe penalties dissuaded repeat offenses.

By the time he was in his mid-twenties, Hugo Navarro had left the barrio and relocated to Ensenada. He was still a very young man. The coastal city seemed to wash away the filth of his earlier years and offer the promise of a gentler tomorrow.

Running a drug cartel was not without its trials. What made Navarro different from his competitors and those wishing to challenge him was his utter detachment and ruthlessness when meeting out punishment for even the slightest transgression.

Many opposed the young entrepreneur during the early years, but none were up to the task. For that matter, none of them lived. It was said that *you only have one opportunity when you go up against Hugo Navarro. If you are not successful, there will not be another.*

Navarro never, ever let anything he considered an offense go unanswered. Even a hint of disobedience was met with overwhelming violence and lethality.

His drug empire had expanded beyond Mexico City to most of northern Mexico and much of the southwestern United States. Finding places to put the millions of dollars his enterprises raked in became paramount. It was one thing to generate mountains of cash but keeping it and hiding it was an entirely different animal.

As time passed, his competition increased, and his margins were impacted. He became more focused on preserving and investing his already substantial ill-gotten gains.

His initial foray into the Pacific Northwest market with that dipshit car dealer was a disaster. That he was out several million in fentanyl wasn't the end of the world, but it had to be recovered. It could never be acknowledged that someone had bested him.

While Herrera was attempting to locate his purloined drugs, Navarro was focused on locating one Peter Hall, the cocksucker who had disappeared with his twenty million dollars.

It seemed that even when Hugo Navarro attempted to slide into the mainstream of legitimate investing, violence was not consigned to the back seat for long. It became apparent that the search for Hall was going to require a hands-on approach.

TWENTY-FOUR

Sunshine was an anomaly around Seattle. The number of cloudless days in April could be counted on three fingers, but apparently, the stars had aligned for a nice day.

Kevin and Jenne O'Malley had boarded the 9:30 Mukilteo ferry from the island to spend the day in the Bellevue area on the east side of Lake Washington. The air was a chilly forty-eight degrees but was predicted to warm up to the low sixties, and with the northern sun, it might actually feel like seventy degrees by the afternoon.

It was Wednesday, and Kevin was looking forward to his weekly contest on the links with his buddy, Bill Owens. Jenne too, was anticipating a fun-filled day with Shelly. At Nordstrom's.

After the day's events, the four of them met at Kelsey Creek to share a bite to eat.

"So, should we ask who took the money today?" Jenne grinned, needling the two men.

"As you can see, darling, I'm holding a tumbler of that expensive Dalwhinnie that my good friend Bill here has sought to provide."

A shake of the head and a roll of the eyes from Owens ensued as he added, "Yes, Jenne. Your husband is correct. What he didn't say is that the reason I'm buying his booze is because he stunk up the course today. Since I won so much money, I felt it only appropriate to provide necessary imbibements for him. Also, if I didn't pay for his drinks, he probably wouldn't show up next time, and I'd have to look for another pigeon."

Both women gave each other a knowing look while the men continued acting like juveniles. That the four of them were close friends was not lost on any of the other diners.

"Kevin, did you ask Bill about Jake's problem with that St. George project?"

"Damn, I forgot. Bill, a friend of ours on Whidbey, put a few million into a spa development in Utah. Same place we lived for a bit. We even did a little preliminary spec work on the thing. Anyway, it seems the principal ran into some issues with the site, and he's disappeared with the funds. I told him I'd ask you if you knew of any recourse for him."

With a deep sigh, the detective replied, "You *are* aware that I'm a cop in the state of Washington, right? And that this sounds extremely messy. We're talking lawyers, SEC folks, AGs, all kinds of people with initials."

Kevin nodded, fully expecting the direction in which Owens was headed. "Yeah, I figured as much. I guess I'm wondering what you'd do, though, if it happened to you."

Bill let out a laugh. "Firstly, I don't have millions to invest. Yes, I know my wife may, but not me. And secondly, well, I don't know. Maybe his best bet is to hire a detective agency to attempt to locate the guy."

"How does that help him get his money back?" This from Shelly.

"It doesn't. But at least if he can find out where the guy is, then maybe he can sic the state of Utah on him. For that matter, if he's now in some other state, then *they* might be able to do something. This stuff is really out of my league, guys."

Kevin was looking down at the single large ice cube in his drink while he pictured Jake Early at home in his wheelchair. "Thanks, Bill. I'll pass that on to him. I just wish there was some other help we could offer."

"The only thing I might be able to do is send his picture to our state law enforcement groups to notify us if he surfaces. I'll need a complaint from your friend as to what he is being accused of. Also, a picture if you can get one.

"Strangely enough, these things have a way of rearing their ugly heads again. My guess is that you'll be hearing more about this guy in the future. Maybe for now, patience is the best way to go."

Back on Whidbey for the weekend, Kevin once again found himself at the Star Store for provisions. And once again, he saw Francis Early, who was perusing the fine wine section.

"Hey, Francis, what's up? You trying to find something to add to your brother's cellar?"

At first, startled because of his concentration, a warm smile spread across his face. "Hey, Kev, good to see you. Nah, I may not drink, but I do like to see what's new on the shelves here. Every once in a while, I'll come across something that Jake has never heard of. It's kind of a challenge, but he gets a big kick out of it when I bring it home. Say, did you happen to run Jake's situation by your friend, the cop?"

"I did." Kevin proceeded to fill Francis in on the less than promising prospects. "He said if Jake files a complaint and there's a picture of Hall, he can send it out to the state law enforcement groups."

"I guess that helps a little, but otherwise, it looks like we're on our own. Maybe I'll do a little research on him myself. You said you did a little work for that outfit?"

"Yes. For about a month is all."

"You think you can email me anything you have on this outfit? Also, whatever contact info you had for Peter Hall?"

"Sure. We had no NDA or anything, so I'll be happy to send you what I can find."

"I sure appreciate it. I'll start going through some databases and also touch base with a couple of guys I knew from McNeil."

"McNeil?"

"Of course. It's not like there were *just* sexual predators there. I'll admit that's where most of them were housed. But there were a few of us that fell between the cracks. The low-security facilities were overpopulated, and we ended up on the island. We were druggies, sure, but that was all. The guys I keep in touch with have cleaned up their act, and a few have gone into IT work. That's how I got started with the computer stuff. I get stuck every so often and go to them for a bit of help.

"Anyway, I may not get anywhere, but I owe it to my brother to at least try. He's been very good to me."

It was difficult to fathom how different Kevin felt about Francis now compared to their first confrontation.

"He's lucky to have you. I'll get that stuff to you when I get home."

TWENTY-FIVE

Even when Francis Early wasn't playing video games with his ex-prison mates, he was always on the computer.

He spent hours researching. No subject was too arcane, no site too hidden to access. If it wasn't looking for cult wines for his brother, it might be searching for old classmates. With very few friends and, really, no face-to-face contact with other humans on the island, it was no wonder his social skills had atrophied.

Now that he had spent some time with the O'Malleys, he found he liked them. A lot. He was happy, too, that Jake seemed to be coming out of his shell, if only sluggishly.

He felt terrible that his brother had lost so much on that Utah deal, and he vowed to do his best to track down whoever was responsible. Kevin had emailed over the contact information he had used for the developer when he had worked for the guy. At least Francis had a place to start.

First, he started with Peter Hall. Francis found there was scarce information on the public sites. He managed to log into the State of Utah public records network, where he located the corporate documents for CP Ltd. They listed Hall as the president and showed four other officers and board members.

There was *some* information on the web regarding the development company. While they didn't have a website per se, there was plenty of data available on Facebook and some other social networks.

Early was able to see many of the successful projects the company had done as well as the Oakville debacle. The Snow Canyon project was listed only as "under construction." There was even a photo showing Hall with the mayor of Ivins, the town in which the spa was being developed. Francis thought Hall looked like someone from a movie he had seen some years ago, but he couldn't recall which one. At least he could use the photo to accompany the complaint.

Previous investors had many comments—all positive save for a few who had lost money on the Napa deal.

After consuming whatever else he could find on the company, he focused on the St. George project. One of the comments alluded to conflict with one of the Native tribes from the area and how it had halted progress on the construction.

In fact, much of the adjacent property was home to a vast collection of petroglyphs created by the Anasazi. Local archaeologists had pegged their age at over a thousand years. Francis wasn't much of a developer, but even *he* thought it would have been prudent to check out this shit *before* pissing away millions of dollars.

Francis found that the Hopi in Southwest Utah were thought to be descendants of the Anasazi. Several of their Elders were leading the resistance to the Snow Canyon Spa. The local newspapers listed the names of the tribal leaders who were prominent among those featured on the tribe's website.

One of these Elders, a fellow named Adisa who, judging by his Facebook photo, appeared to be well into his eighties, seemed to be the principal protagonist against the spa development.

Octogenarian or not, the fellow was computer literate. In hours, Francis had initiated an email dialogue with him.

Adisa—the Hopi moniker meaning *the lucid one*—was adamant that the development be stopped. He had riled up enough of the locals to encourage the county to halt the project until the BIA reviewed the entire situation. As it stood now, nothing would happen until hell froze over or until the government decided something, whichever came first.

While Francis may have been awkward in face-to-face social encounters, the email ethos was made for him. His immediate rapport with the Hopi resulted in Adisa forwarding everything he had accumulated that had anything to do with Peter Hall or CP Ltd.

The trove of documents, articles, and files was so voluminous that it was necessary to download them from a cloud storage application. The sheer bulk of materials ensured that Francis would see little daylight for many hours. He owed his brother that much.

Most of the forwarded data were various files from one government agency or another. Francis was much more interested in any personal information regarding the missing president of the development company.

Adisa had been prescient enough to include several local newspaper articles highlighting the past successes of CP Ltd., and these included glimpses into Hall's personal life.

One particular story appearing in the *Spectrum* detailed Hall's journey from a failed investor to Home Depot employee and finally to successful entrepreneur. While there was little about his early family life, an older brother was mentioned.

Francis moved on to the public records for Salt Lake County and spent hours poring over birth and death registers. Hall's parents had passed away. The obit mentioned they were survived by three sons, Peter, Mark, and Bobby.

Although Francis was exhausted, he still noted the discrepancy between the newspaper article and the death records.

Shuffling between three computer screens, he quickly found what he was looking for. The article, picked up by the *Spectrum* from the AP, was written by Jay Phillips of the *Salt Lake Tribune*.

A phone call to the newsroom of the *Tribune* turned out to be futile. The message saying Phillips would love to take his call but was on assignment and could the caller please leave a phone number offered little satisfaction.

Again referring to the *Spectrum* story, Francis located an email address for the Salt Lake City reporter. Choosing his words carefully, he related why he was interested in Hall and explained his efforts to find him. He suggested that a real estate developer making off with millions from innocent investors was perhaps of even greater public interest.

He hit *send* and trudged up the stairs to say goodnight to his brother.

The following morning, Francis was surprised to see a response from Phillips in his inbox. The only message in the body of the email was a phone number. It was different from the one he had called yesterday.

"Phillips here. What can I do for you?"

The brusque phone response took Francis by surprise, but he recovered quickly. He supposed big-time reporters didn't have any time for bullshit.

"This is Francis Early. I'm the one who sent the email about Peter Hall."

"Thanks for calling. I wrote that article when the Snow Canyon project was just getting underway. The guy was from Salt Lake City, so there was some interest here. I guess the local St. George paper picked it up. Now I hear the slimebag disappeared with the money."

If Francis had thought Phillips wasn't going to be forthcoming, he was mistaken. The guy was just like his articles—*just the facts, ma'am.*

"Yes. That's correct. I'm doing some research. My brother is out several million dollars. I'm trying to figure out where the guy could be. You said he had only an older brother in your article, but the county records show that he had two brothers. Do you know why?"

"No, I do not." Phillips hesitated a moment as if trying to recall his facts. "Okay. Got it. Before I went to press with that thing, I did a short interview with Hall over the phone. When I asked about his family, he told me his folks were dead, and he had an older brother. Billy or Bobby, something like that."

"Just the one?"

"Yup. It wasn't that important at the time, so I didn't bother to check any public records. It's just what he told me. If the county's documents say there were two brothers, then they're probably correct."

"The brothers' names are Bobby and Mark. Supposedly they're still alive. Doesn't it seem odd he wouldn't mention Mark?"

"Odd, yes. But I've been at this a long time, and there's way odder shit than that in this world. Here's what I'd say. If you manage to get anywhere with this thing, then get back to me. My plate's full right now with all the LDS shenanigans, but I would be thrilled to do a follow-up. Good luck."

Francis heard the disconnect and stared at his phone. He had to admit; the guy *was* direct. He supposed if he could find anything out, Jay Phillips would be an excellent resource.

Francis was a persistent fellow. Spending five years in a maximum-security prison on an island was excellent training in the art of patience. It was what had allowed him to sit for hours, then days on end searching for a green Explorer with Utah plates.

This subtle yet enviable talent enabled him to meander through hours of Facebook and Instagram posts, newspaper articles, classmate postings, obituaries, and birth records.

Francis learned that Bobby, the older brother Peter Hall had acknowledged, had relocated from Salt Lake City to New England. A small blurb in the University of Utah alumni magazine mentioned that Bobby Hall was to be a guest speaker at the spring meeting of the Four Corners Artists Symposium.

This small organization of New England artists was based in Little Compton, RI, and was considered essential for anyone hoping to connect with local and national galleries and agents.

Following up with the group's newsletter, Francis was able to find out that Bobby was a watercolorist and was well known, at least locally, for his distinctive style. The publication also listed his contact information.

"Is this Robert Hall?"

"If you're calling for Bobby Hall, then you've reached him. If you're selling something, goodbye."

"No, wait. I'm not selling anything, Bobby. I'm calling because I'm trying to locate your brother."

After what seemed like a full minute of silence but probably closer to ten seconds in reality, Hall responded. "You're talking about Peter?"

"Yes."

"I haven't heard from him since a Christmas card a few years ago. We were close until we went to college. We hung with different crowds then. Peter always wanted to be with the high rollers. Why are you trying to reach him?"

Francis went through the narrative about his brother, yadda, yadda, yadda, and when he'd finished, he asked, "Also, Bobby, do you have any idea where he might have gone? I realize he is family, but all I'm trying to do is help my brother get his money back."

"Look, if he broke the law or stole some money, I don't care if he is my brother. The last time I saw him in person was at our parents' funeral."

"It said in your parents' obituary that you had another brother. Was that Mark?"

Now it *was* closer to thirty seconds of silence. Bobby answered with an audible sigh, "Mark was our older brother. He was much older. Now he would be in his seventies.

"When the Vietnam War reared its head, Mark became obsessed with opposition to it. When his draft number came up, he moved to Canada. He never came back, and Peter wanted nothing to do with him.

"My mother became pregnant when she was still in her teens. Being members of the LDS Church, she and our father were encouraged mightily to get married before the baby was born. They did, and Peter and I weren't born until much later.

"I've thought about this a lot. Our parents were very conflicted about their religion and eventually left the Church. It took them a very long time, though, and I think Peter and I were in their efforts to bring children into this world that were unencumbered by religious beliefs of any kind.

"At the time Mark left the country, we were toddlers. I only ever saw him one other time. Before Peter and I left for college, our parents insisted we take a family trip up to Canada. We met with Mark in Vancouver. We had lunch and visited for a while, and then drove back to Utah.

"I corresponded with him for a while when I was in college, and I know he stayed in touch with our parents up until they passed away. Peter said he couldn't be bothered reaching out to someone he never knew. He just considered him not a part of our family."

Francis had a sinking feeling he was at another dead end. "Is it possible Peter might have tried to get in touch with Mark?"

"Possible, I guess. But highly unlikely. I'm not even sure if Peter knows where he is."

"Do you know where Mark is?"

"No, not really. About ten years ago, my folks died in an auto accident. I recall my mom saying something about Mark the week before. She said she had received a photo postcard of the view from Mark's apartment. She said it was across from Stanley Park. It only stuck in my mind because it was the last time we talked on the phone. She was dead the next week."

"That must have been awful, Bobby. I'm sorry."

"Thanks, Francis; I appreciate the thought. You sound like a nice guy, and I wish you well in finding my brother. Peter was always looking for the big score. I was a bit leery of his tactics. If I think of something that might help, I'll get back to you."

Living in the Northwest, Francis knew that Stanley Park was in Vancouver, BC. Hell, he'd even been there several times. The fact that Mark Hall lived across from Stanley Park at one point, and there was only the remotest chance he knew where his brother was, did not bode well for his search.

There must be some other way, he thought.

TWENTY-SIX

Navarro's concern for the fentanyl sitting in a barn in Washington State was not overly immediate. Albert had taken care of Burns, and if the stuff hadn't been found by now, then it was indeed well hidden.

The twenty million he'd invested with CP Ltd., though, was giving him a royal pain in the ass. That fuckstick Hall had to be made an example of. The trouble was, he had no idea where the sonofabitch had gone.

He'd gone through some of the documents he'd signed when he had loaned the money to Hall and found that they listed other prominent investors. He was the largest but coming in second was someone named Early.

Sure, he was in first position on the note, but now that the local tribes had made such a stink about things, the dirt was worth a fraction of its pegged value.

He copied the guy's address and opened Google Maps to see where he might have to go to visit the fellow. He didn't know where Hall was, but maybe this Early did.

Shit. He lived on some island. *And* it was back up in Washington State. *What were the odds?*

He knew Albert wasn't gonna like this, but he'd have to send him back up there to see if Early knew anything about Hall. Albert was probably overkill for a job like this, but he'd rather send him than have to go way the fuck up there himself.

This time Herrera *flew* up to the Evergreen State. If he *had* to go there—and he did—then he'd make sure it would be a quick trip. Hugo had given him strict instructions to maintain a low profile.

How he would meet up with this Early fellow and discuss his investment in CP Ltd. was still a plan in the making. Maybe he'd bump into him in a bar or something.

He landed at SeaTac at noon. And, no surprise, it was raining. *Damn, these people must have webbed feet*, he thought. *Late April and still gray skies and rain.* He was glad it would be a short trip.

Hugo had given him an address, but that was all. After getting into his rental, a Chevy Silverado, he plugged it into the nav system on the pickup. The driving directions showed a three-hour trip. This was a surprise.

Upon closer inspection, Albert noticed that the guy lived on a goddamn island. A very strangely shaped one at that. *And* he had to take a fucking *boat* to get there. *No wonder it takes so long. Is nothing easy in this state?*

He slogged through the midday traffic on I-5, which ran through the center of the city of Seattle. Arriving at the ferry terminal in Mukilteo—*where do they come up with these names?*—he attempted to try to understand the instructions on the fifty or so signs before the entrance to the terminal.

Judging by the blaring of horns and the flipped birds, he figured he must have misunderstood the lanes or directions or something. After a rebuke from the toll booth attendant, he was directed to the end of the line.

"Pay attention to the signs this time and turn off your engine when you stop." He wanted to wipe the smirk off the bitch's face with a backhand, but he was sure Hugo would have frowned upon such indiscretion. God, he hated Washington.

Albert was a killer and a tough motherfucker. He was also nervous as hell trying to maneuver his large pickup with its extended mirrors through the twists and turns necessary to get on the ferry. He'd already pissed enough people off and, with no option to retaliate, he felt emasculated. It was like being in the first grade with all the kids laughing at him.

Ending up in the outside lane on the starboard side of the *Tokitae* ferry, he dutifully set his parking brake and turned off the engine. He'd managed to avoid any severe damage to the vehicle but did sustain a smashed passenger-side mirror when he got a little too close to one of the support beams. He thought he saw a couple of the crew looking his way and smiling.

It was one thing dealing with drug dealers and murdering competitors. He wanted nothing to do, though, with the folks in fluorescent yellow slickers telling him what to do and where to go.

He managed to depart the vessel with no more damage to the truck as the ferry poured its stream of vehicles into the tiny town of Clinton on Whidbey Island.

The rain had stopped, and the late afternoon sun began poking through the marine layer. There appeared to be only one major road on the island. The map showed the landmass as quite long but also very skinny in places.

About a mile from the dock was the turnoff to Langley, the principal city on the south end of Whidbey Island. Albert figured it made sense to stop there, get the lie of the land.

Langley was little more than a village. With one general store, a half dozen or so eating establishments, numerous coffee stands, and no red lights, it was a dead ringer for a Hallmark Channel movie set. Tourists and locals alike meandered through the gift shops, gazed out over Saratoga Passage hoping to see a gray or an orca, and generally smiled at one another. It was as if there were no religions or politics to argue about.

Albert figured these people *had* to be smoking something. No way they could be this happy. After three or four smiles and nods from passersby, he found himself reciprocating. He just *had* to get back home, where being permanently pissed off was much more the norm.

The town was too small for any chain restaurants or bars, and there appeared to be no central gathering place to initiate conversation.

With no alternative but to track down Jake Early, Herrera proceeded with a more direct approach. According to the nav system in his rental, Early's home was only three or four miles away. Albert figured the sooner he took care of business, the sooner he could vacate this strange little place.

"Jake, I'm gonna go into town to pick up some groceries. Anything you need?" Francis donned a vest as he headed for the door.

"I'm good, thanks. Hey, you get anywhere on your research, looking for Hall?"

"Nothing definite yet, but I did find a picture of that asshole. Thought you could use it to file that complaint with Kevin's buddy. I'll get it to you when I get back, and we can at least make sure the crook gets stopped if he crosses state lines."

Not five minutes after Francis had left, the doorbell buzzed. The Ring app on Jake's phone showed a medium-sized male, probably in his late thirties, with several days' facial hair growth. Hispanic-looking and wearing a Padres baseball cap, the guy either had overdeveloped shoulders or his Carhartt jacket was several sizes too big.

"Yes?" Jake spoke through the mic on the doorbell as he wheeled his way toward the door.

"Is this the Early residence?"

"It is. What can I do for you?"

"I'm sorry to bother you, but my boss wanted me to ask you some things about the Snow Canyon Spa."

The words were barely out of the killer's mouth when the heavy fir door swung open.

"I'm Jake Early."

Jake never went anywhere anymore, but he still recalled the reaction some folks had when they were surprised by a person in a wheelchair.

"Um … er … hi. My … um … my name is Albert Herrera."

Jake stuck his hand out. His visitor grasped it with some reluctance. *Maybe he thinks whatever put me in this chair is contagious*, Jake surmised.

When the caller finally returned his clasp, Jake was taken aback by the strength of the man's grip.

"Come in, Albert, and have a seat. Please tell me why you're here."

Herrera gingerly stepped into the great room and cautiously sat on one of the upholstered leather chairs. He seemed still taken aback at the presence of the wheelchair. Jake had seen some strange reactions, but this guy's was slightly over the top.

"Maybe you should tell me why you're here."

Still with his eyes glued to the wheelchair, Herrera began his spiel.

"My boss—his name is Navarro—invested some money with CP Ltd. It was for the Snow Canyon Spa development. The guy running the thing disappeared with the money, and nobody knows where he is.

"Hugo came across some documents that showed the other investors, and you were listed as one of them. He wanted to know if you had any idea where this Hall guy had gone."

"Well, Albert, I'm trying to find him as well. He's got a bunch of my money, and I'd like to get it back. I have two questions for you. Why didn't you or Navarro call me and have this discussion? And secondly, is my appearance in this chair making you uneasy?" Jake was seldom this confrontational, but something about the man caused him concern.

Herrera blushed a little. "Um, about the chair. When I was a kid, I spent some time in one. It just brought back memories. That's all.

"The reason I made the trip is cuz my boss wanted me to. He likes to do things in person. He put a great deal of money into this thing."

Jake thought this a bit odd, but he let it go. "Well, it sounds like we both would like to find Peter Hall. My brother is trying to search for him on the internet. You leave me your contact info, I'll reach out to you if I hear anything. You can do the same for me."

As Herrera stood to leave, Jake followed him to the door. He was looking forward to filling Francis in on this developing situation.

Herrera turned, and this time, he extended a hand. "Thanks, Jake. I'll fill in my boss on what we discussed. I appreciate you getting back to me if you hear anything."

With another incredibly firm handshake, he turned, closed the door, and left. Jake sat facing the door, unsure what to make of his visitor. There seemed to be a vulnerability there, but that was overpowered by a menacing quality that could not be disguised.

"We had a visitor while you were gone." Francis had just walked into the house with two bags of groceries in his arms.

"A visitor?"

Because of the rural nature of the island, there were no door-to-door salespeople or religion peddlers. It was one of the benefits of living in a place surrounded by water. Very, very rarely did a *visitor* stop by unannounced.

"Yup. This guy—kind of an odd duck, by the way—has a boss who sent him up here to see if we knew where Hall took off to. The guy had put big money into the deal."

"How do you mean, odd?"

"I don't know for certain. He wasn't overtly threatening or anything, but there was something scary about him."

"Tell me what he said."

"It was straightforward. He asked if I knew where Hall was. I told him no. He left me his contact information, and I told him if *he* heard anything to let me know as well. Told me his boss's name was Hugo Navarro."

Francis rubbed the top of his shaved head like a crystal ball that might enlighten him. "So, his boss was screwed on the deal too."

"Yes, it appears. Though by the way the fellow acted, he isn't going to give up searching for him anytime soon."

"Well, at least we're not the only ones looking for him. Maybe we'll hear from him. In the meantime, I'll keep looking."

TWENTY-SEVEN

"Jenne, I sure wish there was some way we could help Jake locate that real estate guy who disappeared with all the money," Kevin said as he put on his raincoat. It was a drizzly day at the end of April, and Kevin was headed out to the hardware store to pick up some plumbing supplies.

"Me too. I think Francis is focusing on it full time, though, and I can't imagine we can do any better."

"I think I'll stop by their place on the way home to see how they're making out. You need me to pick up anything?"

"Nah, I'm taking off to meet Shelly. We've got some things to take care of. Liz Burns is selling her ranch, and we're helping her stage the place for photos."

"Where's she going?"

"She's not sure yet. Probably stay in the area as long as the kids are in school. She just doesn't want all the headaches and the upkeep for that big place. That was all Robbie's idea."

"You know she's selling the dealerships to some national outfit, right?"

"I heard. I don't blame her. She'll be set for life and have none of the management headaches to worry about. I wish her the best."

"Hi to Shelly. See you tonight."

Once again, Jake Early opened the door even before Kevin had reached the doorbell.

"Geez, Jake, you love that Ring app, don't you?"

"I'm just surprised you don't have more sympathy for a poor wheelchair-bound shut-in."

"Good one. You're certainly not poor, and you're only a shut-in out of choice. I'll agree that you're stuck in that chair, but that's the only slack I'm cutting you."

"Ouch, I think I'm beginning to like you. At least you treat me like you treat everybody else. You know, like shit."

"Hah, another good one. How about asking me in?"

Jake quickly maneuvered his chair away from the door to make way for Kevin.

"To what do I owe the pleasure?"

"I was out getting some toilet repair crap from Ace, so I thought I'd stop by and see how Francis was making out trying to find Peter Hall. Any luck?"

"My brother has been down in his office for what seems like weeks. Let's get him up here and grill him."

Francis arrived after several shouts from Jake. With scraggly facial hair almost reaching the bags under his eyes, he looked in desperate need of sleep.

"Hey, Kev, s'up?"

"Francis, you kinda look like shit."

"Yeah, I've been at it for a while."

"Can you fill us in on what you've found?"

"Sure." Francis brought them up to speed on his efforts, including Adisa, the reporter, Phillips, and the brothers Bobby and Mark.

"I've covered a lot of ground, it seems, but I'm not sure I'm making any progress. I think I'm gonna see what I can find out about that Navarro person. Did you fill Kevin in on your visitor?"

"No, I didn't have a chance yet." Jake proceeded to relate his experience the previous day when he'd received a visit from Albert Herrera.

Kevin held his tongue until Jake had finished and Francis had chipped in with a few comments.

"Well, it sounds like you two aren't the only ones looking for Hall. Maybe this Navarro will figure out where he went."

"Yeah, maybe." Francis wasn't overly confident in anyone else succeeding where he hadn't.

"Good to see you, Kev. I'm gonna go hit the hay for a few hours before I get back to it."

After Francis had gone, Kevin looked at Jake. "Is he always this focused?"

"When he gets into something, he's like a Pitbull with a pork chop. He won't even come up for air. If I didn't bring him sandwiches and water, he'd probably expire down there. I'm surprised he even takes a break to hit the head."

"It looks like he's made *some* progress. At least he's gotten further than anyone else. Are you going to keep your visitor abreast of what you've learned so far?"

"I think the less we have to do with him, the better. If I think it'll give us a better chance to locate Hall, then maybe. I'd like to see what Francis finds out about the guy first."

"Good luck. Let me know if there's anything we can do," Kevin offered as he made his way out the door.

TWENTY-EIGHT

"So, this Early, he has no idea where Hall is?" Navarro started interrogating Herrera as soon as Albert was able to reach him. The cell service on Whidbey was notoriously unreliable.

"He said he was trying to find out, but so far, he hasn't gotten anywhere."

"Do you believe him?"

"The guy's a cripple. His house is pretty cool, but I don't think he ever leaves it. I'm sure he doesn't know where Hall is. Said his brother was doing some stuff on the computer to try and find out where he is."

Albert was on his way to Clinton to catch the 6:30 boat to Mukilteo. He couldn't wait to get back to San Diego. This place sucked.

"There's not much for you to do here, Albert. Maybe you should hang out up there for a while; keep an eye on things."

Fuck me, Albert thought. He knew when his boss suggested something . . . it wasn't a suggestion. What could he do hanging out in some hotel in the rain in this shithole of a state?

"Are you sure? It doesn't look like anything's gonna happen anytime soon."

"Yes, I'm sure. Check on that barn where the fentanyl is supposed to be if you can manage it. If that doesn't work out, keep an eye on Early and his brother. Maybe they'll get lucky."

Albert was frustrated. He was confident Navarro had no idea what a tiny place South Whidbey Island was and that there was no place to hide with any degree of anonymity. He also knew better than to try to change his jefe's mind.

"Okay, boss, I'll stick around in case something comes up. Please let me know when I can return to San Diego."

Herrera managed to navigate his way through the toll booths and ferry lines without incident. It wasn't easy to see, even though it was only half-past six. Getting used to the lack of daylight in Washington was difficult for him.

He found an upscale hotel halfway between Mukilteo and Carnation in the affluent city of Redmond. Hugo was adamant that Albert be comfortable if he needed to be on the road. He felt it essential to keep his people happy. Unfortunately, Herrera spent the balance of the evening trying to figure out how to spend the rest of his time while marooned in this depressingly damp and dismal climate.

Twenty-Nine

Jenne and Shelly had spent most of the week helping stage the Burns property in readiness to put it on the market. The land and trees didn't need any boosting. It was stunning, even from the road, and once you got up by the house, it was a marvelous oasis.

As an interior designer, Jenne's decades allowed her to visualize what made sense and what didn't. Since she was a close friend of Liz Burns, Shelly served to buffer any conflict that might arise.

Frequently what a homeowner thought was "just perfect" was more a reflection of their tastes, not necessarily the current style or something that would appeal to most house hunters.

"It's not anything close to what I would have thought to do, but I've got to admit it looks stunning." Now that everything had been pulled together, Liz was blown away by the finished product.

"If this place doesn't sell in three or four days, I'll be shocked. When does the listing go online?" Shelly, too, was impressed.

"They said it would go on next Thursday. Just in time for 'open house' over the weekend."

Jenne was pleased with the result. "The house is going to be well received. I'm certain of that. But anyone looking at this place would have to be a horse person, especially since you've got several million sunk into that barn. Is it in good enough shape to walk people through it? I realize it's not finished, but still, folks are going to want to see it."

"I've had some contractors clean up the place as much as possible. The drywall is mostly finished, and much of the trim work has been done. The painting hasn't been started, and the viewing booth just off the loft is still just framed in," Liz offered hopefully.

Jenne looked pensive for a moment before she spoke. "Why don't Shelly and I do a walk-through? It should be okay if it's clean and folks can visualize the finished product. It doesn't make sense, though, to put the ranch on the market unless prospective buyers can understand exactly what they're getting."

"Makes sense to me. Why don't you and Shelly take a look? I'll finish up a few things in here before they come to take photos. I appreciate all your help. You two have been wonderful."

The two friends made their way to the vast structure. The rain had finally stopped, and a few sunbreaks had even begun to materialize. They slid open the massive barn doors and managed to find most of the switches that controlled the lighting.

"Sheesh, this place is ginormous." Shelly voiced the same thought that was running through Jenne's mind.

The arena was bathed in light, as were the stalls and whatever ancillary areas could be seen from their vantage point. The arena surface, a combination of silica sand mixed with a rubber component, was combed tidily.

"Well, if they stopped right here, the buyers would love it. Let's take a walk through the rest of the place." Jenne led the way past the stalls and up the wide staircase. The only sounds in the cavernous structure were their footfalls on the steps and the occasional creak of a windblown door.

At the top of the stairs, another bank of switches controlled the upper lighting. When Jenne flipped the controls, the reception area and viewing platform were illuminated.

"Liz was right. The only area not drywalled is half the back wall of the viewing platform and the side walls. Wonder why they left off there."

Shelly was still gawking at the Brazilian cherry floors and just now noticed the anomaly. "It does seem a little strange. Let me give Liz a call, and I'll ask."

While Shelly was on the phone, Jenne wandered over to the viewing platform. The entire arena bathed in light below was a spectacular sight. If someone with plenty of money and a love for horses was looking for a one-in-a-million ranch, this was the place.

The lack of drywall on the sides and back gave her the feeling of floating twenty-five feet above the ground.

"Yikes, it's a little scary up here." Shelly had ambled over after her phone call.

"Liz said she doesn't know why they stopped there. Robbie hired a contractor to finish the drywall shortly before he was killed. He told them to hold off on the platform area until he returned from his Napa meeting. Course, he never made it back."

While Shelly was speaking, Jenne wandered around the twenty-by-fifteen viewing area, just off the large gathering area.

"Huh, looks like this back wall is double studded, almost like a plumbing wall. I don't remember that in any of our drawings."

"Could the contractor have done that on his own?"

"Not without us or the owner telling him what to do. Maybe Robbie needed it done for something. I'll check with Kevin just in case. At any rate, I can't imagine this area that's not drywalled being a problem for prospective buyers.

"I'll suggest that Liz put a couple of traffic cones up here just to warn folks that it could be dangerous. Other than that, I think she should be able to publish the listing."

THIRTY

Francis had started looking into Hugo Navarro immediately after Kevin had left their house. He began by using Check Them, Google, and Spock, three of his favorite search engines for finding people.

No luck. He wasn't surprised; it was rarely that easy. It was time for him to pull out the big guns.

His fellow gamers were well versed in computer searches. Two of them even offered it as a service to ex-cons searching for estranged family members. He sent a group email to his former jail mates and asked if they knew the name, or if not, would they try to find it. In their spare time, of course.

Francis knew that if there were anything anywhere on Hugo Navarro, his buddies would find it. Right now, he *had* to get some rest.

After his first good night's sleep in weeks, Francis once again found himself at his computer. His office was a measly ten-by-fifteen closet of a room compared to the rest of the spaces in the house. It was adjacent to the wine cellar of which his brother was so fond.

After his run-in with drugs and the law, he'd sworn off anything that might muddle whatever remaining brain cells he had. His proximity to several thousand bottles of wine was more ironic than it was a temptation.

Even though Whidbey was an island, it had outstanding internet capabilities. Both Comcast and Whidbey Telecom offered download speeds of up to one gig per second, which was more than enough for research purposes.

For his gaming, he had recently installed a Dell Alienware Aurora Ryzen Edition R10 desktop. Coupled with two additional monitors and his wired keyboard, the hardware took up all the available desk space.

His only concession to manual communication was a half dozen legal pads and a box of pre-sharpened Ticonderoga No. 2 pencils residing on the desk return to his right. Occasional scribbled notes haphazardly appeared on them.

The darkened room resembled more the cockpit of the *Starship Enterprise* than a residential office. On this day, refreshed by seven hours of shut-eye, he was eager to get going.

He felt stymied at this point, finding nothing more than cul-de-sacs. He'd learned patience while at McNeil, but that was wearing thin. There *had* to be some way of stirring the pot.

He thought of the old Hopi, Adisa, and how he had successfully put a stop to the Snow Canyon project. Then he had another thought.

He rifled off a quick note to the Elder, including his phone number, and asked if he could speak with him. He wasn't sure how lucid the guy would be—he was in his eighties, after all.

Francis had muted his ringtone when he'd originally purchased his phone and had never turned it back on. He was not a big talker, and the only calls he ever received were from his brother or some unfortunate telemarketer.

If some poor soul could connect with Francis, trying to sell something turned out to be the last thing on their mind. Neither the caller nor the company would bother him again. Francis had a foolproof way of avoiding any future contact.

He neither threatened nor lied. He simply and quietly told them the truth. "I used to be an inmate at the penitentiary on McNeil Island, and I'm never going to prison again. Goodbye." It always seemed to work.

When his Galaxy S-10 began vibrating and skittering across one of the legal pads, he answered it immediately.

"Hello?"

"Is this Francis Early?" a high-pitched but clearly spoken voice inquired.

"It is. Who is this?" Francis asked cautiously, thinking he might have to explain his past again.

"This is Adisa. You wanted to speak with me." The man's voice was rock-steady. He could have narrated books on tape for a living.

Francis stumbled for a few seconds, nonplussed at the old Hopi replying to his email so quickly. "Th-thank you for calling me so soon."

"I will tell you, son, it's not like I have many things to do here. Visiting with people on the phone and spending time with my family fills most of my days."

"I … I appreciate you sending me the information on the Snow Canyon project. As I told you in my emails, Peter Hall has disappeared with the money from the investors, including my brother's."

"I am sorry about that. I was not a fan of that Hall fellow. I just tried to tell him that if he could find a way to avoid our sacred prayer grounds, then I wouldn't care about his spa. Our tribe here is impoverished. Those religious grounds are all that is left of our ancestors.

"He did not want to change any of the plans, said it would be too expensive. I do not regret my actions, and I'm glad the BIA agreed to review things. There's not much I can do to help you."

"Yes, I'm sure I would feel the same way if I were you. I think there might be a way for me to find out where Hall is hiding out, but I'm going to need your permission for something."

"What would you need my permission for?"

"I thought if I could post a story on Facebook about you dropping your opposition to the spa, then we might hear from Hall. I have some friends who might be able to trace his email to a location."

"I told you. We will not drop our objections to the project."

Francis hurried to get his message across. "Yes, I'm not suggesting you do that. I would like to post a phony story that says you will. We just need him to respond or inquire about it." He rushed to continue. "Adisa, I will put together a legal document that says you have no intention of letting the development go forward and that the responsibility for any misrepresentation is all mine."

It was silent for so long, Francis wondered if the old man was still alive. "Adisa?"

"Yes, I am here."

"Do you think it'll be okay if I do this?"

"I think you are an honorable man, but I need to be certain that this in no way jeopardizes our holy ground."

"How about if I get something written up and get it to you? If you're comfortable with it, then I can move forward. If you aren't, I'll forget about it."

"Do you think this will help?"

"I don't know. All I do know is that now we're at a dead-end, and I sure hate to let this guy get away with millions of dollars."

"Okay. I'll look forward to seeing what you propose."

Francis spent several hours writing and rewriting what he thought made sense. One of his gaming buddies, also a graduate of McNeil, had begun to study law while incarcerated. Although he would never be allowed to take the bar exam, he had more than enough hours to qualify.

Francis emailed his marked-up version of the letter to James, the pseudo attorney, to ask his opinion.

"I think most of what you have here is fine, Francis. Remember, you're just posting a story to Facebook. Nothing is binding about it, and half the shit on there is made up anyway."

"Yeah, I know. I just want the old guy to feel comfortable enough to let me do it. If there's any response from Hall, he might end up touching base with the tribe down there, and I'll need him to back me up. Frankly, I'm glad they stopped the fucker from building near their land. I'm just trying to find him to get my brother's dough back."

"Well, this looks good. I've added a few legalese terms that should make your friend comfortable. Bottom line is, they're safe. There's nothing you can say or do that will change their situation."

"Thanks very much, James. Talk to you later."

"Francis, wait, hold on …"

"What?"

"Mickey's got something for you."

"What something?"

"He was digging into that name you gave us to find out about."

Francis was trying to remember what name he was talking about. He knew he'd been tired. "I got nothin'. What name?"

"Navarro, remember? You passed it along to see if the Hackers could find something."

Things finally clicked into place. "Shit, yes. I'm sorry, I forgot. I was pretty exhausted that night."

The hackers were three McNeil alumni who were more proficient with computer searches than most kids working sixty hours a week at Microsoft. Mickey, Otis, and Sparks had begun their tutelage while in the prison. Because they were *only* drug abusers and dealers yet still thrown in with killers and sexual predators, they received some leniency when it came to their freedom.

They were allowed to use laptops but initially under supervision. When it appeared as though they were behaving, the guards grew bored and finally let them do whatever they wanted. They had more serious felons to attend to.

Eventually, the three found a way in to the prison's router, thus allowing them to roam freely on the Internet. Twelve hours a day scouring the World Wide Web for four or five years provided a vastly superior learning experience than that of any college or tech school program.

Francis had attempted to keep up with them but to no avail. He told them it was due to the lack of dexterity in his stubby fingers. Deep down, though, he knew the three were far quicker and brighter than he was when it came to technical issues.

"What did he find out?"

"Call him. He wants to talk to you."

After they'd said their goodbyes, Francis immediately called Mickey. "Mick, it's Francis. Whatcha got on that Navarro guy?"

"Before I tell you what I found, I gotta ask, why are you looking into this guy?"

"He's an investor in the same deal my brother's into. He sent one of his employees here to ask if we knew anything about a Peter Hall. He's the developer, and he disappeared with all the money from the investors. Nobody knows where he went."

"It wasn't easy finding out anything about this guy. Know why?"

"Just tell me, Mick."

"Hugo Navarro very quietly ran the biggest drug-smuggling operation in the Western US."

"Huh, you're kidding!"

"I'm not. I had to get into some old articles from *El Universal.* It's all in Spanish, but my Word program does a good job translating. Also, Otis, being Mexican, did most of the work."

"Why would he be investing in a development in St. George, Utah?"

"Word is, he's been trying to get out of the drug business for a few years now. He's putting his money into real estate, casinos and making hard money loans to legitimate developers.

"This guy was, and probably still is, one ruthless motherfucker, Francis. He's killed competitors and cops alike. The murders are always violent. He likes to set an example.

"The cops in Mexico *and* the DEA agents have never been able to lay a glove on the guy. It seems whenever they get close, somebody either dies or disappears. They also say he's relentless when it comes to payback. There's no slight too insignificant for him to ignore. Guy's a really bad dude.

"One other thing. He has a right-hand man, an enforcer, name of Herrera. He's no one to mess with. According to what we found, he comes across as your average Joe, but word is he's a vicious sonofabitch."

"That sounds like the guy who showed up here trying to see if Jake knew anything about Hall's disappearance."

"It probably was. If I were you, I'd stay as far away from Navarro and his crew as I could. These are not nice people."

"You've been a big help, Mickey. Thanks for doing all the legwork."

"One thing, Francis. Do not piss these guys off. Just stay away from them."

THIRTY-ONE

Two days after Francis had emailed the letter explaining that he understood the local Hopi tribe was in no way lifting their objections to the Snow Canyon Spa, he heard from Adisa.

"Francis, this is Adisa. I have received your letter."

When nothing more was said for at least ten seconds, Francis responded. "Thank you for calling, Adisa. What did you think of my letter?"

"It looks acceptable."

Another ten seconds. "Um, does that mean I can post something on Facebook?"

"Yes, but I've been thinking."

The old-timer had a way of making Francis feel uncomfortable. "Yes?"

"I think this story you are going to make up will make more sense if I post it on *our* Facebook page. If you intend to get this Hall fellow to respond, he is more likely to do so if it comes directly from the tribe. Does that make sense?"

Francis was moved that the tribe Elder would think to extend himself in this manner. "It makes a lot of sense, Adisa. I would greatly appreciate it, but I don't want you, folks, to go to any trouble. You have had enough in dealing with this man."

He wasn't sure, but he thought the old man chuckled. "Francis, when you have lived as long as I have, you see many wonderful things. Unfortunately, you also see many injustices. When an individual has an opportunity to right an injustice, it is incumbent upon that person to make it so. I have a contact at the BIA. I'll inform him of what we are doing to ensure this will not affect their review of our situation. He is a good friend—I trust him. We would be unhappy if you do not let us assist in this endeavor."

Francis began to wonder: When he was as old as Adisa, would he even be half as wise or as caring?

"That is very kind of you, Adisa. Thank you."

"When you have put something together that you think will be effective, just email me. I'll post it. Until then, I wish you well."

Francis disconnected the call and sat at his desk for another five minutes. It was such a small thing, but because of it, he felt just a tad bit better about the human race.

It took him two days and several hours of consultation with his brother before he was happy to send it off to Adisa.

The Hopi Tribe has objected to the Development of the Snow Canyon Spa in St. George, Utah. Our concern has been the damage that would be done to our holy ceremonial grounds. We have consulted with our tribal council and the Bureau of Indian Affairs.

We understand the need for responsible development and the desire to share the beautiful geography and culture that southwest Utah offers. Snow Canyon may be smaller, but it is no less beautiful than Zion or Bryce. It would be a shame not to expose it to a greater number of people.

If we get concrete assurances from CP Ltd. that no harm or damage will come to our land and they will respect our traditions, we will lift our objections to the development. Please get in touch with us if you would like to discuss this.

Francis began checking the tribe's Facebook page the day after he forwarded his statement. When he checked on the third day, it was posted right alongside a spectacular photo of Snow Canyon at sunset.

When his email notification chimed, he saw the message from Adisa.

Hope you liked the photo (smiley face). If I hear anything from Hall, you'll be the first to know.

Francis would continue to do his research, but he felt he could relax, if just a little.

THIRTY-TWO

Peter Hall pulled a two-by-three folded card from his wallet. It had been folded over ten years ago and had never been unfolded. Even so, the folds had cracked, and one of the corners became detached.

He laid it on a table and, after reattaching the section, read the note he had received over a decade ago.

Peter, I know you've never acknowledged Mark as part of the family, but he is your brother, after all. This postcard was included in the last letter I received from him. It's from Stanley Park, which is near where he lives. Try to find it in your heart to connect with him someday. It would mean a great deal to me.

Mom

Hall stared at it for a minute, thinking. He had received the postcard the week after his parents were killed. At the time, his grief, coupled with his new company, had caused him to simply fold the thing up and stick it in his wallet. He'd held on to it more as a keepsake from his mother than with any intention of contacting his brother.

He was hiding out in another country because he was a crook. The twenty million he had absconded with was now in an untraceable numbered account in the British Virgin Islands. He had enough money for the rest of his life, but what kind of a life would it be?

Several weeks passed, and even though it was late spring, the rain persisted. Hall was more depressed than anyone with twenty million in the bank should have been. He had no friends, no plans, no future. He pulled out his wallet, unfolded the card for the second time in many years, and opened his laptop.

He opened CheckPeople.com and typed in Mark Hall. There were plenty in the Vancouver area, but isolating his brother was a simple matter. It cost him one hundred dollars in the end, but the app lived up to its reputation. Within five minutes, he had the address and phone number he was looking for.

Rather than calling Mark, he chose to pay a visit to his older sibling. His quest was a twentystory high-rise just off Lagoon Drive. The condo building boasted the best view of Stanley Park in the city, and after exiting the elevator on the nineteenth floor, Peter had to agree.

He slowly approached the specified unit number, still unsure why he was there or what he would say. The stylish bronze door knocker, including a peephole, beckoned him. He knocked.

Brisk footsteps echoed on concrete from the other side of the door. Then silence and a slight shadow across the peephole. The door opened, and a slightly bald, slender man with kind eyes and reading glasses appeared.

The two brothers looked at each other for a moment until one of them said, "Please come in, Peter. It's been a long time."

The high-ceilinged loft was essentially a great room, including a stylish kitchen and two en suite bedrooms. The concrete floors and simple yet elegant furnishings spoke of the owner's excellent taste. A wall of bookcases filled with hundreds of volumes and accented with memorabilia and tchotchkes hinted at a well-traveled and educated occupant.

The floor-to-ceiling gas fireplace comfortably warmed the place, and two welcoming upholstered chairs beckoned.

"Have a seat. Can I get you something? It's around cocktail hour; perhaps a scotch? I'm having one."

"That sounds very good, Mark. Thank you."

Mark retrieved two crystal tumblers from one of the open shelves and placed one large, square ice cube in each. Two fingers of eighteen-year-old Glenmorangie single malt were poured gently over the ice. All the while, there was silence.

He walked back to the fireplace, handed Peter a glass, and raised his. "Here's to seeing you again, and here's to our parents. Mom would be glad you're here."

As Peter touched his brother's glass, he said, "You're right—she would."

Still not sure what to say, Peter let his brother start.

"I know you haven't felt any reason to stay connected, Peter, but I've always kept up on what was happening with my two younger brothers. Bobby likes the East Coast, and from what I hear, he's become extremely good at painting. I've followed your business and saw that you've made quite a name for yourself with some very successful projects."

As Mark continued with his narrative, Peter looked into his scotch, thinking, *Sure, very successful. Lost a bunch in Napa, then tried to screw over some Indians, then took off with all the investors' money. Yeah, really successful.*

"I also read something about you disappearing with your investors' money. Is that true?"

"I have to hand it to you, Mark—you don't beat around the bush, do you?"

"Hey, I'm twenty years older than you. I don't have the time or patience to beat around the bush." His smile suggested he wasn't above zinging his younger brother.

"I got married to a wonderful woman about eight years ago. After Mom and Dad died, I was a little depressed. My work here is editing manuscripts for publishers, and I can do it from home. For some time, I hunkered down and let life just pass me by.

"Then, one day, I got a call from the author of one of the books I was editing. She was upset about some changes I thought she should make, and she wanted to talk about it. She asked if we could meet since she too lived in the area.

"She was a widow and a few years younger than me. After I explained my suggested changes, she smiled and said, 'I understand why you've advised me to make these, but I disagree. I think we'll leave it as I wrote it.'

"I told her sure, she was under no obligation to change anything, but the publisher hired me to edit the book, so that's why I made the changes. You know what she said?"

Peter had no idea where this was going, but all he had was time, so he listened. "No. What did she say?"

"She said, 'Fuck the publisher. If they don't like it, I'll go somewhere else. Also, I kinda like you. How about dinner?'

"The publisher didn't give a shit about either my changes or her not wanting to make them. Her novel was published, became a bestseller, and she sold the movie rights. After that first night, we were never apart for more than a few days.

"We got married a year later. A year after that, she was diagnosed with cervical cancer. She fought it like a trooper for a long time. She died two years ago."

Mark stopped talking and stared into the fire. His eyes teared over.

Peter was at a loss for words. He had disowned his brother, and here the man had gone through a tremendous loss without any family for support. He had felt shitty before he'd come here, and now he felt worse. There was silence for several minutes.

"So, Peter, how about those M's?"

Peter now had no idea what to say. His mom had told him about Mark's fondness for the hapless Seattle Mariners and how he continued to follow the team even though he lived in Canada.

"Huh?" was all he could muster.

"You know that sorry-assed excuse for a baseball team. The Mariners. Whenever I start feeling like shit, I think of those poor bastards, and it perks me up. Just a crutch, Petey, but it picks me up."

He hadn't been called Petey since he was a little kid. It made him feel like the younger, less wise brother that he was.

"I fucked up, Mark. After the Napa mess, very few people wanted to invest anything with me. I got a chunk from a previous investor and a little here and there from folks who thought the wine country deal was an outlier.

"We needed a lot more money than we had, and I made the mistake of accepting a loan from a questionable source. It was a hard money loan, but I was certain the spa project would be gobbled up quickly as soon as we broke ground. Then we ran into problems with the local tribes."

"I read somewhere that you were trying to build on property adjacent to some ceremonial grounds. Is that right?"

"Yes. They put up such a stink that we had to abandon the deal. I'd already pissed away several million in developmental costs, A&D fees, and so on.

"When things came to a halt, I panicked. After losing a bunch in Napa, then this disaster in St. George, I couldn't see a way out. The others in the group bailed, and I was left holding the bag. I couldn't even afford the interest on the loan."

"Couldn't you reach some accommodation with the lender?"

"After things got going, I discovered what I feared all along. This guy, Navarro, was a major player on the drug smuggling scene. He has some serious muscle, and he's notorious for exacting revenge on people who cross him."

Mark's eyes widened above the glasses perched on the end of his nose. "Let me get this straight. You borrowed money from a drug kingpin who kills people he doesn't like. Then you took his money and left the country. That about right?"

Peter just stared into his now empty glass. "Um, yeah. When you put it that way, it sounds foolish."

"Shit, Peter, what are you going to do?"

"I have no earthly idea. I guess that's why I looked up my big brother." A tiny smile escaped his lips.

"Is there any chance he could find you here in Vancouver?"

"Suppose anything is possible, but I think for a while I may be safe. I'm not in touch with anyone from the States, and I keep a pretty low profile here. Been paying cash for everything, even my rent."

"If you could pay him back, would he forget about it?"

"Maybe, but I doubt it. I also owe a bunch to one of the other investors. I don't think that guy's a killer, though."

"Well, good news finally."

"It's a fucking mess, isn't it?"

"Yes. I'd like to help you out, but I can't imagine how. Why don't we let it settle for a few days? Maybe after I think about things, I'll come up with something that makes sense, at least in the short term."

"Mark, I appreciate it. Here I am on your doorstep after pretending you don't even exist. It's probably best if we just text each other for the time being. The last thing I want is for you to be an accessory."

"I agree, Petey, but I think that horse is already out of the barn."

THIRTY-THREE

"The Burns ranch listing hits the market today, Kev. After Shelly and I got through staging the place, it looked terrific. I think Liz had second thoughts about selling the place."

The O'Malleys had made the trip back to their Whidbey home after a long day on the mainland. They enjoyed cooking together and were in the process of building a savory mushroom risotto with roasted chickpeas, one of their favorites.

"I'm sure you two did a fabulous job. Based upon what I see on the market, it should move quickly."

"Yeah, I think so. Only thing is, the place needs to attract a pretty unique buyer with that outrageously large barn and all."

"I agree, but there's no shortage of millionaires, even billionaires, in this part of the country."

"That reminds me, why did you have them put a plumbing wall on the back side of the upper viewing platform?"

"What are you talking about?"

"Upstairs. The back wall of the platform. It's double studded like you'd do for a thick plumbing wall. Although I probably would have spec'd two by sixes instead."

Kevin had a mystified look on his ruddy Irish face. "I'm certain I would have remembered something like that. There's no plumbing in that area, and no chase is needed for anything down below. The fact that it's double studded suggests that it was an afterthought. Maybe the contractor or Burns did it after we quit."

"Well, it's there, and I thought it was a little odd." Jenne paused while chopping a huge shallot. "Anyway, the listing's gone public, so I guess it's no big deal."

Kevin, too, hesitated while checking the chickpeas for crunchiness before turning the oven off. "You remember when we found Burns at the Meadowlark?"

"No, what are you talking about? Burns?" Jenne's mischievous look was enough to cause Kevin to purse his lips, just now realizing what a stupid question he'd asked.

"That was rhetorical, dear. Don't you know the difference?"

"Kevin, either get where you're going with this or shut up and finish the goddamn chickpeas."

The banter was familiar and comfortable. Kevin smiled, reflecting upon times when folks had thought they were at each other's throats when they were just playing a game.

"What I was *going* to say was about the note that the detective found. Remember? It said something about him needing to talk to me about something. I'm just wondering if there's anything there or it's just a coincidence."

"You know what Bill says about coincidences."

"Yes, there aren't very many."

"I promised Liz I'd stop by before the open house just to touch up a few areas. Why don't you come along and you can take a look for yourself? I think it doesn't matter since the place will be sold soon, but you can maybe figure out if that's why Robbie wanted to talk to you."

Kevin thought for a minute while taking a bite from one of the now very crunchy chickpeas. "I think maybe I'll do that, coincidence or not."

That following Friday, the O'Malleys found themselves approaching the gravel driveway to the Burns ranch. As the tires crunched, they saw that Shelly had also arrived.

While they parked off to the side of the red sports car, Jenne offered, "Why don't you go see if you can figure out what that plumbing wall was for? I'll go in to see what needs to be done."

"Sure thing, hon, but it's dark in there. I'll be *ascared*."

"Oh my. So sorry to hear that. How about turning the goddamn lights on and acting like a grown-up? And it's *scared*, you moron." Jenne was grinning from ear to ear.

"Did I ever tell you how hot you are when you abuse me like this?"

"Arrgh, I'm going in the house. You check the barn." She walked through the gate leading up the flagstones to the house, still shaking her head and smiling.

Kevin slid the fifteen-foot-high barn door open and flipped the lights on inside. There was the faint smell of sawdust mixed with drywall mud even after the hiatus in the work schedule. The only sound was a distant creak of timber, possibly just expansion or a sudden breeze, he thought.

Turning to the right, he found the switches for the upstairs rooms and turned them up. Even though they had done most of the plans for the place, he still marveled at the size of it as he negotiated the story-and-a-half staircase.

He walked directly to the viewing platform and immediately saw the uncovered back wall that Jenne had asked about. He was confident the thickened wall was an afterthought by the owner. There was no other answer.

The studs were sixteen inches apart, and there was blocking four feet above the floor to accommodate the screws for the drywall. As he approached the back wall, he noticed an orange string line attached to one of the drywall screws in the blocking.

Often electricians would use the string to pull up wires to a switch or thermostat after the wall had been completely covered. The odd thing here was that the wall was still uncovered, *and* there was nothing electrified below.

Kevin took a step closer, unwound the string from the screw, and tugged at it. Whatever was attached wasn't very heavy or restricted in any way. After pulling up six or seven feet of string, he came to a yellow nylon rope; the kind used to tie down loads in pickups or trailers.

He gave the line a tug, and there was some serious resistance after three feet or so. It took both hands now. He figured there must be fifteen or twenty pounds of weight on the other end.

The platform was twenty feet above the arena floor. If whatever was on the other end was inside the wall of the lower floor, then he had at least two dozen more feet of rope to retrieve.

There were coils of yellow line strewn about his feet when he could no longer pull. Whatever was on the other end was probably stuck on a drywall screw or framing nail.

Kevin was committed now. He was also working up a healthy sweat. He was certain there was a ladder among the collection of contractors' equipment on the lower level—a tall one.

Although he was moving up into his fifties, he considered himself in reasonably good shape. Still, the prospect of scaling a twenty-foot ladder was distinctly unappealing.

Screw it, he thought. *I've come this far, and I have a sneaking suspicion of what might be on the other end of the rope.*

First, he paced off the location of the wall bay in which the retrieval line was located.

He quickly returned to the lower level and then paced off to get to the same spot beneath the viewing platform wall. After scratching a mark with a dropped screw at the location, he went to confiscate the ladder he had seen.

"Jesus, this thing is heavy," he muttered as he half dragged it to the mark he'd made. The wall had been completely mudded, but he could still see the screws indicating where the studs were.

He tipped it up against the wall, making sure the legs were on solid footing. Back at the tool staging area, he located a drywall hole saw. The pointed six-inch serrated blade looked positively lethal.

After climbing fourteen feet of aluminum ladder rungs, Kevin again questioned his sanity. Setting the thought aside, he took a deep breath and plunged the saw into the drywall about a foot below the ceiling. He worked hard to saw out a hole big enough to fit his hand through.

Reaching through the hole up to his elbow, he was able to feel a heavy plastic wrapper. It had the consistency of one of those blue tarps people used when their roof sprung a leak.

Well, I'll be damned, he thought. With renewed energy, Kevin carved out the drywall to the ceiling. By the time he was finished, he was dripping with sweat.

With a firm tug at the final corner, the twelve-inch square of sheetrock clunked to the floor. The opening now exposed a densely packed cache of what he was certain were the drugs that Tom Mahoney had told him about.

This is what Robbie Burns was killed for.

Kevin reached the rope holding the package and cut it with the drywall saw. He gingerly climbed down the ladder, cradling the illicit drugs.

With the entire effort taking the better part of an hour, he hoped his wife and the others were still busy inside. It dawned on him that the ranch was now on the market, and there was a gaping hole in the wall.

Shit. He hustled back to the collection of tools, found some scraps of backing and a screwdriver, pocketed a handful of screws, and returned to the ladder.

It took another twenty minutes, but he managed to replace the section he had cut out. He rationalized that it was up so high on the wall that it was out of the direct lighting. With any luck, no one would see it.

Kevin was absolutely certain that Bill Owens would be royally pissed at him for messing with a crime scene. Again rationalizing, he figured Robbie was already dead. The drugs were important, but how did they help find the killer?

If he told Bill right away, there would be blue-uniformed bodies and yellow tape all over the place. Better to be quiet right now. Let Liz Burns have an opportunity to sell the home and fill his buddy in later.

He took the package of fentanyl or whatever it was and lifted the spare tire compartment in his SUV. And he figured tucked in with the tire was good enough for now. He could fill Jenne in later. No sense in upsetting Liz right now, either.

As he walked to the house, he was struck by a sudden realization. Now he knew why Burns had left him the note. To create a cavity for the drugs, Robbie had double studded the walls on both levels of the barn.

The only possible way was to remove the top and bottom plates where the floors came together. In doing so, Burns removed a section of the rim joist, creating a structural deficiency.

The deceased car dealer was an idiot. He'd sacrificed the integrity of the building, and he wanted Kevin to figure out a way to fix it. What he needed was an engineer, not an interior designer.

How would he break the news to Liz Burns that she would need to disclose the concern to any prospective buyer?

THIRTY-FOUR

Albert grew bored with nothing to do but hang out at the Archer Hotel in Redmond town center. The hotel, only a few years old, was very comfortable. His two-room suite overlooking the shopping complex included a den with a sixty-inch HD TV and a delightful bedroom complete with a king-sized bed and, of course, another sixty-inch TV.

He was still miserable. He was a man of action. Hanging out in a hotel room, regardless of how nice it was, created more stress than he was comfortable with. He needed to do something—anything.

Thinking it was prudent to check on the ranch in Carnation, he hopped into his pickup and headed out to Union Hill Road. When Burns had confessed that the drugs were in his barn, it had been a simple matter to track down the address. In this age of information on demand, very little couldn't be found on the internet.

The rain petered off to a slight drizzle as he crossed the Snoqualmie River about a mile north of the tiny town of Carnation. The clouds began to recede, and it took a few seconds before the enforcer realized that the bright shining globe in the sky was indeed the sun.

Despite his dislike of the Evergreen State, he had to grudgingly admit that this pastoral setting just might have one or two redeeming qualities.

The road to the ranch headed east off the Carnation–Duvall road. It was paved and striped for the first three miles, then deteriorated into an oil and gravel passage winding through acres and acres of white-fenced pastures.

Rounding a copse of cottonwoods, an enormous white structure appeared. To call it a barn was a disservice, he thought. The damn thing looked like something out of "Lifestyles of the Rich and Famous." Off to the side of it was a tidy board-and-batten ranch house that appeared tiny in comparison but was probably bigger than most houses he'd been in.

The driveway was still several hundred yards away when he noticed a signpost just off the road.

Shit. The goddamn thing is for sale. This was gonna complicate things. He was certain Hugo was not going to be happy.

Slowly cruising by, he could see several vehicles in the courtyard area. A Cadillac Escalade, a fancy Mercedes convertible, a Subaru Outback, and an older Explorer were parked facing the white pasture fence on the north side. From the looks of things, there would be plenty of people coming and going, at least in the short term.

It wasn't possible to check out the barn, but maybe he could see what was happening. He drove another half mile to where the road ended in a rutted turnaround. Approaching the property from the east, he stopped behind a row of katsura trees.

His truck would have been unnoticeable at this distance. The trees provided good cover, and the thick firs on the south side helped to obscure the dark truck. He pulled his Maven compact binoculars from his pocket and settled in to observe.

Nothing moved for over half an hour. He began to think it was a wasted effort. Just then, he saw an older guy wearing a black ball cap emerge from the huge barn. He had wisps of gray hair sticking out the sides of his cap and appeared to have a weathered face. He was also holding a package wrapped in plastic under his right arm.

Herrera was instantly alert. Could this be . . . ?

He watched intently as the man walked over to the Explorer and carefully put the bundle into the back of the SUV. *Fucking Hugo would be ecstatic if he could get his hands on the drugs.*

As much as he wanted to drive in, break open the car, and just take the package, he didn't. Navarro had been adamant that he draw no attention. They'd waited this long. An opportunity would present itself.

All he had to do was find out who this guy was and get to him before he turned the stuff into the cops.

He'd seen enough. Rather than risk being exposed, he drove to the nearest cross street and positioned himself where he could observe any traffic coming from the east. It wouldn't be much. He had only passed one other house before getting to his present location.

After forty-five minutes, the Mercedes drove by. Shortly afterward came the Outback, followed very closely by the Explorer.

Over the years, Herrera had become adept at doing all that enforcers needed to do. Killing? Yes. Threatening? Yes. Maiming? Yes. Tailing victims to perform all the aforementioned tasks? Certainly.

He followed the Explorer, which seemed to be following the Outback. They took Woodinville–Duvall Road, winding along until it ran into the 520. From that point on, following them on the freeway was far easier. Both cars merged onto I-405 north.

Albert wasn't yet familiar with all the roads in the area, but this trip seemed all too familiar to him.

Sure enough, the 405 turned into the Mukilteo Speedway, leading to Whidbey Island's ferry terminal. *No fucking way. Does everybody live on this goddamn outpost?*

Albert wasn't sure about getting on the ferry and following them once they got off, but he could see no other way. *Remember, no attention, no killing unless it's necessary.* Hugo's words rattled in his brain.

He took the time to call Navarro while waiting for the *Suquamish* to make the twenty-minute crossing over Possession Sound. He left an update on his boss's voicemail, letting him know the good news.

Because of the haphazard way they emptied the goddamn boat, Herrera lost his quarry. Since there appeared to be only one main road on the island, he followed the long line of commuters until the first light at Langley Road. Several cars made the right turn toward town, and although he was a half dozen cars behind, he managed to pick up his targets.

Most of the traffic had turned off before reaching Langley. Now there was only one car between his pickup and the Explorer. Amazingly, the SUV and the Outback were still next to each other.

The little parade made its way through town and picked up Saratoga Road, heading north. Now there was no one between them. Albert slowed down until he could just see the cars ahead. At four in the afternoon, there was plenty of light.

After several miles, the road branched off onto Little Dirt Road. *Where do they get these names?* As the name implied, it *was* a little dirt road and so tiny that Herrera passed it by. It wasn't worth the risk. At least now he knew where his boss's drugs were, and he had an idea how to find out the identity of the people he'd been following.

Albert was able to find a room at a fifties-style motel in the town of Freeland, several miles away. The place was cheap, not too sleazy, and reasonably clean. Judging by the guests he saw, it was a favorite for visiting contractors and salespeople.

After checking in and picking up a sixpack of Bodhizafa and a pizza, he turned on the TV to catch the Mariners game. They weren't the Padres or the Dodgers, but they were on TV, and any baseball was better than no baseball. Next, he fired up his Surface and opened the attached keypad.

The Island County website was amazingly complete. He managed to zero in on Little Dirt Road using the interactive satellite map. After selecting the appropriate layers for the display, he was able to see the separate parcels of land beside the road. There were only four, and only two had houses on them.

Clicking on the first, he saw that the owners were some trust out of California. He disregarded it and went to the second occupied one. The name and address appeared, and Albert nearly choked on his beer.

O'Malley? Really? The same O'Malley I found two years ago? Holy shit, what are the odds?

Herrera had come here from San Diego to do his employer's bidding. Now he was on an island in the middle of Puget Sound where two individuals could make him look like a hero in the eyes of Hugo Navarro.

The drugs were undoubtedly here. Of that, he was sure. He just had to figure out when, where, and how to get them. The cripple in the wheelchair might not know where Hall was, but he was worth watching.

The Mariners had just given up three runs in the first inning. Herrera shut off the TV and tried his boss again.

THIRTY-FIVE

Kevin had been uncharacteristically quiet when he came back in from the barn. All the finishing staging elements had been added, and the house looked ready for prime time.

"Could you figure anything out about that rear wall?" Jenne looked up from straightening out a throw as he entered.

"Um, no, not really."

Jenne looked surprised. "Not really? So you can think of no reason for that change?"

"Nah, it must've just been something he was planning for later. So, hey, you guys have done a great job in here. Looks fantastic. Should sell this weekend." Looking directly at his wife, Kevin widened his eyes and nodded toward the door.

It appeared Jenne knew her husband.

"I think we're great here, Shelly, Liz. We're gonna head back to Whidbey before the ferry line gets ridiculously long. Make sure to call me if there's something you need or if you have any questions about where stuff should go."

After the O'Malleys had got into their respective cars and headed west, they got on their cell phones. When they were off-island and in separate vehicles, they often chatted to pass the time in traffic. Being hands-free, it seemed like they were sitting next to each other.

"So, Kev, what the hell was that charade at Liz's all about?"

Kevin had to smile at how well they knew each other. "I found the drugs that they killed Robbie for."

Jenne was just ahead of him, so he could see her swerve ever so slightly.

"Hey, easy there, kiddo. Don't run off the road."

"You found the fucking drugs?"

"Yup. They were hidden down in the lower wall. There was an electrician's line that you could barely see tied off on some blocking. I pulled up the rope that was attached. Then the damn thing got stuck in the wall."

"So that's why you were out there so long."

"I didn't think you'd noticed."

"Of course I did. I just didn't want to say anything. Did you leave them there for Bill? Have you called him yet?"

"No. It's kind of a long story." He took a deep breath, anticipating what was coming.

"You haven't called the chief of detectives? Kevin, he's been all over that barn several times. You've got to let him know."

"I know. I know. Just hear me out first."

He proceeded to tell her about cutting out the drywall and taking the drugs. It had been a couple of years since the murder, and it didn't seem all that urgent. He told her they were now in his car.

If Owens got involved, he reminded her, the cops would be all over the place, and the chances of Liz selling the house quickly would be nil.

He also told her about the structural issues with the barn. And he was sure that was what Robbie had wanted to talk to him about.

After his explanations, there was silence.

"Jenne? You still there?" More silence.

"Jenne? Hello?"

"I'm here, Kevin. Just thinking this through. Is that why you were so pitted when you came in the house?"

"I've got millions of dollars of fentanyl in my rig here, and you're concerned about me sweating?"

"Easy, big fella. Just trying to buy some time here. Lots to get my arms around."

"Yeah. I know. I'm sure Bill's gonna be pissed, but, as I see it, I don't see the harm. More problematic, though, is the structural integrity of that barn. Liz won't even know about it if they sell the ranch quickly. Then we'll tell her, and she'll have to disclose and maybe screw up the sale."

"I agree on the Bill thing. He'll be royally pissed off. What are your thoughts on the barn?"

"Well, it's not the end of the world. We can get a structural person in there and have them develop a remedy. It'll probably require a little demo, some hardware, maybe a new post, and some hangers. Then they'll have to redo the drywall."

"So, what do you think? Couple grand?"

"Maybe. I'd say no more than five."

"Kevin, that place will sell for at least five million. They have ten acres. It's listed at five, and the way things are going, they'll surely get at least that. I can't imagine five grand is going to make a difference."

"I agree. It's just that we know, and she doesn't. I don't think it makes sense to tell her right now. Then she would have to disclose it, do the repairs, and pull it off the market. When it goes under contract, I'm sure they will have inspections. We can point it out to them at that time. It's an easy fix, and I can't imagine it killing the deal."

"I guess that makes sense. Hey, look, no line." They had just come down the hill to the terminal.

"Hey, Jenne. Let's table this until we get home. Then we can figure out how to tell Bill."

THIRTY-SIX

Mark Hall had been content as an ex-pat living in Vancouver. He considered himself incredibly lucky to have been married to a woman who made every day special. That the experience was cut short by a deadly disease only made the memory more intense.

After the death of his wife, he drifted from one day to the next. When the days turned into weeks turned into months, his awareness of the passing of time was missing.

Recently, after throwing himself back into his work, the numbness had started seeping away little by little. Then Peter had knocked on his door.

Although the shock of seeing him was diminished by his extended mourning period, he was still mildly curious about where this particular intrusion into his quiet life might lead.

He had read about the missing developer from Utah. News reports had established the missing funds as more than twenty million dollars. He thought it ironic that even this sizeable fortune couldn't or wouldn't secure happiness for his brother.

By the time Peter was in high school, Mark had already lived in Canada for over fifteen years. He had kept up with his brothers' lives via letters from his mom. She would speak of both of them as doing well, but she occasionally expressed concern over Peter's insecurities, including his choice of friends.

Mark correctly surmised that the need to show others his success had fueled his current predicament. That Peter had sought him out offered a glimmer of hope that even this deep in the weeds, there might be some way to turn the ship around.

He thought it crucial to come up to speed on all things related to the spa at Snow Canyon. This included the local Native American tribes, the local county and township regulations, and the investors' backgrounds. If it were possible to alleviate his brother's situation, this research would reveal it.

Three days later, Mark saw a potential life raft. After a review of the initial offering and all other public documents for the project, he perused the local government regulations regarding permit requirements. Following that, he considered the Hopi culture, including their ceremonial traditions. The complaint that had been forwarded to the BIA was reviewed as well.

He spent some time going over the backgrounds of the two largest investors. Jake Early, while oddly reclusive, appeared to be a legitimate investor with a sparkling military history.

The majority investor was listed as Peter, but that was misleading. The twenty million he had invested was the hard money loan supplied by Hugo Navarro. Mark noted, too, that Navarro's name was listed in the first position on the deed as security for the note.

Unfortunately, with the project going sideways, Navarro's security was worthless. This meant the most significant contributor had only one recourse for recouping his money. That would be Peter.

Mark had a much more difficult time finding any history on Navarro. Eventually, though, his dogged persistence produced results. And it proved ugly. Very ugly.

The guy was a goddamn drug lord, a smuggler, and a killer. What the hell was his brother thinking? It became apparent that if this man found out where Peter was, he was truly fucked.

Then he stumbled upon a small article posted on the Facebook page for the local Hopi tribe in St. George, Utah. The last paragraph suggested a possible opportunity to resurrect the project. If assurances were given to the tribe that no harm or damage would come to their sacred grounds, they would perhaps allow the project to continue.

Mark immediately texted his brother, telling him to stop over.

He had copied the posting from the page, and he presented it to Peter as he came through the door.

"Look at this."

After reading and rereading the small blurb, Peter looked at his brother. "This is interesting."

"That's all you can say? I've spent three days wading through reams of shit. I've come up with maybe an out for you, and you call it interesting?"

"Please, Mark, don't think I don't appreciate it. I do. It's just that there are way too many things to work through. First, there is no guarantee that if I give them assurances, we'll be able to restart the thing. Secondly, Navarro surely wants his money right away and probably wants to kill me. Also, the project will probably be another ten percent higher because of the elapsed time. It's a real long shot."

"Okay, so what's the alternative?"

"I don't have one."

"So, you can either inquire about this and see where it goes, or you can stay here and hide out until you die. That sound enticing?"

Peter just stood there, hands by his side, bags under his eyes, and a pasty, depressed expression on his face.

"Petey, how the hell did you ever get involved with this drug dealer?"

"When I met him, I didn't know about that. He was just some guy at a casino bar. The owner introduced me to him. He had lent them a bunch of money, and they seemed happy, so I figured it was okay. He was just some rich guy. I guess I had some suspicions, and it felt a little odd, but I was hard up for money. It wasn't until I ran up against the Hopi that I realized who he was. That's when I left the country."

"Jesus."

"Yeah, I know."

"What if you could convince Navarro that instead of the twenty million, he could have twenty-five or thirty?"

"How could I do that?"

"If you could get things going again, maybe you could sell it quickly. From what I read, things are going gangbusters down there. You'd have to give up anything you were going to make, but hey, at least you'd be alive."

"That's an awfully big if, and there's still that smaller investor."

"Don't you have some verbiage in the prospectus that says there's no guarantee of any return?"

"Yes, but—"

"No buts. That person will just end up a casualty of a bad investment. Shit happens."

"Mark, there are a lot of moving pieces here. I'm gonna have to give this some thought."

"Sure. But maybe it would make sense to email these people to find out what they would require. Just in case."

Peter put his arm over his brother's shoulder as he started toward the door. "I'll take this with me, Mark, and I'll think on it. Thanks for all your help."

A week later, the originator of the Facebook page for the local Hopi tribe in Southern Utah received an email. The message was a request for further information on what might be required to allow the resumed development of the Snow Canyon Spa.

Adisa immediately forwarded the email to Francis Early.

THIRTY-SEVEN

"Jake, Adisa got a reply to his Facebook post. It's from Peter Hall. He's asking what the tribe wants in the way of assurances. He's considering it."

"That's good to know, but how does that help me get my money back?"

"Well … it doesn't . . . yet. I'm going to forward this to the Hackers and see if they can isolate the IP address. If Hall has an Apple device, we may be able to locate it. I guess the MAC address is hardware-specific and globally unique depending on the communication format."

Jake looked at Francis as if he were speaking Klingon. "Who are you, and what have you done with my brother?"

Francis just sat there smugly.

"No, really, Francis. Did you just make this shit up?"

"Nah. I'm just repeating some stuff my buddies told me. The gist of it is that depending on the message format, we may find out where Hall is. I should know better this afternoon after they've had a chance to look at it."

"And then what?"

"Not sure. I guess if they get a location, I'll visit the prick. You're not going anywhere."

Jake reddened a bit and looked down at his withered legs.

"I'm sorry, Jake. I didn't mean anything about your injuries. It was maybe a little dig about you being an agraphobe."

"It's agoraphobe, you dunce." Jake rallied a little, even showing a tiny smile. "You're probably right. I keep thinking I'll work on that, but it's just so damn easy to do nothing."

Francis looked away. He had no idea what demons his brother had to deal with. He felt bad about putting him down.

"Listen, Jake. Let's see what the Hackers turn up. Mickey said he'd get back to me by dinner time. Then we'll figure it out."

"He's up in Vancouver. Somewhere near Stanley Park." Francis had just taken the stairs two at a time and burst into the great room. "Mickey says that's as close as they can get."

"Didn't you tell me something about an older brother who also lived there?"

"Yes. It was Mark. Hell of a coincidence, doncha think?"

"I do. Too much so."

Francis paused for a moment. He tilted his shaved head to one side, like a border collie trying to remember where his favorite toy was.

"You know, we're not sure where Peter is, but I bet I could find out where his brother is."

"How?"

"The guy's been up there forever. Nobody can stay in one place that long without leaving a trail. I'll tell Mick to have the boys do a search for Mark Hall. I'll bet we get a hit."

"And then?"

"Don't know. I'll be there by then. I'll figure something out."

Very early the following morning, Francis made his way north. The two-lane meandering highway heading off Whidbey Island went over Deception Pass. The skinny two-lane bridge almost 200 feet above the raging current always gave him a shiver. Another hour to the border, and then he was in another country.

By the time he had reached Vancouver, he'd already gotten a text from Mickey. It was an address for Mark Hall.

THIRTY-EIGHT

As Kevin came down the stairs of the stylish Dutch Colonial, the sun streamed in through the small-paned windows. Their two-story home sat high on a bluff with a spectacular view east over Saratoga Passage.

Today, the first of May, brought bright blue sky and sunshine, a rarity for this time of year in the northwest. The strange glowing ball of fire, as most Northwesterners referred to it, had just risen over the Cascades. Both Mt. Baker and Mt. Pilchuck could be seen, each still covered with many feet of snow from the winter storms.

Upon debarking from the ferry the previous evening, all hell had broken loose. Their next-door neighbor, Tim, who frequently took care of Emma while they were gone, had taken her out for a potty break. Just as the German Shepherd was finishing up, a young fawn proceeded to hop across the small orchard.

Emma, sensing a serious game of "chase me," accelerated to her top speed of thirty miles per hour in two seconds. The fawn already yards ahead disappeared into the forested area across the street.

Emma followed at the same time as a small Prius came up over the hill. With a screech of brakes came a thump and a whimper.

Tim rushed to the emergency clinic and immediately texted the O'Malleys. "We're at the vet's. She's okay. A cracked rib, but okay."

They were exhausted by the time they had gotten the dog settled and themselves to bed.

Jenne had already risen and was busy making coffee and puttering about the galley kitchen. It was 6:30. Emma was now wide awake and ignoring her tightly wrapped chest.

"Hell of a night, eh?"

"Yeah, Kev. I'm still a little wasted. I need coffee, please."

"Looks like nothing happened to her, except for the bandage, of course."

"I think she's fine. She ate like a horse. I feel bad about Jim. He thinks it's his fault."

"Ahh, that could have happened to anyone. He took care of her at least as well as we could have. The vet said if he hadn't gotten that rib taken care of, it might have caused serious damage. She was lucky, and we're fortunate Tim took care of things."

"I know. Still, we need to let him know he was the hero, not the bad guy."

"Got it."

"With all the excitement, we didn't even discuss what's in your car and what we're going to do about it."

As Kevin sipped the coffee handed to him, he furrowed his brow. "Yeah. While I was getting up, I was trying to think of how to break the news to Bill. I'm sure he's gonna go apeshit."

"No argument here."

"Wait, I got an idea."

"Boy, can't wait. I'm sure it's a doozy."

"Not very encouraging, darling."

"Sorry. I'm sure it will be fabulous."

"That's the spirit. Encouragement is always preferred."

"What is preferred is that you quit stalling and tell me what you've got."

"Okay. Can we agree that us not reporting this immediately really isn't going to make any difference in finding the killer in a two-year-old crime?"

"Yes."

"Can we also agree that if we hold off, Liz will have a better chance to sell her place?"

"Yup."

"So, how about this? Next Saturday is Cinque de Mayo. We throw a party, have Bill and Shelly up, and ask the Earlys too. We get Bill half in the bag and tell him then. Good one?"

"You're an idiot sometimes."

"You don't like it?"

"I didn't say I didn't like it. I just said you're an idiot sometimes. Right now, I'm not sure. It could go either way."

Kevin saw an opening. "Look, I know it sounds stupid. Truth is, he's gonna be upset one way or another. I just thought it would be fun to get the Owenses and the Earlys together. I think they'd like each other. By then, maybe Liz's ranch will be under contract, and we can spill the beans."

"Much better. Now you're making some sense. How do you expect to get Jake over here? We don't have an accessible home here, and he still won't leave his house."

"Shit, yes. I didn't think about that."

"What if you told Jake and Francis your idea? Maybe they'll volunteer their place. Pretty sure you can lay some guilt on them."

"That's terrible, Jenne. Okay, I'll try."

THIRTY-NINE

The buzzing of Herrera's phone startled him. It was past seven a.m., and he'd slept soundly. He looked at the number. It was Hugo.

"Albert, I got your message. Are you sure about my cache of fentanyl?"

"I saw that designer guy walk from the barn with a duct-tape-and-plastic-wrapped package and put it in his car. Remember, the guy I killed in Napa said the stuff was in there. He also said he had to talk to the designer. This guy."

"And where are you now?"

"I'm in some shitty motel on this island. I followed the guy to his street, but I didn't go down there. You said to keep a low profile."

"And you're certain it's him?"

"Yeah. I looked it up in the county records. That's him for sure."

Albert heard only breathing on the other end. He knew better than to interrupt his boss while he came up with a plan.

"And this is the same island where that other investor in the spa lives?"

"Yes."

"Fucking amazing."

"What I thought too."

"Okay. If he were going to turn them in, he would have done so already. He's either going to try and sell them or do something else with them."

"I don't know, boss. He doesn't look like a dealer."

"Then why does he still have them?"

"Don't know."

"Okay. Stay there. I'll be up in a few days. Keep tabs on him, and don't do anything unless we talk. Call me if it looks as though he's planning to unload them. And Albert?"

"Yes?"

"Do not draw any attention. Remember, low profile. But Albert?"

"Yes?"

"Get something to shoot people with. Just in case. I can't bring anything on the plane."

"Got it, boss. But where? They have laws up here where you have to wait a while."

"Don't they have military bases up there?"

"Yeah, but …"

"Just find out where one is and go there. There are always pawn shops around military bases, and they always have guns. Bring cash and grease the owner really good. Always works."

Herrera thought about it for a few seconds and remembered something he'd seen on the map of Whidbey. The northern half of the island was home to a Navy base. "Okay, boss, I'll try."

"Albert, do more than try."

When Hugo spoke in that way, it gave him the chills, even after all these years.

South Whidbey Island was small geographically, and it was very sparsely populated. Modest farms and ranches were scattered throughout, while the historic town of Langley was home to less than a thousand slow-moving souls.

Keeping tabs on O'Malley wouldn't be difficult. Keeping unseen was another matter. Herrera drove past the turnoff to Little Dirt Road several times a day.

On one occasion, he passed as the Outback was returning. He assumed that was the wife. Another time the green Explorer pulled out before him, and he followed it into town. The driver went to the post office, picked up something from the vet's office, and stopped at the Star Store. Albert saw all this from his parking spot on the east side of Second Street. It was a very small town—not even a red light.

O'Malley headed back on Saratoga, and Albert didn't bother to follow. There was no place for the designer to go but home. Unless he decided to leave the island or do something with the fentanyl, Herrera felt sure he had things under control.

Navarro always kept his distance during any operation involving the law or requiring wet work. He had not avoided prosecution this long by being careless. Whether cause for concern or not, the fact that his boss was coming to see him left an unsettled feeling in the enforcer's stomach.

FORTY

Francis arrived in Vancouver late morning and continued northwest until he reached the Stanley Park area. The thousand-acre park extended well into the Burrard Inlet and was a must-see for tourists and residents alike. Stanley Park was to Canada as Central Park was to the US. The high-rise condo buildings with views of the park were as highly sought after as those surrounding Central Park.

Driving his Ram pickup down Lagoon Drive, he parked a half block away from the address he'd been given. He knew where Mark Hall lived, but he still wasn't clear how that might help him find his brother.

He wasn't even sure whether Peter had touched base with him. He felt, though, that the chances of them both being in another country and in the same city and not connecting were remote.

Francis eased his six-foot-four frame out of the pickup and strolled over to the lobby of the building. He was aware that passersby might possibly remember a 260-pound man with a shaved head and tear tattoos, so he acted as nonchalantly as possible.

The lobby was small, with a key fob access control system for added security. Tenant traffic was light during the late morning, so Francis bided his time by sitting on a small concrete bench just to the side of the entry.

After an hour or so of playing Candy Crush on his phone, he saw that an older woman was exiting the lobby elevator. He moved to the entry door as casually as possible and managed to catch it just as the tenant left the building. He congratulated himself on his stealthy move, even managing to avoid a glance from the old lady.

Once inside, he studied the tenant directory, confirming that Mark Hall was a resident here at the Stanley Tower. He immediately left the building and returned to his vehicle. With very little else to go on, he committed to observing the front of the lobby during the busiest times of the day.

If he were going to watch over the entrance from an acceptable location, he would have to do something to mitigate his noticeable physical appearance.

A block away, while thirty gallons of diesel were pumping into his truck, he walked into the souvenir-laden convenience store. His goal was to acquire anything that might help make him somewhat less noticeable.

A Canucks baseball cap and a triple-X Henrik Sedin jersey looked like the obvious choice. Half the population wore testaments to their favorite team in this hockey-crazy city. Sedin, a Hart Trophy winner, was still the most popular player in history.

With remnants of the pandemic still of some concern, plenty of the Vancouver citizenry had donned surgical masks, Francis couldn't do much about the tears, but the mask he selected did a decent job of obscuring all but one on each side. It, too, had the Canucks logo.

He busied himself during the afternoon by finding a place to stay for a few days. He returned to the tower just before four to observe the foot traffic before the dinner hour. Now in his new hockey disguise, he wandered over to a nearby espresso stand, picked up a latte, and pretended to read his phone while returning to the bench.

With plenty of tenant traffic , Francis was sure he'd never know if Mark Hall was one of them. What he had seen was that picture of the groundbreaking in Utah, the one with Peter Hall in it. He had enlarged the article, and even though it was a bit grainy, he felt sure he could recognize him.

By seven, the traffic had thinned, and a fine drizzle had started falling. And it was fucking cold. The hockey jersey was a great idea, but the paper-thin polyester did little to warm him. Time to head for the hotel and report back to his brother.

"Francis, good to hear from you. Figure anything out?"

"Got a bunch of new hockey shit to wear. These people are nuts about the Canucks."

"You know, you coulda got that on Amazon. You didn't need to go all the way to Canada to buy it."

"Funny man, bro. You're a laugh a minute. Nah, I bought the stuff to blend in; as much as possible, that is."

"So, what's up?"

"I found the place where his brother lives. Pretty fancy, great views, yadda, yada. Since Peter's IP address is here in the city, the only thing I can think to do is stake out this place for a few days. I can't hang around forever, cuz even with my excellent disguise, I think folks would begin to notice."

"I'm pretty sure you're right about that. What are the odds he'll look up his brother?"

"No idea. But as we talked about earlier, too much of a coincidence to ignore. If nothing happens in a few days, maybe I'll have to go and knock on this guy Mark's door."

"Well, don't do anything that'll get you in trouble. I know sometimes you try to make things happen rather than let them happen."

"No fear, Jake. I got things under control. I'll let you know if I get anywhere."

"Um, Francis?"

"Yes?"

"What will you do if you do find this guy?"

"I don't know yet. I'm just focusing on finding him first."

"Okay, but the cops up there take things very seriously, especially if you're not a citizen."

"Jakie, I got this. I'm not gonna do anything stupid. I'll talk to you tomorrow."

FORTY-ONE

Navarro did his best to avoid any situation that might threaten his freedom. He had managed to stay ahead of the law this long by staying out of the news. That, of course, and killing witnesses, including several undercover detectives who had tried to infiltrate his organization.

With the balance of his drug enterprise now fragmented and fought over, he made sure to distance himself from the mess. He left it to younger thugs and gangsters to attempt to prosper in that futile and dangerous business model.

He had made millions, and he had managed to keep it unlike most drug lords. His portfolio was diversified. A sizeable amount was in cash in offshore accounts. There was a substantial portfolio of hard money real estate loans, each returning a minimum of ten percent. Additionally, there were safe deposit boxes containing gold and diamonds spread over several financial institutions in several countries.

Hugo never forgot where he came from and had vowed never to experience any degree of poverty again. Many drug kingpins had built lavish estates and surrounded themselves with dozens of security personnel.

Navarro preferred to live comfortably but modestly as far as the public was concerned. His avocado orchard in the hills east of San Diego sprawled over thirty acres. It was plenty big enough to provide safety.

His field hands were members of his security team. Should there be any trespassers or unannounced visitors, they would not get past the gate. CCTV cameras spread generously throughout the groves of avocados and staffed 24/7 enabled him to live a carefree life.

Still, from time to time, Hugo's restlessness got the better of him. Albert Herrera had been his second in command ever since he had saved his life in that sleazy bar in El Centro. Other than having a quick temper, he was as dedicated and dependable as he could hope for.

Now that he no longer considered himself an illegal drug purveyor, his risk tolerance for prosecution had ebbed considerably. His last connection to the drug trade seemed to be on some obscure little island in the middle of Puget Sound. He trusted his right-hand man to accomplish the mission, but getting it done quietly and inconspicuously was still up for grabs.

Hugo may have put off going after the fentanyl Burns had stolen, but he still wanted to get his hands on the seven kilos that were neatly packaged and bound with duct tape. The street value alone was close to ten million.

A more annoying thorn in his side was the fact that Peter Hall had made off with twenty million dollars of his hard-earned money. He had yet to pay for this disrespect. Navarro treated every affront with lethal force. It was why he was still a free man.

He had no illusions that he could easily find Hall, but he felt he might be able to question the other investor a bit more thoroughly than Albert had.

That both of these matters would somehow come together on this stupid island was too much to accept. He had never been to Washington State before. He even felt a tiny bit of pleasure at the thought of seeing somewhere new and different.

FORTY-TWO

The gravel courtyard was bathed in sunlight as O'Malley pulled into Casa d'Early. As expected, the front door was opened before he could reach the doorbell, and Jake greeted him effusively.

"Hey, Kev, what are you doing here?"

"Hi, Jake, glad I caught you at home, hah."

"Good one, Kev. I think you should work on some new material, though." His smile gave away his acceptance that the dig was accepted as the endearment it was intended to be.

Kevin grinned and moved on to the reason for his visit. "Jenne and I wanted to have some folks up this Saturday for Cinque de Mayo. We thought you and Francis would enjoy meeting our friends as well."

"That's very kind of you, Kev. I'm sure we would enjoy them. Unless, of course, they're anything like you."

"Touché, good one. My wife reminded me that even if we could convince you to leave your estate here, we don't have a way to get you up the stairs. Here's where I'm supposed to say: 'Damn, I guess we'll have to call it off if we can't have the Earlys over.' And then you're supposed to say, 'Well, gee whiz, Kevin, why don't we have everyone over here? There's plenty of room, lots of wine, of course, and the place is wheelchair accessible.'"

Jake was shaking his head from side to side as he laughed. "Gee whiz, Kevin, why don't we have it over here? How's that, knucklehead?"

"Wow, terrific idea, Jake. We'd love to. Seriously, are you sure about this?"

"I'm sure. It sounds like great fun, and I'm looking forward to meeting your friends."

Kevin looked relieved. "Say, where's your brother? Down at the computer?"

"Uh, no. Francis came up with some plan to find the guy who ran off with my money. I don't know the particulars, but he figured out some way to isolate the guy's IP address. It was up in Vancouver, BC, and that's where he is. He's trying to find Peter Hall."

"Suppose he does, then what?"

"I don't think he knows yet. He said he'd figure it out when the time came. My brother is a great dude and loyal as hell, but sometimes he can be a little heavy-handed."

"Really? You don't have to tell me about it, remember."

"Don't remind me. I think I get to share a little of that one."

"You think he'll be back?"

"Whatever he plans on doing, I think he'll be back before the weekend."

"Great. Let me know what to bring. I'll have the Owenses come to our place, and we can drive over together."

FORTY-THREE

After drinking lattes and loitering in the neighborhood adjacent to the Stanley Tower, Francis began to think he was pissing up a rope after a day and a half.

What was I thinking coming up here with no plan? He knew the email had originated in the city, but he had no backup other than hoping Hall would contact his brother.

Wednesday morning arrived with overcast skies threatening imminent rain. Francis once again donned his Canucks disguise and headed over to his station outside the Lagoon Drive condo building.

As he settled in with his first latte of the day, he noticed an older gentleman with longish gray hair leave the condo lobby. The man walked right past Francis almost as if the big fella was part of the shrubbery.

Concentrating on his phone, the guy turned into the espresso stand that Francis had just left. Bored as he was, the Canuck fan continued to watch him as he ordered a drink and then pulled up a chair to one of the three small bistro tables.

Francis turned back to the hotel lobby and just missed seeing a balding, portly fellow wearing glasses enter the coffee shop and slide into the chair opposite Gray-Hair.

Foot traffic had thinned out as the morning commute dwindled. Francis stole another bored glance at the man drinking coffee at his table and sat bolt upright.

The lighting was poor, and the shop's windows were tinted, but he was sure he was looking at Peter Hall. Indeed, he looked disheveled and sported dark circles under his eyes, but Francis knew this was the man he had seen in the picture of the groundbreaking ceremony.

He watched as the two got up and walked back over to the lobby. They both got into the elevator and disappeared. Jesus, what to do?

Francis was shaking, overcome with adrenaline. He'd taken a chance by coming up here but hadn't given much thought to what he'd do if he found the crooked developer.

Breathe, he told himself, *breathe. Think it through.* What would his brother do?

He figured he had a little time because they wouldn't have gone up to the unit if Hall left immediately. He remembered Kevin saying his friend, the cop, had been told it would be difficult to do anything until they found the guy.

Well, I've found him. Now what? Francis was not aware of the laws of Utah or any applicable federal laws. And he damn sure didn't know anything about the laws in Canada when it came to US citizens.

What he brought to the table was determination and physical strength. That would have to suffice until he could get some advice. However, what he was not going to do was let Hall out of his sight when he left the building.

He drove the pickup to a Home Depot that he had passed after leaving his hotel. He made stops in the electrical department, the paint department, and the plumbing department. A half-hour later, he was back at the Stanley Tower. Waiting.

FORTY-FOUR

Peter and Mark Hall had spent the better part of the day coming up with scenarios and options that might work. The biggest hurdle was Navarro. Finding a way to convince him that the Snow Canyon Spa was still a viable option would be tricky.

"Thing is, Mark, we're assuming I can come up with enough of a guarantee that will satisfy the local tribe in St. George. Even if that flies, I'll certainly have to do something about the law."

"How many people have money in this deal?"

"Only a dozen or so. Navarro has the most, then Early. The rest only have a small piece—less than a few hundred thousand each."

"It seems if you could get the investors not to press charges, you might skate."

They sat at the dining table with copies of the Snow Canyon documents strewn haphazardly on the quartz tabletop.

"That's a big if, Mark. Still, it's Navarro I'm worried about."

"Is there any way to feel him out?"

"Before I go there, let me see if I can even get this thing off the ground again. I'll start putting something together, get it off to the head honcho of the Hopi down there, then see where it goes. Last thing I want to do is give Navarro a heads-up as to where I am."

"Sounds like a plan. I'll be here whenever you'd like to bounce some ideas around. Just give me a call or text me, and we can get together."

Peter struggled into his down vest and headed back to his car. It was late afternoon, and he was tired. As he began the drive to his apartment in North Vancouver, he failed to notice the dark Ram 3500 truck following him.

Twenty minutes later, he reached his small apartment on the ground floor of a two-story fourplex. Because he was using an alias and paying cash for the place, neither callers nor mail were ever even a possibility.

He grabbed a beer from the fridge, popped a frozen dinner in the microwave, and turned on the TV. Anything was preferable to mentally rehashing his situation over and over again. There would be plenty of time for that tomorrow.

Halfway through a rerun of *Cheers*, there was a knock at the door. Hall jumped out of his chair, knocking over what was left of his Swanson chicken pot pie.

No one knew he was here. It had to be a misguided delivery driver or someone with the wrong address. He peered through the side window and saw the back of an uncannily large man in a hockey outfit. *What the fuck?*

Still convinced that the caller was making a mistake, he left the security chain attached and cracked the door a few inches—a terrible miscalculation.

A split second later, the cheap entry door was slammed into his face, the chain snapping, the jamb splintering, and screws flying like tiny missiles.

The Hockey Man slammed the door shut, quickly grabbed Hall by the shirt, and threw him onto the cheap sofa. He started to yell just before a meaty fist drove his top lip through his front teeth. The caller put his finger to his lips, indicating no words were required.

Hall could now fully appreciate the thug's size. The shaved head and prison tears did little to mitigate the perceived threat.

The man pointed to his Canucks jersey pocket, where the black barrel of a pistol peeked out. He again put a finger to lips, making sure the message was obeyed.

"Stand up and turn around."

Shaking and barely controlling his bladder, Peter Hall followed his instructions.

"Hands behind your back."

He did as he was told and felt several plastic zip-ties clamp over his wrists.

"Now turn around and sit down."

The blood from his perforated lips had dripped down his chin and was now making tiny red teardrops on his white T-shirt.

"Sorry about the split lip, but I can't have you talking right now. Just to be sure, let me fix that for you."

Francis pulled a roll of two-inch green painter's tape from another pocket.

"I was gonna use duct tape, but that shit's too hard to remove. I know I can be nasty, but I'd hate just to pull your lips off. This stuff will keep you quiet for a while without causing any permanent mutilation. Nod if you appreciate that."

Hall nodded like his head was hinged. Was this guy here to rob him? Was he here to kill him? That couldn't be, or he would have already done that.

With his hands behind his back and his bloody mouth plastered with green Frog Tape, he perched on the edge of the sofa, looking up at his assailant.

"My name is Francis Early. My brother is Jake Early."

Peter's eyes widened in recognition as the heavyweight pulled up a small wooden chair, still glaring at his trussed-up prize. The chair creaked and groaned under Early's weight. Peter was hoping the thing would collapse.

Francis reached into his pocket and pulled out the six-inch black nipple he had picked up in the plumbing department.

"Nice pistol, eh? You should know they don't allow guns in this country. What the fuck's wrong with you? I know you're not wondering why I'm here. Are you?"

Hall shook his head, *no*.

"Well, that's just great. We don't have to dick around lying and shit. So, we know you fucked my brother and probably some other people. Do you have the money somewhere?"

Peter hesitated, trying to come up with something that would appease the fellow.

Francis rubbed his right fist with his left hand. Spending five years in the slammer was excellent schooling in the art of intimidation.

"I imagine you've got a pretty sore mouth right now. I can make it much worse, you know. Should I ask again?"

167

Peter shook his head furiously from side to side.

"Where's the money?"

Peter rolled his eyes around in his head.

"What does that mean? Is it here?"

A head shake—no.

"Somewhere else?"

A nod.

"Far away?"

Another nod.

"Can you get it for me?"

Peter hesitated. How could he explain to this man his plans for reviving the project? He had to try. Maybe he could convince Early to let him continue the development.

"Mmm emm mmmemm emm em."

"You want to talk?"

A nod.

"You know what happens if you yell, right?"

Hall looked at the enormous right fist and nodded again.

"Okay. Close your eyes and hold your breath."

The tape was ripped away in a split second, pulling off bits of lip and semi-coagulated blood.

He yelped as quietly as he could, still eyeing the ham hock of a fist. Blood started dripping more heavily.

"Can I have a tissue?"

Francis looked into the kitchen and salvaged a roll of paper towels. He wadded up several sheets and gently patted Hall's mouth. "There, that will have to do. Now, what were you trying to say?"

Hall hurriedly explained that the money was in offshore accounts and not easily retrievable. He then proceeded to tell Francis of his plan to resurrect the project after getting the blessing of the local tribe.

While he explained the situation, he noticed the tiniest of smiles beginning to form on his attacker's mouth. He felt a clench in his gut. This guy knew something, and it was probably more bad news.

"Sorry to break it to you this way but, no. You're not going to be building any spa in Utah. That post was a fake to get you to respond. I was able to track your IP address in Vancouver. Then I camped outside your brother's, hoping you would show. I'm still surprised it worked. Pretty clever, eh?"

Peter Hall was devastated. He had a drug lord after him who most likely wanted to kill him. And he had this giant bald-headed Neanderthal who was much sharper than he appeared. And now he had nothing to fall back on. *Shit.*

FORTY-FIVE

Francis's hand hurt like hell. After his time at McNeil, he'd vowed to avoid violence unless absolutely necessary. He figured this qualified as necessary. It was amazingly effective to punch someone in the mouth, but it was impossible to do without getting a few teeth punctures in the knuckles.

Watching Hall realize he was screwed was worth the trip.

The crook deserved what he got. It would have been nice to find some way to get Jake's money back, but he'd always thought it was a remote possibility.

Francis didn't know the intricacies of international banking, nor did he know what laws had been broken and what jurisdiction they fell under. What he knew for sure, though, was that he had this guy. He could see no other option but to get him back to the States, where people more knowledgeable about these issues could deal with him. Maybe Jake could figure something out.

It was challenging to get back into Washington without getting stopped by the border patrol at the Peace Arch. It would be impossible to do so if he had a trussed-up and gagged crook sitting in the passenger seat. Jake had mentioned that the AG in Utah had initiated a BOLO for Hall, which could be a problem.

His brother was his go-to guy for everything important. Jake was a straight shooter, and at no time would he consider an act even remotely unlawful. Francis did not doubt that forcing an individual into another country against his will, regardless of his being a thief, was absolutely against the law.

He didn't care. Jake had taken care of him when he was strung out on heroin, and he'd taken him in when he got out of prison. The least he could do was to try to bring Hall back to the States to face the music.

But he couldn't tell Jake. He would not go along with what Francis had planned. But first, he needed some help.

"James, I've got a situation here, and I need some advice."

"Every time I hear someone say 'I've got a situation,' Francis, it never turns out well." His prison-educated attorney sounded cautious.

"I know, I know, but I couldn't see any other way to do this. Here's my question. Is it possible to get a reluctant passenger over the US–Canada border without any trouble?"

"By reluctant, what do you mean?"

"Sorta like tied up, you know, with tape across his mouth."

"Yeah, I'm not surprised. Tell me what's going on."

Francis proceeded to explain to his former prison mate his current predicament. He let him know how effective the Facebook post had been in flushing out his quarry, making sure to credit his buddy.

"I just need to get him back to the States. There's gotta be some way to do it."

"Well, there are ways, but none are legal. Any road that has a border crossing will have attendants or border guards. Even the ferries that go from BC to the US check the passengers, either in Canada or when they make port in Washington."

"How about smaller boats?"

"The border patrol uses radar to track the smaller boats. Sure, sometimes they get through, but they can get pretty nasty if you get caught. Especially if you've got a prisoner with you."

"Is there any way to avoid them?"

"You can make your way through the San Juans and some of the smaller islands. Make yourself harder to follow. There are no guarantees, though."

"You know where I can get a boat?"

"Do you know how to pilot a boat?"

"No. Can't be that hard, though, right?"

"Francis, the Puget Sound waters can be rough this time of year, and the currents up there are brutal."

"Let's just assume I can do it, for shits and giggles. Now, do you know where?"

"First of all, you want to spend as little time on the water as possible. That means you'll need to get as close as you can to the US before you attempt your boat ride. Take a ferry to Vancouver Island. They take hundreds of cars, so no one will be checking anything.

"When you get there, drive south to Victoria. At least you won't have to spend as much time on the water if you leave from there."

"What then?"

"Then call me. I need to make a few calls to see if I can line something up. If you take the ferry first thing in the morning from Tsawwassen to Swartz Bay, you should reach Victoria by noon. I'll talk to you then."

After disconnecting from James, Francis looked down at Hall, who was looking very worried. The bloody lips had started to clot, creating a brownish smile almost like that of the Joker.

"It looks like we'll be spending the night together. How about I take the sofa, and you can snuggle up right here on the floor. You like?"

"I guess I don't have much choice. I need to take a piss, though, and I can't do that with my hands behind my back."

"Well, you can, actually, but I don't want to be sleeping next to some clown who's pissed his pants. Here's what we're gonna do. I will tie your hands in front of you so you can go to the bathroom. We'll throw some cushions on the floor, and you can sleep there.

"When I was checking out at Home Depot, they had these really neat little bicycle locks on display. Thought I might be able to use one, and lo and behold, I can.

"I'm gonna wrap this cable around your newly zip-tied ankles and hook you up to the sofa leg. If you try anything stupid, your lips are probably gonna start bleeding again."

With a defeated look and a slump of his shoulders, Hall shuffled off to the bathroom.

FORTY-SIX

Albert was going batshit crazy. He'd been on Whidbey Island for two days with nothing to do but make sure O'Malley didn't leave the place.

On the second day, after seeing that O'Malley wasn't heading for the ferry, he headed up the two-lane country highway with more eggs for sale signs than pawn shops and finally reached Oak Harbor. Where his boss was right. There were a half dozen pawn shops scattered around the Naval base town.

He selected the sleaziest-looking one and went inside. There was an entire case of handguns. He asked to see two of the more expensive Glocks. After looking at each side carefully, he told the owner they were fine; he'd like to buy them. The total came to just under 900 dollars.

"You'll have to fill out some stuff and then wait ten days, sir."

Albert mustered his most menacing glare and said, "I don't think so. Here's two grand. Do I still have to wait?"

With a visible gulp, the owner shook his head. "No, sir, I was mistaken. Let me get you some ammunition, and you can be on your way."

As he started for the door, Albert did a double-take at a display case exhibiting all manner of knives. The Kershaw Leek pocketknife had long been a favorite of his. Because he had flown up, he hadn't been able to carry anything threatening. The gleaming stainless-steel blade of one reflected the display lights. "I'd like to buy that as well," he said, nodding at the case.

"The Kershaw?"

"Yes."

The proprietor reached into the case, retrieved it, and passed it. "Take it. You've more than made my day."

173

Most of his activities on behalf of his boss were done alone. It was rare for Hugo to be present for any enforcement action, and he had *never* accompanied him when he was out of town.

The drugs were no big deal. Albert could easily have taken care of that on his own. His jefe must think that Early, the other prominent investor, had some insight into where Hall had gone.

Herrera thought the money that the developer had split with was less important than the fact that Navarro had been taken for a fool. Hugo was a proud man with zero tolerance for any affront.

If his boss thought he could get more information from the guy in the wheelchair, then okay. Albert wasn't stupid, but he recognized Hugo was much more sophisticated. He could possibly learn more from Early. It wouldn't surprise him.

The recent voicemail instructed Albert to pick him up Friday morning at Paine Field located in unincorporated Snohomish County between Mukilteo and Everett, merely twenty miles north of Seattle, which bypasses the ever-growing traffic jam. The nonstop from San Diego would arrive in the late morning.

In the meantime, Albert spent his hours walking the beach at Double Bluff, sitting on the bluff in Langley watching the gray whales cavort, even hand feeding the famous bunnies.

His life's twists and turns had not prepared him for what he faced daily in the little town. People were friendly. Hell, even the tourists—they were easy to spot—were friendly.

And the bunnies: The damn things were all over the place. These weren't your average wild brown rabbits. Some were black, some red or brown or even white. More diverse than the people. These furry guys were the kind that pet stores sold to innocent little kids.

Yet the little fuckers roamed the streets indiscriminately. He'd read something about a few escapees from the local fairgrounds years ago. They bred like, well, like rabbits, and now they were town mascots. They were getting handouts left and right. Even more astonishing was the absence of squashed fur and entrails on any streets. Somehow the tiny beggars managed to avoid the traffic.

He'd be happy when he got back to San Diego. Back where things were *normal*.

FORTY-SEVEN

"Can you believe it? It's only Thursday. The Burns' property went live yesterday, and they've already got an offer."

Kevin had just come in from mowing the grass. "You're kidding."

"Nope. Some millennial just sold her company to Microsoft. She's a horse person."

"Four legs? Can she speak?"

Jenne was shaking her head as she turned away. "I've got better things to do if you're going to act like a doofus."

"Ooh, you mean she likes horses, the animals. Sorry, I missed the connection."

"Remember when I said you were an idiot? You're being one now."

"Okay, I'm sorry. It was the best I could come up with. Did she get what she listed it for?"

"Nope. She got an extra five hundred thou if she accepted the deal before they had the public open house. Seems as though the buyer really wanted the place. She told Liz she'd been looking for over a year in Carnation Valley and that she just had to have the property. Also said she'd be making some changes to the barn, so I don't think that wall under the platform is going to be an issue."

"That's fantastic. At least when we bring Bill up to speed, there shouldn't be any repercussions. Sounds like someone with that kinda money won't blink at a few grand."

"Speaking of Bill, I just got off the phone with Shelly. It's where I got the news on the ranch. She said they'd love to come up on Saturday. Maybe when they come here first would be a good time to break the news about your little drug discovery."

"I'm afraid there won't be a good time, but I agree with you. I'll fill him in then. When I stopped by yesterday to talk to Jake, he said Francis was out of town. Said he's trying to find the fellow who made off with Jake's money. The spa deal."

"Any luck?"

"He didn't seem to know. He did say he thought he'd be back in time for the weekend, though."

"I hope so. I think Bill will get a kick out of him, and I know Shelly will."

"Hopefully, he'll at least find out where the guy is. I gotta finish up outside before it starts raining. Oh, and don't holler at me while I'm on the lawnmower. I won't hear you, and you'll go hoarse yelling."

FORTY-EIGHT

Neither Francis nor Peter Hall had slept well. The sofa was built for someone much smaller than Francis. His captive, on the other hand, found it impossible to nod off with both his hands and his feet bound tightly.

At five a.m. on Thursday, Francis finally gave up. "Okay, Peter, here's what we're gonna do. You go into the bathroom and take care of whatever you need to do. I'm gonna take that lock off, so you don't have to hop around, but don't get any crazy ideas. When you're done, we are gonna hit the road."

"Where are we going?" A look of genuine fear crossed Hall's face.

"You let me worry about that. Just behave, and we'll get along fine."

With a full tank of fuel and a tired and frightened passenger, Francis headed south to the small town of Tsawwassen. Just north of the border from Washington State, it was home to the largest ferry terminal in North America.

Francis expected Hall to behave himself simply because of the threat of physical violence. Even so, the man was subdued to the point where he was concerned for his well-being. He hadn't uttered a word since leaving the apartment and stared straight ahead as they passed through the toll booth. His fears that Hall might try something with the attendant were unfounded.

The 9:30 a.m. sailing to Swartz Bay was aboard the *Queen of Cumberland* ferry. A smaller boat than the one generally used on the route, it had a capacity of only 115 vehicles. The journey across the Strait of Georgia and through the Gulf Islands lasted just over ninety minutes.

Francis decided to stay in his truck. No sense in giving his prisoner any opportunity to cause a stir.

"Something bothering you?" The silence proved unnerving for the big man.

"Ya think? I've been punched in the mouth, tied up, and now kidnapped. Yes, something is fucking bothering me."

Francis considered this for a moment. "You do know that you are a crook. You stole money from people and left the country. That's wrong. I'm taking you back to fix things."

"Sometimes stuff doesn't work out. People lose money on deals. That's what happened here."

"I understand. Sometimes investments go south. But in this case, you took all the remaining money instead of refunding what was left over. That makes you a bad guy. That's why you're going back."

"If it was just your brother's money, we could work something out. My problem is with the twenty-million-dollar loan I got from an individual."

Francis nodded, then broached the elephant in the room. "Is it Navarro you're afraid of?"

Hall snapped a glance at his captor, eyes bulging. "You know about him?"

"Yup. One of his people came to visit my brother. Wanted to know if we knew where you were. Course, we didn't at the time. My brother said the guy was a little odd, so I had some buddies do some research on him. Fucker's a badass dude. I'd hate to piss him off."

"Then you know why I can't let him know where I am."

"You had some successful projects. At least according to my brother. Why did you go to this drug lord for money?"

"I got greedy. Was hurting for funds. I knew he was sorta shady, but I had no idea to what extent. If he finds me, he'll kill me."

"That's too bad."

"Too bad? That's all you got? He's gonna kill me."

"Yeah, I heard you. Sorry about that, but my brother wants his money back, and you're coming with me. It's on you for doing business with douchebags."

For a few minutes, the only sound was the throbbing of the huge diesels powering the ferry. Francis was considering the journey ahead, hoping James would come through. He assumed his reluctant passenger was trying to find a way to stay alive.

"Look, I'll make a deal with you." Francis had given some thought to this during his failed attempt at sleep the previous night. "We've got a bit of a complicated trip ahead of us, and I can't be worried about you always trying to get away. If you promise to behave yourself, I'll get my buddies to try to come up with some way to give you a new identity. Something that'll keep you hidden from Navarro. Keep in mind that even if you did manage to get away, I know where your brothers live—both of them."

"He's a killer. You couldn't do that. They're innocent."

"Yeah, so's my brother."

"What kind of buddies could help me with a new identity?"

"My ex-con friends."

"You were in prison?"

"Look at my face, moron. You think they do these at the mall?"

"Perfect. A drug kingpin wants to kill me, and I'm being kidnapped by an ex-con with permanent tears who's now offering an olive branch."

"Hey, take it or leave it. I want my brother's money back. You can take your chances with Navarro or with me."

Hall's silence and look of resignation confirmed his acceptance of the lesser of two evils.

After the ferry eased into the dock at Swartz Bay, the Ram 3500 began the twenty-mile journey south to the quaint city of Victoria, on Vancouver Island. Francis made the call to James.

FORTY-NINE

"Okay, Francis. Take this down." James had answered on the first ring.

Francis put the phone on speaker and motioned his reluctant passenger to take notes. He pulled out a pencil and pad from the console and threw it to him.

"There's a place called West Bay. It's south of town, a little to the west. You should have no trouble finding it. When you get there, call the number I'm gonna text you. Perry will answer the phone. He's an old friend from McNeil. Who got out before you arrived. He runs a small marina there, and they do bareboat charters. They have a Grand Banks thirty-six that should be perfect for your trip.

"I told him you'd probably need a refresher on driving the thing, so he'll take you out for an hour or so and teach you the ropes. I also told him about your passenger. He's cool, so no worries about that.

"Remember what I told you about the border patrols. They have ways of seeing whether the international traffic stops at the customs locations. Be careful."

"I owe you big time, James. Thanks for doing this."

"Thank Perry. He owes me. I told him, you're good for all the fees, and you'll take care of him once you get to where you're going. Eventually, you'll have to get the boat back to him. Of course, you'll have to pick up your truck too."

Francis was focused on getting back to Whidbey Island. He wasn't concerned at the moment with any of the logistics.

"No worries, James, I'll get it handled. Thanks."

After the disconnect, he felt Hall staring at him. "We're taking a small boat to Whidbey Island from here?"

"If we go through customs, we run the risk of you getting caught. My brother got the folks in Utah to put out an alert on you, but I'm certain you were already in Canada by then. If that happens, you'll be sent back to Utah, and Navarro will know exactly where you are. Also, that doesn't help get my brother's dough back."

"Yeah, but a small boat?"

"It's a trawler, a thirty-six footer."

"It's Puget Sound, not Lake Washington. Shit can happen."

"We'll be fine." Francis covered his uncertainty with bravado.

Peter Hall just looked worried.

"Is this Perry?"

"It is."

"This is Francis Early. I got your number from James."

He could hear the smile over the phone. "How is my good friend James? It has been some time since we were together."

Francis heard the distinct accent of one of the Caribbean Islands. He had no idea which one.

"He's great, Perry. He sends his regards. Said you have a boat we can charter?"

"Yes, mon, I do. He told me you might need a bit of a refresher on the vessel."

"He's right. We're about fifteen minutes away. Is now good?"

"I'll see you then."

The small office structure at the front of the dock sported a small wooden sign: West Bay Charters.

A tall skinny gentleman with deep black skin, short-cropped gray hair, and a two-foot-wide grin approached them.

"Aye, you must be Francis. A pleasure to meet you." Perry offered an extended hand.

"Thanks, Perry. James spoke highly of you. This is my, uh, my friend, Peter."

Perry nodded knowingly in Hall's direction. "Nice to meet you, Peter," he said quietly with no offer of a handshake.

"Follow me. We'll get right to it. James said you were anxious to get going. There's a small craft warning now, and they're saying perhaps it will last into the evening. You'll be fine unless things get nasty."

They left the dock and spent most of an hour moving slowly in and out of the bay. The boat was equipped with twin screws and could be piloted from inside the cabin or up on the flybridge. While he lacked any boating experience, Francis was adept at most things mechanical and fairly agile for his size.

"You should have no trouble handling this craft, Francis." Perry congratulated him as he brought the boat nicely into the slip. Hall contented himself with sitting on the settee inside the cabin.

"Just remember, sir. Stay near the land if you would like to remain unseen. Watch the tide charts too. There will be a very low one this evening, bringing many submerged rocks into play. Pay heed to the charts in the galley as well."

"I'll do that, Perry. It looks like we have a seven- or eight-hour trip ahead of us. What happens if it gets too rough?"

"It's one-thirty now. You don't want to be out there during the dark: too many rocks and big ships. The seas should be roughest around dinner time and into the night. I would aim for Fisherman's Bay on Lopez Island. You can spend the night there and continue at high tide in the morning."

"That's what we'll do then. Again, thanks, Perry. I'll make sure to take care of payment when this is over."

"No, no. There is no payment. James has done so many favors for me. This is on me."

"Well, we'll see about that." Francis wasn't sure what to say, so he shook the gentleman's hand. Then he and his traveling companion headed out into the sound.

The trawler, heading east, crossed into US waters approximately ten miles from West Bay. Travelers going from Canada to the US via pleasure craft were required by law to stop at the designated customs office, located on San Juan Island in the quaint village of Friday Harbor. They would not be stopping there.

Silly Sally seemed an odd name for a boat, but Francis didn't care. As long as the Grand Banks got him where he was going, they could call it anything they wanted.

As the gray overcast sky turned to dusk, they turned north, past the southern tip of San Juan Island. Just past the small hump known as Goose Island was the entrance to Fisherman's Bay on Lopez Island.

While there are only a half dozen or so significant islands in the San Juan Archipelago. There are over one hundred named islands and over four hundred individual islands and rocks.

When they approached the bay, the tide was rising and at its mid-point. The entrance to the protected harbor was notoriously narrow and very shallow outside the channel. Any approach made when the tide was out was often met with scraped bottoms and damaged props.

Since Perry had cautioned Francis about the entrance, he found his eyes glued to the depth sounder, proceeding with just enough speed to maintain way. Their trawler had five feet of draft, and the sounder was registering eight feet. The last thing they needed was the attention a grounded $150,000 boat would garner.

After twenty stress-filled minutes, they made it safely into the marina's guest slip.

"Thanks for all your help, Peter. Much appreciated," Francis yelled caustically down to Hall, still hunkered down in the cabin.

"Hey, this is your show. I'm just the person you kidnapped." Peter seemed a little grumpy now that they were out of Canada.

The boat rocked back and forth as Francis jumped onto the dock and tied off the dock lines to the large cleats. It rocked again as Francis climbed back aboard and entered the teak-lined cabin.

"Let's get something straight here, Peter." Francis towered above the overweight thief, arms crossed and a severe frown on his face. Even with the Canucks jersey proudly displayed, he projected a menacing look. Hall retreated further onto the banquette on the far side of the small dining table.

"We've still got a ways to go, and I'm not babysitting your fat ass the whole time. I don't need much help driving this thing, but I'll need a hand from time to time.

"Here are your choices: You can shut the fuck up and do what I tell you without complaining. Or you can continue to be a pouty, annoying little asshole. If you choose option B, I will immediately contact your buddy Navarro and tell him exactly where you are. Your choice is . . . ?"

Hall paused a moment, then stretched his arms and legs. "Okay. I seem to be screwed either way, but maybe your pals can help me disappear again. Please don't tell Navarro where my brothers are."

"Nah, I wasn't gonna do that. Just trying to scare you. But I will kick your ass if you try anything like running. And I will tell Navarro where you are. We clear?"

"Yes. I'm hungry too."

"I was right; you are a pain in the ass. Stay here, and I'll go get us something to eat."

FIFTY

In the past, Hugo Navarro had rarely left his compound. Now that there was nothing but a few loose ends to clean up to get completely out of the drug business, though, he considered himself a legitimate businessman.

He had kept his most-trusted employees as farmhands. They worked very little, were paid handsomely, and preferred the safety and security of the large avocado farm.

Albert, his most trusted and capable, was highly effective when it came to murder and intimidation. He was less so when the task required a more civilized approach.

Hugo boarded the Alaska Air 737 bound for Paine Field on a crisp, clear seventy-degree San Diego morning. He sat in first class with the other well-to-do travelers headed for the Pacific Northwest. He was looking forward to seeing this part of the country he had never been to.

He was also looking forward to a quiet chat with one of the other investors in the Snow Canyon Spa. If there was any information as to the whereabouts of Hall, he was confident he could find it.

Flight 3330 touched down at two p.m. on Friday, April 4th. The temperature outside was forty degrees. It was overcast, and an intermittent fine mist clouded the air from time to time.

Navarro had worn only a blue blazer and was already questioning his decision not to carry an outer coat.

One of the first to deplane, he walked briskly down the jetway and covered the small concourse in short order. He immediately recognized his employee standing by a column on the far side of the luggage carousel.

Herrera wore his turd-brown Carhartt jacket and had a Mariners cap pulled low on his head. "Boss, good to see you. How was the flight?"

"Fine, Albert." He shivered a bit as a cold blast blew in through the automatic doors. "Is it always this fucking cold here? It's May, goddamn it. It's springtime."

Herrera seemed to suppress a smile. "Boss, no, it's not always this cold here. Lotsa times, it's way fucking worse. Really.

"Let's go get in the truck, and I'll turn up the heater."

"Why do people live here?" Hugo was still curious as they walked through the short-term parking to Albert's pickup.

"I don't know, honestly. But there sure are lots of them. This little airport here is way north of the city, but if you go south, it's wall-to-wall people. Fucking freeways are a mess. It takes forever to get anywhere. I've been up here twice, for over ten days total, and the sun's been out once."

"Sounds like hell."

"Yup, but where we're going is completely different. You won't believe it."

"Is there sun there?"

"Nah. Sometimes there's a little more, but it's not that far away, so I'm not sure. Anyway, let's get to the ferry."

The lot in Mukilteo was packed, and the cars went halfway up the hill. Friday afternoons were famous for long ferry lines.

"What the fuck is this? Where are all these people going? I thought you said nobody lives here." Navarro was having difficulty with the ferry culture.

Albert, being an old hand at it now, attempted to explain. "Half of the people in line live on the island but work in Everett or Seattle or somewhere in the area. The other half have second homes there, and they come over for the weekends. Friday is the worst day of the week. You've also got Cinque de Mayo tomorrow so that probably means more people."

Navarro just shook his head, amazed at the things people would put up with just to live on some stupid little island.

"Do we at least have a decent place to spend the night?"

Albert smiled. "You do. I'm still staying at the same shithole I've been at. I was able to get you a room at the inn at Langley. Nice place, right on the water."

This, at least, seemed to mollify Hugo. "How about the nightlife?"

Albert guffawed. "Hah. No and no. There isn't any. It's quiet there. It's best to pick up whatever you want for dinner at the Star Store and eat in the room."

Hugo was starting to think he'd made a mistake coming to this place. "What is a Star Store?"

"You'll see. You'll like it."

With that, the two busied themselves listening to a Mariners game while observing the locals and eased down the hill and through the lines at the dock. Navarro still couldn't get over how these people lived in this sunless world, waited in line to get on a boat to go home, and then did it all over again.

After his visit the next day with Jake Early, he'd be able to get the hell out of Dodge. He didn't have an appointment, but there was no question of his not being home according to Albert.

"Let's drive by that O'Malley place in the morning. I'd like to see what we're dealing with. There's gotta be something we can come up with that will allow us to get the fentanyl without raising holy hell."

"Sure thing, boss. If it's still in his car, maybe he'll park it somewhere, and we can get at it."

Hugo frowned, thinking that the scenario was unlikely. "I'm tired. Get me to the hotel."

"Oh, boss?"

"Yes?"

"Here. You asked me to pick something up. You were right about the pawnshops."

FIFTY-ONE

After Francis's "come to Jesus" meeting with Hall, the swindler seemed to accept his fate. At the very least, the possibility of him running off seemed remote. There was no place to go, after all.

Since the low, low tide was at seven a.m., it made sense to wait until after mid-morning to depart Fisherman's Bay. The stress of entering the harbor yesterday was still fresh in his mind, so he opted for several more feet of water under his keel.

With nothing to do but wait, he called his brother.

"Francis. I was worried about you. Tell me what's going on."

"I found Hall."

"What? Where are you? What are you going to do?"

Still reluctant to fully disclose his plans or sea voyage, he fell back on skills learned as a drug addict and refined as a prisoner. He lied.

"I was able to find him by staking out his brother's place. Now that I know where he lives, I'm going to visit him in just a little while."

"And do what?"

Since the "what" had already been done, he quickly thought of a plausible scenario. "I'll tell him we're going to turn him over to the cops unless he refunds your money."

"He'll just say it was a bad investment on my part. Tough shit."

"He might, but I'm still gonna try. At least we've got a location on him. I'll see what happens. At any rate, I'll be back tonight—tomorrow at the latest."

"Good thing. I volunteered our place for a Cinque de Mayo get-together with the O'Malleys and their friends the Owenses."

"That the cop friend?"

"It is."

Francis thought that the cop being there could work out to his benefit. "That sounds like fun. I'll look forward to it. I'll see you when I get there."

"Francis?"

"Yes?"

"Your meeting. With Hall …"

"Yeah?"

"Don't do anything stupid, please."

"Jake, I promise you that I won't do anything stupid. See you, mañana."

He disconnected, just now noticing that Hall had overheard things.

"What's that about a cop?"

"It's just a friend of a friend. They're having a little get-together tomorrow. Looks like we're gonna crash the party. Should be fun, eh?"

"This doesn't sound good for me."

"If you find a way to get Jake's money back to him, things will work out just fine. You'll still be on the hook to Navarro, but that's a personal loan—the cops don't care. Besides, what other choice do you have?"

Peter was quiet while they stowed things away to prepare for the next leg of their journey.

The sun was shining brightly in a cloudless sky. It was a rare day in spring that conditions were this good. There was still a small craft caution in effect from the front that had passed through the previous day, but otherwise, the voyage around the north end of Lopez, then over to Deception Pass looked straightforward.

At the suggestion of the marina manager, they had chosen the northern route to the pass rather than going around the south end of Lopez. They were told that the winds blowing straight through the Strait of Juan de Fuca made for brutal conditions, even in a boat as seaworthy as the Grand Banks.

With winds out of the northwest and the currents against them, they topped out at only five knots until they reached Canoe Island, just south of Shaw.

The short three-and-a-half-mile leg between Shaw and Lopez was over quickly, and the twenty-mile-plus easterly trek to Deception Pass began. Except for their circumstances, it would have been a spectacular day on the waters of Puget Sound. The temperature had climbed to sixty-five degrees, and a hatless Francis Early was beginning to sport a blush of sunburn on his naked dome.

Even Peter Hall's spirits seemed buoyed by the rare sunshine. He had joined Francis on the bridge and appeared to have found a tiny modicum of peace and acceptance despite his challenging immediate future.

Deception Pass separates Fidalgo Island from Whidbey Island. The 180-foot rocky cliffs on both sides of the pass form a channel almost 150 feet wide. The current speeds approach ten miles per hour during tidal changes from high to low, making it incredibly difficult to navigate.

The bridge, built in 1935, was recognized in 1982 by being placed on the National Registry of Historic Places. The surrounding park spans over 4,000 acres and is the most visited park in Washington.

None of these facts were even considered by Francis. They approached the pass at its maximum tidal current and were immediately rebuffed.

Its two engines supplying 240 horsepower, the trawler was no match for the tumbling, swirling, frothy current. Seeing no other choice, Francis maneuvered the craft around Lighthouse Point and spent an hour in Bowman Bay on the Fidalgo Island side of the pass.

"No way we're gonna make it back tonight. After we get through the pass, we'll have to find someplace to put in for the night. Make yourself useful. Look at those charts and see where we can anchor or moor or find a marina somewhere."

Hall grunted, turned, and went below.

Their second attempt at getting through the fierce current was still turbulent, although with less white water. After a half-hour of fighting the current, they found themselves coming abeam of Strawberry Island. It was the entrance to Skagit Bay.

With an hour or so remaining until sundown, they needed to find a place to spend the night. Francis's exhaustion from his day at the helm was thrown into overdrive by his battle at Deception Pass. His depleting adrenaline left him socked with fatigue.

"Peter, we need to find a place, now."

Hall hustled up to the bridge carrying one of the books of charts. "The closest place is called Shelter Bay, near a town called La Conner. We have to go a little way up this Skagit River, and then it's on the left."

"That's where we're going, then. Get on the radio and see if they've got a guest slip for the night. We should have just enough daylight to make it. If we leave early enough in the morning, we can make it to Langley shortly after noon."

FIFTY-TWO

Kevin, standing on the edge of the deck, never tired of seeing old sol peek over Mount Pilchuck. "Wow, check out that sunrise, Jenne."

During the summer months, rain in the Northwest was scarce. However, throughout the balance of the year, cloudy skies were the norm. A spectacular sunrise in mid-spring was to be celebrated.

"I agree. Looks just like a Roy Vickers painting. I never get tired of it." Jenne referred to the well-known First Nations artist from Tofino on Vancouver Island.

"Should be nice tomorrow too. Maybe we can force Jake out of the house. Get him in a cornhole tournament." Kevin was half-serious.

"Don't push him too much. You don't know what demons he's battling."

"I agree, but he's such a gregarious fellow that it seems like he would enjoy getting out and meeting folks. He said he expected Francis to be back from his trip to Canada."

"What are the chances that he'll get anywhere?"

"He's pretty good with the computer stuff, and he has some buddies that are very good. Jake said they found a way to track Hall's IP address to Vancouver. I still think it's a needle in a haystack, though."

"Why don't you go see Jake and ask what we can bring for tomorrow?"

"I could just call."

"No. I've got stuff to do, and I'm better off doing it by myself. Now go."

"You're being hurtful, you know."

"Get out. Go pester Jake for a while." She was grinning as she shooed him out the door.

Kevin was beginning to think that the weather cleared every time he paid a visit to the Early residence. This day, Friday was no exception.

Once again, the door opened just as Kevin reached the front step.

"Don't say it. I know you're dying to use some clever little insult, so I'll save you the effort."

"First, my wife kicks me out of the house, and now you, my closest friend on the island, find a way to abuse me."

"Shut up and get in here. It's cold with the door open. What's up?"

"Jenne says I'm to ask you what we can bring tomorrow. So here I am. What do we bring?"

"Nothing I can think of. We got food and wine. Pretty sure that covers all the bases."

"If I don't tell her what to bring, she'll say I didn't insist. This is me insisting."

"Okay, tell you what. It's Cinque de Mayo, so bring some margaritas. Will that get you off the hook?"

"I guess. Hey, how is your brother making out in Vancouver?"

"Believe it or not, he found him. Hall. I just got off the phone with him."

"You're shitting me."

"Nope. Said he followed him from his brother's place and was going to have a meeting with him."

"And do what?"

"I don't know, and I don't think he does either. If nothing else, we know where he is, and we know what alias he was using."

"That's great news. Maybe Bill Owens can come up with something when we see him tomorrow."

"Maybe. We'll see. It sure would be nice to get some of my investment back. Francis said he'd be back tonight or sometime tomorrow, so we'll have to wait until then to see what's what."

"I can't wait. I'll fill Jenne in on things, and we can prep Bill on our way here tomorrow. See you then. With margaritas and whatever else Jenne's making. You know she will."

"I do. I still don't see why she has anything to do with you."

"Bye, Jake."

FIFTY-THREE

Francis had slept later than he had planned. He looked at his watch, still hearing the snores of Peter Hall in the forward stateroom. It was eight a.m.

"Let's go. Rise and shine," he shouted as he clanged the bell on the post in the galley. "C'mon, Peter, get your ass in gear. It's late."

Whatever remaining hair Hall possessed looked frazzled as he stumbled past the bulkhead. "How come we slept so late?"

"Don't know, maybe sea air. Don't give a shit either. We need to get going. If we leave now, we should be in Langley a little after noon."

"What's the rush?"

"The rush is, I'm tired of being on the water. That and I told Jake I'd be there. Pull up the fenders and untie us. There's some bread and peanut butter from last night. That oughta hold you until we land."

They made their way out of the marina and headed south down the Skagit River. The river would open to Skagit Bay, which would lead them into the Saratoga Passage, the body of water between Whidbey and Camano Islands.

The passage was home to abundant sea life. Cutthroat trout, salmon, and Dungeness crab, as well as oysters and shrimp, were plentiful. Gray whales and orca pods were known to visit during certain times of the year.

With the morning sun glinting off the water and the small craft warnings now diminished, the southward trip down these more protected waters of the sound was almost pleasant.

Francis wasn't sure what would happen when he brought his captive home to celebrate the 5th of May with his brother and friends. He felt confident of one thing. With Jake, Kevin, Jenne, and the cop and his wife present, Hall would have a tough time refusing to give up the money his brother had invested.

As he pictured the scene when he arrived at his home, he realized he wasn't driving his truck. He would need a ride from the Langley Marina to his house.

That meant confiding in someone. His brother sure as shit couldn't drive, so that left only Kevin.

FIFTY-FOUR

"What time did you say Bill and Shelly were arriving?"

"They should be here in a couple of hours, Jenne. I thought we could spend a few minutes here breaking the news to Bill about the drugs. After all the yelling and screaming dies down, we can head over to Jake's. I told him we'd be there early afternoon."

"Sounds good. You think Bill's gonna be pissed off?"

"Jenne, of course, he will be. I guess I don't blame him either. It's a case he couldn't solve, and I know they searched that place from top to bottom, even with the dogs. The only reason I found it was because I looked closer at that double wall upstairs. I guess because the stuff was stuck inside the wall, the dogs couldn't smell it either.

"Anyway, he'll settle down after he blows off steam. If he doesn't, Shelly will straighten things out."

Just then, he heard the familiar sound of the Chieftains., It was his cell phone. Kevin looked at the caller, then at his wife.

"It's Francis. Wonder why he's calling *me*?"

"I know how to find out," Jenne said with raised eyebrows.

"Hey, Francis, how are you? Jake told me you found where Hall was hiding out. That's great news."

"Um, yeah. I got lucky. Listen, Kev, I need a favor."

"Sure, anything. What?"

"I need you to pick me up at the Langley Marina. About one-thirty or two. Can you swing it? I know there's that thing at our place. I just need a lift to get home from the dock there."

"Well, sure. No problem, but why there? Why don't you just drive home?"

"I don't have my truck right now. I had to make some other arrangements. I'll fill you in on everything when you get here."

Kevin had a million questions, but he deferred, sensing Francis was in a hurry. "Okay. I'll take Jenne and the Owenses over to your brother's place; then, I'll swing by and pick you up."

"You sure it's all right?"

"Not a problem. See you then."

Jenne had heard just the one end of the conversation. Still, her curiosity was piqued. "What the hell was that all about?"

Kevin, too, was trying to figure things out. "I guess I don't know. Francis asked me to pick him up at the marina in Langley. He needs a ride."

"What did he say when you asked why he didn't drive?"

"Said he doesn't have his truck. I have no idea what's going on. He seemed to be distracted. I guess we'll just have to wait."

FIFTY-FIVE

"When do you want to talk to Early?"

Navarro appeared to give it some thought. "Why don't we see what we can do about getting our merchandise back first? You know where O'Malley lives. Let's head over there, park somewhere out of the way, and just observe for a bit. If an opportunity doesn't present itself, we may have to force the issue. I'd prefer not to, though."

Albert knew his boss wasn't familiar with the island. He wasn't aware how rural the place was and that there were no places to park "out of the way" from which to observe. He knew better than to voice these concerns, however. Hugo would find out soon enough.

They drove north on Saratoga Road and slowed down as they passed Little Dirt Road.

"That's where they live. Down that little dirt road."

"What, these people are comedians? That's how they name their streets?"

Having spent some time on Whidbey Island, Albert had come to accept the quirkiness of the place. "They do some odd things here," he agreed.

"Where can we park so we can see them? Can we drive down that dirt road?"

"No, boss. There are only two houses down there. They'll notice us for sure."

"Where should we park?"

"Boss, there's no place. There are so few people around here that they notice shit. It's hard to hide."

Albert could see the frustration beginning to mount in Navarro's demeanor.

"How about this? We'll go back down the road. There's a place where people park to walk their dogs through the woods. If they come by there, we'll follow them. I know both their cars."

"And suppose they go the other way?" Navarro wasn't used to not being able to do as he damn well pleased.

"It doesn't go anywhere, just up to the north end of this peninsula. There's nothing there. They have to come this way if they go either into town or off the island. We'll see them."

Navarro grudgingly accepted his subordinate's reasoning. "Okay. Let's try it for a little while. We'll give it an hour or two; then we'll have to do something else."

FIFTY-SIX

Francis and Peter Hall made good time. They were passing Coupeville, close to the north-south midpoint on Whidbey Island. It was ten a.m.

He pulled back on the Ford Lehman diesels just a smidge, confident now that he would meet Kevin at 1:30.

Uncharacteristically, Peter was sitting up on the bridge with him.

"What do you think the odds are that your friends can find a way to hide me from Navarro?"

"Well, they're very good at what they do on the web and stuff. I'm fairly certain they can give you a new identity. Maybe you can go back up to Vancouver and live near Mark or Bobby in New England. I guess you could worry about charges from the State down in Utah, but if they haven't done anything yet, you're probably safe from them."

Hall appeared pensive as he considered his future.

"Besides my brother and Navarro, how much money do you have from the others?"

"There's five from your brother. All the others total up to another six or seven million. Most of those folks have invested in previous projects."

"I'm not a person who gives advice, and I don't like to get it either. It seems to me, though, if you took care of all the legitimate investors, you'd still have twelve to fifteen million dollars. You may not get anyone to work with you anymore, but so what? But the Navarro thing is a real problem. The guy is wanted throughout the country, but they can't get anything to stick to him. He either kills witnesses, or they disappear."

"That's what I'm afraid of."

"They say he's out of the drug trade, and he's trying to clean up his act. If his future paybacks are anything like his previous ones, though,

I'd be afraid too. Maybe you could lay low until they find a way to convict the guy."

"I could be dead by then."

"I agree. You're in a tough spot. Let's focus on the first issue; then, we can look for a way out of the Navarro thing. Unless I'm mistaken, it's not the money with him. It's being taken for a sucker."

"None of this is making me feel any better."

"I'm not trying to. I'm just looking at reality here. Unless somehow the law gets to Navarro, your only fallback is to stay under the radar. Let's see what my friends have to say about that."

FIFTY-SEVEN

For an hour, Navarro and Herrera sat in the parking area adjacent to one of the many hiking trails on Whidbey Island. The sun streaming in through the windshield managed to induce the two into a semi-conscious state.

The only movement was several vehicles, primarily Outbacks and pickups, unloading their dogs and proceeding into the thickly wooded area.

Because they were focused on vehicles heading south on Saratoga Road, they failed to notice the bright red Mercedes S-class Cabriolet heading north.

Hugo roused himself and stretched his arms and legs in the generous cab of the F-150. "We're going to give this another hour or so, Albert. Then we go to plan B."

"What would that be?"

"Then we take a drive up Little Dirt Road, pull out the hardware you scored, and take back my merchandise."

Albert cracked a smile at the thought of finally taking some action. "Sounds good to me, boss. Can't wait."

FIFTY-EIGHT

It was 11:30 a.m. when the O'Malleys heard the sports car turn into the gravel driveway. Emma acknowledged the activity by barking as only a German Shepherd. Loudly.

"Bill and Shelly are here."

"What I figured, hon. It was either them or some army trying to assault the castle here. This oughta be fun."

"Take it easy, Kev. Let's let them get in the door before you start the fireworks."

"Thanks for the tip," came the sarcastic response.

A look from his wife caused Kevin to restate his last reply. "Sorry. What I meant to say was, 'Of course, I will, dear. Thank you for reminding me.'"

Bill and Shelly Owens made it to the front door before any other sparring between the two.

"How was the ferry lineup, Bill?"

"Not too bad, Jenne; just a one-boat wait. Thought it would be much worse on a sunny day."

"Glad you two could make it up. I know you'll like the Earlys. They volunteered their place for the get-together."

Shelly looked at Kevin. "Why their place? I thought it was your idea."

"You'll see. It just seemed to work better."

"What time should we head over?"

"I told them we'd be there around one-ish."

"How come you had us up this early, then?"

Kevin looked over at his wife, both nodding, both knowing that it was time for the show to begin.

Kevin had practiced his delivery several times in his head, but it never seemed to sound very good. *Might as well get it over with*, he thought.

"You remember the Robbie Burns murder?"

"How could I forget? The goddamn case is still open, but it's pretty cold by now."

"You guys looked all over that barn for the drugs, didn't you?"

Bill looked at Shelly, then Jenne, then back at Kevin. It appeared he was showing some anxiety.

"We did. We had the dogs out there, and Houser and I were there several times ourselves. Why are we talking about this?"

Kevin finally ripped the Band-Aid off. "Bill, I found the drugs. They were stuffed inside a double wall that Burns had the contractor modify. I think the reason he came to see me that night at the Meadowlark was to talk to me about the changes and how they would affect the structure."

Kevin let out a deep breath with the air remaining in his lungs.

Both women looked at Bill as a slow flush crept up his face. Even Emma was quiet.

The chief of detectives of the Bellevue Police Department spoke barely above a whisper. "You what?"

"I found the drugs."

"I heard you the first time. I just couldn't believe it." The cop's voice was now certainly above a whisper.

"When did this happen?"

"A week ago."

"A week ago? And you're telling me *now*? Kevin, what the fuck is wrong with you? You know how much time we've put into this case."

"I know you're pissed, and I don't blame you. Just give me a few minutes to explain."

Kevin went into his rationalization for withholding the discovery. He attempted to explain the impending sale of the ranch and how he'd thought that at this stage of the game, what could a few days hurt?

Owens appeared to have his temper marginally more under control at this point. "So, did you just leave them there?"

"Um, no. I sealed the wall back up and put them in my car. They're still out there."

"You *took* the evidence and then tampered with the site?"

"When you put it like that, it doesn't sound so good. I thought it was best for Liz, and who the hell cares about the site? We know it was Burns who hid the stuff there. Sheesh."

Owens looked as though he was processing the revelation before he spoke. "I'll admit that there is probably no evidence to be gained by re-working the site. The drugs, though, are another story. These days , a mass spectrometer can determine the origin and purity of illegal drugs. We compare the findings to similar tests to establish where they came from.

"So, to be clear, we need the goddamn drugs. It might help us determine the supplier, hence the killer of Robbie Burns.

"We'll need a full statement from you too, Kevin, explaining how you found them, what you did, etc. Also, you'll need to detail how you removed them from the site to maintain a chain of custody."

Now that Owens was on familiar ground, he was focused on the process rather than yelling at his buddy.

Shelly looked over at her husband and offered, "Well, Bill, does this help you make any progress on the case?"

"It should, yes."

"So, shouldn't you be thanking Kevin and Jenne here for helping?" Shelly's pixieish smiling face reminded Bill how much he enjoyed her.

"It's a good thing I'm a cop, Shell. I don't think anyone else could keep you in line."

"As if."

"Jenne, thank you for helping your idiot husband solve the whereabouts of the smuggled drugs. I'm certain he couldn't have done it on his own." While Bill's graciousness was directed at Jenne, he looked directly at his friend.

The tension level had decreased precipitously in the house when Bill put on his police cap once more.

"Kevin, let's get that stuff out of your car. I'm sure you don't want millions of dollars worth of fentanyl with you while you're driving around. You'll feel better when it's gone."

"You've got that right. I was scared to death I'd get pulled over and searched."

"You watch too many movies. You're white. I'm the type who gets pulled over."

"Touché, buddy. Sad but true." Kevin marveled at his friend's ability to smooth things over, even if the subject was a volatile one.

They transferred the plastic-wrapped package to Shelly's convertible and tucked it into what little room there was in the trunk. "Let's take both cars to your friend's place. I'll feel better knowing the contraband is with me. I'll get it to the station as soon as we get back to Bellevue."

They loaded up their margaritas, and the dessert Jenne had made and headed down Melody Road in a two-car convoy. Kevin insisted on taking the refreshments. The aroma of frozen tequila and lime juice did wonders for his sinuses. On the remote chance of a flat, he would be prepared.

FIFTY-NINE

"Hugo, there's the car. O'Malley's heading out." Navarro had just started nodding off when Albert startled him.

They took off, following a convertible that was behind the green Explorer.

The Explorer turned off Saratoga onto Lone Lake Road. The red sports car followed, as did the Ford pickup. Goss Lake Road crossed Lone Lake about two and a half miles south. The two cars took a right while Albert held back a half-mile. Except for the three vehicles, there was no other traffic.

Goss Lake Road was a hilly stretch that wrapped around Goss Lake itself. After they crested the top of a hill, the O'Malleys, followed by the Owenses, turned onto Melody Road.

The pickup slowed, then drove by.

"I don't fucking believe it," Herrera almost shouted.

"What? What is it?" Hugo showed some concern as if his enforcer had lost it.

"You know the cripple, the guy I talked to about Hall and the money he stole?"

"Yes?"

"That's his fucking house. These people with your drugs are at the same house where the other investor lives. What the fuck is going on here?"

Hugo was quiet for a moment, then said, "Pull over here. Let's talk this out.

"Is it possible that this place is so small that everyone knows every-one else? I don't think so. Could O'Malley be doing something with this cripple with my merchandise?"

207

"Boss, it doesn't make any sense. Maybe they're just visiting, and maybe he left the fentanyl back at his house. And who's in the little red car?"

Just as the two smugglers were discussing possibilities, the green Explorer came back onto Goss Lake from Melody.

"Follow him, Albert. Let's see where the sonofabitch is going."

SIXTY

Kevin and Jenne waited for Bill and Shelly to get out of their car before going up the pavers to the front doors of the log structure.

"Yikes, this is some place, guys." Shelly was clearly impressed with the log home.

"Wait until you see the inside, Shelly, and watch—we won't even have to ring the doorbell." Kevin had come to expect Jake's all-seeing Ring doorbell.

As expected, the door swung open just before Jenne could reach the bell.

"Welcome, Jenne, Kevin, and these must be the Bill and Shelly I've heard so much about. Please come in."

If Bill and Shelly were surprised by a host in a wheelchair, they hid it well.

"You have a beautiful place here, Jake. The O'Malleys have told us all about it, but they didn't do it justice."

"Thanks very much. Come on in so we can get this show on the road. Francis isn't here yet, but I expect we'll see him soon."

Kevin held back near the entrance until the rest of the party made their way into the spacious great room. As Jake turned his chair to make sure everyone was following, Kevin gave him a nod.

"Be with you in just a sec. Folks, make yourselves comfortable." Jake then made his way back over to Kevin.

"What's up, Kev? Come on in."

"Um, Jake, I need to leave for a little while. I told Francis I'd pick him up."

"Huh? I spoke with him yesterday, and he said if he weren't here by last night, he'd make it sometime today."

"Well, he was certainly right about that. He'll be here in an hour or so."

Jake was still confused. "Where are you picking him up and why?"

"He told me he'd meet me at the dock in Langley, and I said I'd be happy to pick him up. I don't know anything else."

Kevin could see the confusion on Early's face. "Look, Jake, we'll find out what the deal is soon enough. I'm not sure what the hell's going on either. I'll be back as soon as I can."

Kevin made the four-mile trip to Langley in no time. As usual, traffic was very light. He passed a pickup parked on the side of the road about a half-mile from Melody Road but gave it little thought. Probably just a couple of contractors in between jobs.

The sunshine and clear skies made the trip enjoyable. Kevin had many questions about why Francis didn't have his truck and why he was at the marina. But he'd find out soon enough. At any rate, he was looking forward to the afternoon's festivities. Not having to cart around a fortune in illegal drugs contributed mightily to his comfort level as well.

SIXTY-ONE

"I think he saw us."

"So what, Albert? He doesn't know what we look like. Let's see where he goes."

They swung around and kept the Explorer in sight as it made its way to the tiny village of Langley.

Coles Road turned into Third Street. After a left on Park and a right on First, Herrera closed the distance. When O'Malley took a left on Wharf Street, Albert pulled over to the side of the road.

"Why are we stopping?" Hugo could sense the uneasiness from his driver.

"It's a tiny street, boss. I think once we get down the hill, there's no way out."

"I don't care. It's about time we did something. Follow him."

As Albert drove slowly down the hill, he could see O'Malley pull into a small parking area. The sign above announced South Whidbey Harbor.

"On the right, Albert. Pull over there." Herrera could feel the intensity in Hugo's voice.

They backed into a space that gave them an excellent view of the harbor and its small series of docks.

O'Malley exited his car and walked to the main dock and down the 200-foot-long pier. He then just stood there at the railing.

"It looks like he's waiting for someone. Even with these binoculars, it's hard to see what's happening."

"Let's just sit tight, Albert. We know he's gotta come back this way to his car."

"How about we break into his car and see if our stash is there?"

"Too many people. Let's just see where this goes."

Twenty minutes passed before O'Malley moved from the railing.

"He's going on down to one of the smaller sections, Hugo. I can't see him anymore. He's below the level of the main pier."

"Sit tight. He'll be back."

SIXTY-TWO

Kevin had arrived fifteen minutes early. He had only been to the harbor once before. On this pristine day, with the sun glinting off Saratoga Passage, he wondered how this little corner of the country could remain as remarkable as it was, able to avoid the hordes of tourists that rendered other small towns uninhabitable.

Whatever the reason, he was happy to be here.

While entertaining these pleasant thoughts, a beautiful Grand Banks Classic rumbled up to the outer dock. As it got closer, he could see a sunburnt bald dome high up on the bridge.

He knew then that it was Francis.

Stunned as he was, he watched his friend expertly maneuver the beautiful boat gently alongside the dock, just nudging the fenders as he cut the engines.

Another fellow jumped off the boat and tied the dock lines to the cleats. The guy was short and a little chubby. As he turned to shore, Kevin almost fell over. Holy shit. It was Peter Hall.

He hurried the rest of the way to the *Silly Sally*, still trying to wrap his arms around what he was seeing.

Just as Francis jumped off the boat, he saw Kevin jogging up. "Hey, Kev, thanks for meeting me here. I bet you know this guy."

"Francis, Peter. What the hell? What's going on?"

Francis took the lead. "I found Peter here up in Vancouver. After several discussions, he felt it was the best thing to do to come back with me and make amends. Isn't that right, Peter?"

Hall, looking sheepish, took a few seconds to respond. "Let's just say Francis convinced me that coming with him was in my best interests." He glanced at Francis with a knowing look.

"What's with the boat? Where's your truck?"

"At the time, I wasn't certain Peter would come along willingly. I needed to find a way to get him here without going through customs. If they had a lookout for him, they would have detained us and turned him in. We went over to Vancouver Island and made our way here from there."

"Sheesh, I don't know what to say. I'll bet your brother will be thrilled."

"Yup, that's the idea. Can we get going now? We're hungry as hell."

The three men headed up the dock.

SIXTY-THREE

"Wait. He's coming back. Shit, there are two other guys with him."

"Let me have those." Navarro grabbed the field glasses and took a look. "Jesus fucking Christ. That tubby guy is Hall. He's the guy who stole my fucking money. What's he doing here? Why is O'Malley involved, and who is the big goofy-looking guy with the red head?"

"Um, I dunno, boss." Albert knew better than to address Hugo when he got worked up like this.

"Should we take him now?"

"Too many people. Follow them. I bet I can guess where they're going."

They pulled out after the Ford passed and tailed them back to Melody Road. As the Explorer turned in, Albert drove up to the spot they had previously parked.

"Okay, Hugo. What do we do? They've got the guy who stole your money in there, and O'Malley knows where your drugs are. I don't know how he's in the middle of this, but he is. What should we do?"

"Give me a minute." Albert trusted his boss. They hadn't stayed beyond the long arm of the law this long without Hugo Navarro's cunning and intelligence.

SIXTY-FOUR

Jake was in his element entertaining his guests. Before long, Shelly was peppering him with questions about his house, his brother, and even about his disability. She had a way of getting to the root of things in a disarming way.

Bill was getting a tour of the house, courtesy of Jenne. They were taking extra time in the well-stocked wine cellar.

The doorbell rang. The door opened, and Francis stepped in, followed by Kevin and a short, balding man with glasses.

Jake smiled when he saw Francis and Kevin. When Francis stepped aside and the third man was visible, Jake's wine glass exploded on the concrete floor.

Seeing his brother speechless, Francis walked over, bent down, and hugged him. At the same time, he whispered in his ear, "Told you I'd find this fucker. He's here, and he's gonna transfer your money back into your account."

As he stood, he saw a short perky dark-haired woman stride over to him and offer her hand.

"Hi, I'm Shelly Owens. I'll bet you're the famous Francis I've heard so much about. Your brother says you're a sweetheart."

If Francis's head was red before from the sun, it was now purple.

"Easy, Shelly. Can't you see you're embarrassing the man? He just got in from a tough trip. Francis, ignore her. She does that to everyone. Shelly, maybe we can get these two some food. By the way, this other gentleman is Peter Hall."

Shelly patted Francis on the shoulder and sent a quizzical look Kevin's way.

Kevin knew she had heard the name when he and Bill talked about the developer. He watched as the three made their way into the kitchen.

"Kevin, talk to me. What the hell is going on?"

Kevin filled Jake in on the events. He covered Francis's trip along with his semi-abduction of Peter Hall. He explained how Hall would be transferring all the investors' money back to them except for Navarro's loan.

He also covered Hall's reasoning that even if he could get Navarro's money back to him, the smuggler was a stone-cold killer. Hall was going to rely on Francis's computer buddies to come up with a new identity that would enable him to disappear.

While Jake took some time digesting the happenings, Kevin changed the subject. "Where's Bill and Jenne?"

"She's showing my house to your friend. My guess is they got stuck in the tasting room. Maybe you can find them while I clean up this mess."

After Shelly had made sure the weary travelers were well-nourished, she headed off to find her husband. Peter and Francis headed to the computer room, Francis's office. There was work to be done.

SIXTY-FIVE

Navarro had been quiet for a full ten minutes. He turned to Herrera. "I can't see any other way around this, Albert."

"What do you mean, boss?"

"That house down there has everything we came here for. If they don't have the drugs with them, they know where they are. I'm certain we can convince them to tell us. The guy who stole my money is in there too. I don't know how much or if I can get it back, but I know *he's* in there, and I have a score to settle with him. Nobody fucks me over, Albert. Nobody."

"Yes, boss. I know." Albert knew that it was best to get out of the way when Hugo got like this.

"How do you want to do it?"

"There are seven people in there. Right?"

"Yup."

"What we do is round them up and put them in the same room. If they don't tell us where the drugs are, we grab O'Malley's wife. You will take her somewhere else until he tells us. If he doesn't, there will be screaming. Then he will."

Albert nodded, already warming to the sound of things. "So, after we get the merchandise, what then?"

Navarro shook his head from side to side, acknowledging the obvious.

"Hall's dead no matter what. Correct?"

"Yes, Hugo."

"Nobody knows us here. Correct?

"Yes, boss."

"So, the only people who will know that we were ever here are in that house. Correct?"

"Yes."

"So, then, Albert, they need to stay in that house forever."

Albert had known all along where this journey would end. After they were done, they could go back to San Diego, to the warmth and sunshine where they could pretend to be legitimate businessmen. There would be no one left on Whidbey Island to say otherwise.

"Turn this thing around. Let's take a drive down Melody Road."

SIXTY-SIX

After Jake Early had swept up the last shards of glass and deposited them in the trash, the doorbell rang. Looking at the app on his phone, he could see two men outside his front door. One was familiar.

"Hello. What can I do for you?" Jake spoke through the doorbell using his phone.

Albert spoke up as previously planned. "My boss was in town, and he has a few questions for you. You know, regarding that development project."

If Jake had been concerned when Herrera had first visited, he was doubly so now. Francis had related the information about Navarro that Mickey had supplied.

"Now is not a good time. I have some friends over, and we'd like to be left alone." Jake was sure he had come across bluntly but based upon the information Francis had received from his buddies, these were bad dudes.

Living on the island in such a small community, people seldom locked their doors. Jake was confident the doors hadn't been locked after his brother had arrived. He raced as fast as his chair could move to the door. One of the heavily timbered doors was thrown back into his face as he reached for the deadbolt.

The blow knocked him out of his chair, which toppled over on him.

"Sorry about that, Jake. We need to handle some business." Albert moved quickly, righting the wheelchair. Then, with barely any effort, he lifted Early and placed him back in his chair.

"There. How's that? Didn't mean to knock you over, but we just had to come in."

Jake, dripping blood from a small gash on his cheek, looked from one hood to the other. The previous visitor, the one who had picked him up, was incredibly strong. The short guy with the acne scars had yet to say a word.

"My guess is you're Hugo Navarro." Jake wasn't a young man, but his steely blue eyes drove home his intensity.

The smaller man smiled—a particularly nasty smile. "You are correct, Mister Early. How did you know?"

Jake thought it useless to attempt ignorance at this point. "After your friend here visited me, we did some research on you. It wasn't easy, but we finally discovered who you are."

"That's unfortunate, but maybe we can just get what we came for and leave you and your friends in peace."

Although Jake felt a glimmer of hope, his better sense suggested otherwise.

"What have you come for?"

"Two things. One of your guests has located a package of mine that has been missing for a few years. I'd like to get that back. Also, one of your guests has taken a great deal of money from me. I need to speak with him."

Jake had no idea about any package. The way these two looked, though, just speaking with Hall was the last thing on their minds.

"I don't know anything about any package." The only thing Jake had going for him was that the rest of the group was scattered throughout the rambling structure. Maybe someone would come up with a plan.

"I can see why you wouldn't. However, I know that one of your guests knows where it is. I'm certain if you get him in here, he'll tell me."

"I would like you to leave, please."

Hugo looked at Herrera. He smiled as they both pulled out their Glocks.

"I'm sorry, Mister Early. We cannot do that. Now please call your guests in here."

"We have no intercom, and this log structure doesn't let any sound from room to room. I have no way of doing that except physically going from room to room."

Jake looked from one to the other and saw a slight tic appear at Navarro's eye. The man seemed to be marginally frustrated.

"I see you have your cell phone with you. Please call them and have them come here."

Jake smirked at the duo and shook his head. "You see that white box on the wall over there, the one with the green blinking light?"

Navarro looked in that direction and gave a slight tilt of his head.

"That's a signal booster. The service on the island is spotty. The only way we can get cell service is with that booster, and this room is the only one in the house where you can get cell service." The white box was actually a carbon monoxide detector.

Jake wasn't sure whether they would fall for the ruse, but it was all he could think of to buy some time. He was more certain than ever now that he and his guests were in mortal danger.

The little tic at the corner of Navarro's eye was now more noticeable. "Albert, start rounding people up. Bring them here however you can. I don't care if they're conscious or not. I don't even care if they're alive. Now go."

Albert quickly and silently started down the hallway leading to the rest of the house.

SIXTY-SEVEN

The lower floor was below ground level, thus ideal for a wine cellar. The temperature was a steady fifty-eight degrees year-round. As Jake had suspected, Jenne and Bill Owens were wandering about the wine racks, inspecting the different varietals and vintages.

"Wow, what a surprise finding you two in here." Kevin had just walked through the arched doorway.

"Good, you're back. Did you get Francis?"

"I did. He got to Langley on a boat. He brought Peter Hall with him."

"What?"

Bill looked back and forth at the O'Malleys for several seconds before things clicked into place for him.

"Is this the guy you asked me about? The one who left with the millions from that spa deal in Utah?"

Kevin replied, "That's the guy. Francis is quite the salesman. He convinced Hall to come back with him. Well, it seems at first it was more like an abduction. During the trip, though, I guess Hall learned to see things differently. He's with Francis now. They're transferring funds from some offshore accounts back into Jake's bank account."

"That's terrific news. What happens to Hall now?"

"Well, Jenne, that's a bit murky. He's got some drug smuggler after him. He lent Peter twenty million, and it doesn't look like he'll be able to come up with it."

"That doesn't sound good."

"It isn't, Bill. Thing is, it's not the money. The man's got a reputation for permanently ending any relationship in which he feels taken advantage of. Hall knows it, so he's reimbursing all the other investors.

Francis is working on getting him a new identity so he can lay low until either Navarro dies or the law catches up with him."

"Doesn't sound like much of a life." This was from Jenne.

"I agree. But he'll still be alive, and, if nothing else, he's learned a hard lesson. Don't mess with murderers and thieves. Now, what are you doing in here?"

"Jake said to pick out a few bottles. He said anything we want."

"Really? Anything?"

"Yup."

"Well, shit, let's start looking."

Shelly passed the elevator and saw that it was still on the lower level. It was a good bet that her husband and the O'Malleys were in the wine cellar.

As she turned left to take the stairway down, she felt an unbelievably strong rope of an arm encircle her neck. She scratched and clawed at it, but it was like being in an iron vise. She tried to scream, but there was no air. Then everything turned black.

Jake watched in horror as Herrera walked calmly into the great room. Tossed over his shoulder, short hair hanging down over her face, Shelly was being handled like a rag doll. Navarro barely acknowledged him.

"Don't worry." Herrera addressed Jake as he threw her onto the sofa. "It's just a chokehold. She'll be out for a while, but she's still alive. Bitch has got some nails on her, though." The bloody scratches on his arm were evidence of Shelly's struggle. "That's one of 'em, Hugo. I'll go find the rest."

Herrera sauntered off to complete his assigned duties.

"What do you think, Bill? Do we go with the Opus or the Screaming Eagle?"

Jenne was taking full advantage of their host's generosity. Both cabernets were world-famous and, depending on the vintage, could command shelf prices of over 500 dollars. As a bonus, the Opus was a magnum.

"Kevin, should we dial it back a little? This stuff's expensive."

"If Jake says pick anything, he means it. From the looks of what he's got in here, these two are middle of the road. But I think we should taste them first. You know, because if they're spoiled, we wouldn't want anybody else suffering. Right?"

"Excellent idea, Kev. As luck would have it, we have a corkscrew and some glasses right here."

Bill reached for the wine opener just as someone entered the room. "That you, Shell?"

"No, sir. Shell is otherwise occupied. Don't move."

The three friends turned to see a medium-height man with large shoulders and long arms covered with a long-sleeved sweatshirt. He was of indeterminate age. His ball cap hid whatever hair he had. His weathered skin suggested he was of Hispanic heritage, but he had no accent.

Jenne dropped the bottle she was holding when she saw the gun in Herrera's hand. It was a hundred-point Screaming Eagle that was now pooling on the brick floor.

"I have orders to make sure I get you up to the great room. My boss says I can do it any way I want. It'll be easier, though, if you just go on ahead of me and go up there. That way, there's no noise or blood or anything.

"I can do it the other way too, of course, but that means loud bangs and messy blood and shit. Then I'd have to carry you, and I'm just too tired for that. So how about it? Get in front of me, and fucking get up the stairs."

Kevin and Bill looked at each other, clearly stunned at the situation. Bill was the first to speak. "C'mon, you two. We'd better do what he says. Maybe his boss can tell us what's going on."

The three sidestepped around Herrera and dutifully went up the stairs. As they entered the great room from the hallway, Owens saw his unconscious wife on the sofa. *Shelly!* He turned to Herrera, "What the fuck have you done? I'll fucking kill you." He stepped toward the enforcer,

"Stop." This from Navarro. "Your wife is fine. Albert here is very good at what he does. If he wanted your wife dead, she would be. She should be coming around soon."

Owens walked rapidly to the sofa to check on his wife's condition. Seeing her breathing and otherwise unharmed seemed to settle him down. He sat there and glared at Herrera.

Being the chief of detectives for the city of Bellevue, Bill Owens was required to carry a sidearm while on duty. Like many detectives, "on duty" and "off duty" were relative terms. They merged constantly.

As such, Bill was always armed with one of two service weapons. While supposedly off duty, he carried a .40 caliber Glock 27 in an ankle holster. The compact size of the pistol made it almost invisible, and from a seated position, it was easily accessible.

Kevin, who had just witnessed his friend's anger, knew him as well as anyone. The years spent with Owens, especially those on the golf course, gave him a keen insight into what his buddy might be thinking.

He knew Bill had an ankle holster because he'd seen it plenty of times when they had been together socially. He also knew that his friend was very cautious and conservative when using deadly force. Especially when there was a danger of collateral injuries. Owens was simply biding his time, constantly reassessing the situation and looking for an opening. He had complete trust in the man.

SIXTY-EIGHT

"Hugo, this is O'Malley and his wife. They are the designers I told you about. He is the one with your merchandise."

Navarro looked at Kevin and Jenne with the joy normally reserved for a long-lost puppy's return.

"So, you are the people I've been looking for. Please sit down on the other sofa where I can see you. Albert here has been keeping me informed of your activities. You have something of mine."

Kevin looked at his wife as they did as they were told. He had an inkling of what was to come but couldn't be sure. "And what do I have that belongs to you?"

"Come now, surely you must know. You found something in that barn. Something that belongs to me. I've been waiting a long time to retrieve it."

Kevin glanced at Bill, who was now staring wide-eyed at Navarro. Bill couldn't restrain himself. He spoke up. "The fentanyl. It's yours?"

"It looks like everyone knows about my merchandise, yes? Yes, it's mine. That fucking asshole car dealer stole it from me. He thought he was the brains of the operation—what a fool. My good friend Albert here took care of the stupid man. Didn't you, Albert?"

Herrera looked almost adoringly at his jefe. It was apparent that his thirst for approval was paramount in their relationship.

"I did. And I enjoyed it. It is what I am very good at."

Kevin saw his wife shiver. She thought the man was a monster. He did too.

"Is it still in your vehicle?"

Kevin looked over at Bill, who spoke up. "No, it's not. I have it in my car. I was going to turn it in to the police tomorrow."

Kevin, who could see that Owens was trying to keep his occupation a secret, tried to help. "Bill was headed back tonight, and I wasn't going off-island for a few days. I thought it best to have him take it to the police."

"Why did you keep it with you?"

"It was our friend's house, and she was selling it. We didn't want to complicate things. The police would have wanted to search the barn for additional clues, and it would have delayed the sale." It was an easy sell for Kevin since that was precisely the reason he hadn't given it to Owens earlier.

"Are you telling me the fentanyl is outside in your car right now?" Navarro appeared downright gleeful.

"Yes. It is."

"Excellent. Half of our work here is done. Where are the other two?"

The question was directed at Jake, who did his best to avoid answering.

"Unless you would like to see one of your friends shot, I suggest you tell me where the other two are."

Jake looked at his four unfortunate guests and finally answered Navarro. "They had some things to do. I think Francis wanted to show Peter the studio out back."

Kevin knew what they were doing, and it had nothing to do with the studio in the back. Jake also knew Bill was a cop. He, too, was trying to buy some time.

While Navarro and Herrera were looking at each other, Kevin managed to fire off a quick text to Francis. *Bad men here.*

"Albert, please go bring the other two here." Navarro wanted to close this chapter.

The rambling log home was built on a hill, with the downward slope behind the house. The outbuildings were accessed from the outside door on the lower level or the stairs of the enormous deck just off the great room. Albert elected to go down again to the lower level, then outside.

Francis and Peter Hall had been in the computer office for forty minutes or so. It was decided that Peter would transfer the funds that Jake had invested and the total amount of the funds from the other investors into Jake's bank account.

A single transaction would be more straightforward. Hall would supply the list of the additional investors to the Earlys, who would, in turn, forward them whatever they were due.

Because Hall had placed the funds in several offshore accounts, the transfers took time. They were on the final transfer when Francis's phone buzzed.

Glancing at the text, he wasn't exactly sure what it meant, but he recalled his brother describing the visitor from Navarro. He had no idea how it could have happened, but it had.

"Peter, we've got visitors, and I think it's big trouble."

Hall's complexion paled to a deathly pallor. "Who?"

"Don't know for sure, but a good guess would be your pal, Navarro."

"Jesus, no. How— I mean, why? Did you let him know I was here? Please don't tell me you did. You mother—"

"Stop. No, Peter, I didn't. Think about it. What would be the sense in that? You're no good to us dead. I have no idea how or why, and I'm not one hundred percent it's him, but we have to assume it is. He sent his second in command to visit my brother a few weeks ago, so maybe he's back. The text from Kevin doesn't look good. It was very short as if he was in trouble."

"We need to hide. Where should we go?"

"Slow down for a minute. Let me think."

The little office was on the far side of the cache of wine. The stairs and the elevator were on the other side. It had originally been part of the wine cellar but was converted to an office for Francis when he came to live with his brother.

Never having been in a house with an elevator, Albert was curious. With only two more subjects to fetch, he figured he had plenty of time to complete his task. He took the time to recall the lift to the main floor just for the experience.

The elevator was a residential one to accommodate an individual in a wheelchair. *If only they had had this in my foster homes, I probably wouldn't have been a freak as a kid.* It was only three feet by four feet. This one had two doors, one for the wheelchair to enter and the other to exit. Albert could only imagine the luxury it would have been for a youngster in a wheelchair.

He entered from the main floor and took the short ten-second ride to the lower.

Francis had heard several people walking down the hallway from the wine cellar earlier. He'd assumed it was the O'Malleys and the Owenses returning upstairs with their wine selections. Now he heard the thrum of the elevator as it rose and then again as it descended.

"Someone's coming, Peter. Come with me. Into the wine cellar."

"Won't he look there?"

"Don't think so. I think they already did. C'mon."

The two hurried out of the small office and closed the door. They entered the wine cellar and stood on either side of the archway. If anyone glanced in from the hallway, they couldn't be seen. The lights illuminating the fine and rare wines were still on, the Opus magnum still on the table, and a broken bottle of Screaming Eagle puddled on the floor.

Based upon the evidence, Francis was convinced his friends had been abducted.

As Albert walked past the wine cellar, he could smell the wine that had spilled. *Too bad*, he thought. *That stuff looked good.*

He opened the door to the office. It was empty. He proceeded to open the remaining two doors that opened onto the hallway. One was the mechanical room, with every available space used for heating and cooling equipment. In addition, there were water softeners, pumps, and filters. There were no people.

The last door was a storage room filled to overflowing with items that were obviously from Costco. The Kirkland brand was on everything. Still nobody.

He reached the end of the corridor, where the exit door was located. The thing was locked and had cobwebs covering the jambs.

Albert smiled. He knew no one had used this door in some time. *That fucker in the wheelchair thinks I'm stupid. Those two clowns have to be down here somewhere.*

He returned the way he had come and stopped at the room with the computer equipment. This time he entered. He looked behind the equipment and under the desk. One of the screens displayed a website for some bank he'd never heard of. It said, "We have logged you out for your safety. Please reenter your password to continue banking."

Definitely nobody there.

That left the wine cellar. Albert hadn't gone in when he'd exited the elevator because he had just cleared it twenty minutes ago. He started back toward the cellar.

"He's checking out the rest of the rooms down here," Francis whispered to Peter. "Maybe after he sees we're not in any of the rooms, he'll go outside and check out the old studio."

Peter appeared petrified. "He's gonna kill me, Francis. Where can we hide?"

"Right this minute, right here. Shh, I can hear him opening the other doors."

After three doors opening and closing, it was deathly quiet. Francis put his finger to his lips.

Then they heard footsteps returning.

"He's coming back. I'm dead; we're fucked. Francis, help me." Peter was losing it.

They heard the door to the office open. Whoever it was walked into the computer room.

Francis had led an exemplary life since his stint in the slammer. While he was there, though, he did what he had to do to survive. He was still a tough motherfucker who knew his way around bad guys.

He turned to Peter and whispered, "Look, he's gonna come in here. You need to do what I tell you. After you hear the door next to us close, you go and stand on the other side of the table. So he can see you from outside the room."

"He'll kill me. I can't."

"Listen to me. I know what the fuck I'm doing. He won't kill you because you still have his money. He'll want it. I think it's his enforcer anyway. I can't imagine Navarro doing the legwork.

"Now do this, Peter. It's our only chance."

By the sheer force of the big guy's intensity, Peter nodded. "What are you going to do?"

"You'll see. Now get ready."

The sound of computer equipment being shoved aside paused. Then the door closed.

In pace with Francis, Peter moved to the opposite side of the heavy farmhouse table. Francis quickly reached for the magnum of Opus One, grabbed it, and returned to his position at the side of the archway.

Footsteps echoed in the hallway.

Peter saw a nondescript face with a pulled-down ball cap peer around the corner. Then he saw the gun.

"My boss says he wants to see you. Come with me." Albert waved the pistol toward the stairway.

Peter could only stare at the weapon.

"I said come with me, pal. I still have another person to round up."

As he spoke, he took two steps into the room to further control his prey.

Just as he finished his second step, he cleared the archway.

That was when a five-pound magnum of Opus One, valued at over 1,000 dollars and propelled by a six-four ex-con weighing 250 pounds, slammed directly into the bridge of Albert Herrera's nose.

The sound of broken glass and crushed cartilage and bone was followed by a shower of deliciously expensive cabernet sauvignon. The extra-thick bottle, used by the famous vintner to better preserve the coveted wine, had performed nicely.

Albert's nose was destroyed, a midnight green sliver of glass punctured one eye, and portions of his skull were driven back into his frontal lobe. He was dead before he hit the floor. The blood of the freakish killer was now sullying the deep purply red of the fine wine. His muscular arms and shoulders were drenched in Opus.

Wide-eyed and near collapse, Peter grabbed the edge of the solid oak peasant table to steady himself. "I ... I think he's dead."

"Ya think? Jake's gonna kill me for wasting that bottle."

With his foot, he nudged what was barely recognizable as Albert Herrera's head.

"You know this guy?"

"No. But if Navarro was his boss, then my guess is he's the muscle. Look at the size of his arms."

Francis couldn't have cared less. Many of the inmates he had shared time with would have disposed of Herrera just as quickly. He bent down and retrieved the gun from the dead man's still-impressive grip.

"Stay down here, Peter. I'm gonna go have a look and see what's happening upstairs."

SIXTY-NINE

The great room had been eerily quiet for several minutes. Navarro had moved the wooden dining chair he was using to a position where he could cover both couples and Jake with his gun.

With his back to the wide glass doors opening onto the deck, he now had the O'Malleys to his right. Shelly, now fully conscious, was sitting next to her husband on the matching loveseat to his left. Jake was in his chair between the sofas, directly opposite Navarro.

"Who was that asshole who knocked me out?" Apparently in no way intimidated by the situation, Shelly was still pissed.

"That was Albert. He is a very talented man who has been with me for years. He will be bringing your other friends to me soon."

"Well, he's still an asshole."

"Shut up. If you continue to annoy me, I'll kill you now."

It was not missed by the two couples that Navarro had used the word "now." They exchanged nervous looks.

Another fifteen minutes passed before anyone spoke.

Finally, Bill broke the silence. "Where's your buddy Albert? Do you think he might have run into trouble?"

"Albert is very resourceful. I have complete faith in him." Navarro's assertion was delivered with a tiny bit of concern. "He will be here shortly."

After ten more minutes had elapsed, Navarro shifted uneasily in his chair.

Albert was the most dependable enforcer Hugo had ever had. He *always* delivered. But after almost half an hour with no report and, more worrisome, no sounds, he was concerned.

He knew that Early's brother and Hall were somewhere on the property. They had followed them there from the harbor.

It was difficult to imagine that they could somehow gain the upper hand on his enforcer. Sure, the one with the tears was a big man, but Herrera was stronger than any man Hugo had ever seen. Hall was a soft blob, a pussy. He'd be no trouble at all.

He'd give it another fifteen minutes before making a decision.

Francis chose to exit the lower door rather than risk the stairway, certainly not the elevator. The crack when he shoved it open sounded like a gunshot. Fortunately, being fifteen feet under the main floor in the concrete basement level of the log home ensured the sound would never make it to the great room.

For a big man, Francis could move quickly and quietly. He started up the stairs to the enormous deck, stopping only when he was on eye level with the redwood surface. From this position, he could see inside the sliding glass doors to the great room.

A smallish man with graying black hair, worn slicked back, was sitting in a wooden side chair, facing his brother and the two couples. He felt certain this was the Navarro that Hall was afraid of.

They appeared to be waiting. *If they're waiting for the dead guy in the wine cellar, they'll be waiting a long, long time*, he thought.

Francis felt just storming the room was not an option. Even with the gun he'd removed from the would-be killer, there was still too much opportunity to injure the innocent.

He had just decided to wait things out when he saw Navarro get up from his chair.

Something has happened. Navarro hadn't achieved all that he had by denying reality. As improbable as it was, he had to accept that Albert had run into trouble. Still, there was no way he would let that fucker get away with stealing twenty million dollars from him.

He could offload the fentanyl for something approaching ten million, but those drugs were his originally. It wasn't on the income side of the ledger.

From the day Hugo had taken revenge on the killer of his mentor, he had harbored an overwhelming need to counterpunch with devastating violence. Even a perceived wrong, real or imagined, resulted in bloodshed. It was why he was still a free man.

Peter Hall would not leave this house alive, nor would the rest of this bunch.

He stood from his chair and walked behind the sofa that held Shelly and Bill. The two stared ahead at their friends opposite them.

"You." Shelly jumped as Navarro tapped her on the shoulder with his gun.

A tiny scream escaped her lips. "What ... what do you want?"

"I want you to go out to your car and retrieve the package that your husband put there. Leave your things here. No sense trying to call anyone. If you try anything, your husband will not live."

"Shell, it's in the trunk just to the side where the spare is." Bill let his wife know where he had placed the drug package.

Shelly got up slowly, still a bit woozy from blacking out. She took the keys from Bill and walked out the front door.

It was quiet in the wine cellar. There was only the occasional sound of trickling wine and some random sounds from the dead body. Hall imagined there was some sort of body fluid thing going on.

I can't stay in here. What if Navarro comes looking for me? I have to know what's happening.

He walked past the mess of blood and wine and turned to the stairway. He silently crept one step at a time. It seemed an eternity, but he finally got to the hallway leading to the great room. He could now hear Navarro speaking to someone. He stole a glance around the corner just in time to see one of the guests, the short blonde, get up from the sofa. Navarro was pointing a gun at her.

Peter was no hero. Bobby had always looked after him when they were growing up. He was short and chubby and was frequently bullied because of it. Bobby had done what he could to stop it but wasn't always successful.

Eventually, when he got to college, he had managed to find friends with similarly tortured experiences. He had been able to avoid any conflict or confrontation until this point in his life. Selling real estate and doing deals was all about negotiation—no conflict required.

He knew Navarro was there because of him. He knew he had put these people's lives in danger. Still, he was frozen.

Francis had saved him, but he was a big, strong guy. He was a wimp. A soft, pudgy pile of shit. What would Mark say? His big brother Mark who'd gone out of his way to try to help him.

He couldn't let all these folks die. Could he?

Francis tensed, prepared to act when Shelly walked out the front entrance. She appeared dazed.

He retreated down the steps to the ground level and hurriedly ran up the slope and around to the front, making sure to stay out of sight of any windows.

He saw Shelly walk out to the courtyard and round to the other side of O'Malley's Explorer, where her little red sports car was parked. She used the remote to pop the trunk.

She bent over, reached in, and began moving things around.

"Pssst, Shelly. Don't turn around. It's me, Francis."

Still, in her shocked state, she froze at his voice. "Is it really you?"

"Yes. The one they sent to get us ran into some trouble. He won't be bothering anyone anymore. What are you doing?"

"That guy Navarro. He sent me out here to get a package of drugs. Kevin found them in a barn. They've been there a couple of years. He killed a car dealer over them, and the crime was never solved. Now we know who did it. He's a killer, Francis."

"I know. Listen, just do what he told you to do. Tear a hole in the package and when you get inside the front door, dump the whole thing on the floor. Then move out of the way."

Shelly still seemed robotic in her movements.

"Shelly, you with me on this? If we're gonna get out of this, you need to be focused."

She looked directly at him this time. The look on her face was one of fierce determination. "I got this, Francis. I'm good."

She took the package, ripped a slice across the bottom of it with the tiny Swiss Army knife on her keychain, and headed back into the house. She held the bottom together with her right hand and pushed the front door open.

Peter was still huddled in the hallway behind the corner when Shelly pushed the door open. Unaware of Francis's whereabouts, he watched as Navarro turned the gun toward the diminutive woman holding a taped-up plastic package.

While Hugo was focused on Shelly, Peter quietly crept behind the kitchen island about thirty feet from the seated group. He looked for anything he could use as a weapon. It was foolish to take on the drug lord, but after fifty years of just going through the motions, something had changed.

Maybe it was the trip with Francis, or perhaps it was seeing the dedication the man had to his disabled brother. His two brothers were distant through no fault of theirs. Maybe there was still time to repair the relationships.

He reached into the top drawer and grabbed what was handy, remaining out of sight. The first thing he felt was a thick wooden handle. He quietly lifted what turned out to be a large barbecue fork. *Not a gun, but something,* he thought. He gently eased the drawer shut and watched as Navarro raised his weapon.

He yelled something, then charged into the great room, barbecue fork at the ready in a genuinely desperate effort.

Francis had rushed up to the edge of the entry just before Shelly went in. He watched as she took both hands and split the bottom of the package, sending a snowstorm of fentanyl billowing onto the concrete floor.

Navarro was furious and turned the gun on Shelly. Francis had no clear shot without hitting her, and Navarro was taking aim.

"Hey, asshole." The shout came from the kitchen area from a short, chubby man brandishing a barbecue fork.

Just as Navarro turned toward the shout, Shelly jumped to the side.

Two shots were fired. The first was by Navarro in the direction of the kitchen. The second was by Francis. Directly into the spine of the notorious drug smuggler.

SEVENTY

After the earsplitting shots had ceased, time moved second by second. Bill rushed over to his wife. Although in shock, she was otherwise unharmed.

Jake was on the phone with the police and the island EMTs.

With a glance to one another, Kevin and Jenne hurried to Peter Hall, who was sprawled on the floor halfway to the great room. Still holding the barbecue fork, he was fading out of consciousness. He was bleeding profusely from a hole in his left side. They applied pressure to the wound as best they could, but the blood was unstoppable.

As soon as he'd fired his weapon, Francis ran into the room. He knelt next to an immobile Hugo Navarro.

July, Three Months Later

"You remember the last time we had everyone together up here? How did that work out?" Jenne watched as Kevin slid a portable ramp up to the front steps.

"Well, you can't say it wasn't interesting. That was more bloodshed than Whidbey Island has seen in decades. Even made the national news. The knuckleheads over at Fox even tried to put some sort of political spin on it. Go figure."

"Is this the first time Jake has left his compound since he moved in there?"

"It is. I think everything that happened convinced him that life is short. His little world, as safe as he thought it was, turned out not to be so safe after all. I guess he figured, 'what the hell, how bad could it be?'"

"I think it's funny how things turned out. Two brothers, one a paraplegic agoraphobe, the other a very large ex-con with a heart of gold and tear tattoos on his face, and they're our best friends on the island."

"I agree. If you'd told me that night on the ferry that we'd be in this situation, I would have said you were nuts."

Just then, a red Mercedes convertible pulled into the drive.

"Hey, Bill, Shelly, glad you could make it."

"Thanks, guys. A lot different than the last time we tried to get together up here, eh?"

"You've got that right. Bill, fill us in on things." Kevin and Jenne had shut down their emails and computers since the dust-up at the Earlys' and the publicity following it. They'd had enough. Still, they wanted closure.

"Okay. Albert Herrera was linked to over two dozen killings. One of them was Robbie Burns so that one's put to rest. The autopsy showed massive brain trauma, not to mention a really fucked-up face."

"What a way to go, though, huh? All that Opus on your way out."

Jenne glared at her husband. "Good one, sporty. Shut up and let the detective finish."

"As I was saying … Francis did a thorough job of eliminating the threat. Actually, along with Hall, he was the big hero in this.

"The shot to Navarro didn't kill him, but it did sever his spinal cord. He'll be in a wheelchair for the rest of his life, which, by the way, will be in a maximum-security facility somewhere in Texas."

"Talk about just desserts. Couldn't happen to a nicer guy." After the debacle, sympathy for the drug lord was nowhere to be found.

"I feel bad about Peter. He was a bit of a crook, but he did the right thing in the end. I can still see him charging the room with that barbecue fork." Jenne shook her head at the memory.

They all looked up as the gravel crunched, signaling a new arrival. The modest five-year-old Toyota Camry pulled up to the hedge. Slowly and carefully, the door opened. Out stepped a frailer, paler, thinner Peter Hall.

"Peter, really glad you could make it." Kevin stepped over to give him an assist. "How are you feeling?"

"Much better. The bullet tore up a bunch of shit inside, and there was a great deal of infection. That's why I was in the hospital for so long. IV antibiotics and everything. Doctors said if you hadn't helped at the shooting, I'd be toast. Thanks again."

"So, you're on the mend?"

"Yeah. I guess in a lot of ways. Both my brothers have been to see me. We plan to get together every so often now. I'm gonna spend some time with Mark when I leave here. He's a great guy. I was such an asshole."

"What about the rest of the money? The stuff remaining from Navarro?" Bill was curious.

"Funny thing. When I was in the hospital, I got a get-well card from that old Hopi, Adisa. I sent him an email to thank him, and we got to talking.

"His tribe there in Southern Utah is very poor. They've always gotten the shaft. Lotta drugs, alcohol, no jobs. Anyway, they've got some land, not adjacent to the holy grounds but near there.

"They have a license to build a casino but have never had the funds. Now they do. After I've seen Mark for a while, I'm going to go back to

St. George. That old guy is something. We'll be working on the project together. When it's complete, it's all theirs. I can't wait."

Both couples were speechless for a moment; then Shelly spoke up. "Peter, I've never personally thanked you. You saved my life. Loved the barbecue fork, by the way. What the fuck was that all about?"

Everyone laughed. Then Peter spoke up. "I don't know. Things just snowballed, and I was tired of being a putz. Something snapped, and I charged. Kinda stupid, I guess."

"Peter, we're very happy for you, and we're thrilled that you get to go back to doing what you like. Stupid or not, that gave Francis time to take the shot." Bill was happy to credit the former developer.

"Hey, something's been bothering me." Kevin turned to his friend.

"What would that be?"

"Why didn't you do something with that little gun you strap to your ankle?"

Bill pursed his lips as he looked over at his wife. Shelly looked at the ground.

"Perhaps I'll let the little woman answer this one." He used the term affectionately. "Honey?"

Shelly still hadn't looked up.

"Shell?"

"Okay, okay. It's my fault. I told him it was silly to bring a gun to a Cinque de Mayo celebration. We're on Whidbey Island for chrissakes. What could go wrong?"

She was now looking with chagrin at Bill.

"And what have we learned, dear?"

"I have learned never again to question my all-knowing, always-right husband."

Everyone was grinning as Bill continued. "There you have it, folks. We're in complete agreement."

"That's just about enough, you two. Kevin, that ramp ready?"

"It is."

"Good. Here comes the van."

The customized van stopped at the paved walk, and the side door opened. No one spoke as the hydraulic lift lowered Jake to the ground. He looked at the O'Malleys and smiled while Francis stood behind.

"Thanks for the invite *and* the insistence, Jenne and Kevin. This is a beautiful view you have here. I haven't seen the water in a long, long time. I'll admit, I'm still a little nervous. But I think I know what will help."

"What's that?" This from Jenne.

"Francis, will you please grab that box we brought along? You remember that wine you selected before the shit hit the fan three months ago?"

"We do."

"I just happened to have duplicates of those in the cellar. Let's get this party rolling."

CAST OF CHARACTERS

Kevin O'Malley..............interior designer
Jenne O'Malley..............interior designer, wife of Kevin
Robbie Burns.................auto dealer
Aaron.........................guest services, Meadowlark
George Harmon..............owner, Meadowlark
Fred Decker...................Napa County Sheriff
Bill Owens....................Chief Detective, Bellevue Police
Shelly Owens.................house cleaner, Bill's wife
Julie Houser..................rookie detective
Ilene..........................office manager, O'Malley Interiors
Albert Herrera................enforcer for Navarro
Hugo Navarro................drug kingpin
Tom Mahoney................general manager, Burns Auto
Oscar Salazar................lot kid, Burns Auto
Liz Burns.....................wife of Robbie
Sean and Liam Murphy.......owners of Last Chance Casino
Roberto and Hector Ortega..new owners of Last Chance
Robert and Benny Ortega....son and cousin of Hector Ortega
Peter Hall.....................president of CP Ltd.
Mark and Bobby Hall.........Peter's brothers
Johnnie........................bar owner
Officer Gomez................Mexico City policeman
Daniel and Maria Gomez......kids of Officer Gomez
Eduardo Aguilar...............drug dealer
Eduardo Navarro..............head of barrio drug ring
Jake Early.....................investor in CP Ltd.
Francis Early..................Jake's brother

Adisa............................Hopi Elder
Mickey, Otis, & Sparks........ Francis's prison buddies
James...........................another prison buddy
Perry.............................charter manager, West Bay
Emma...........................the O'Malleys' German Shepherd dog

ACKNOWLEDGMENTS

As always, my wife is my inspiration. Without her help trudging through my first drafts, I'd never finish. Whidbey Island is a special place. Spectacular scenery and delightful people abound.

The inhabitants, some far left, others far right politically, are nonetheless incredibly tolerant of others' viewpoints. On occasion, a bit quirky, downright thoughtful, and giving on others, they make it a wonderful place to live.

Thanks to my golf buddies, Dan Hay, for the IT info and Chris Frost for legal. Thanks to the Star Store for being the center of everything on the island's south end.

This is a work of fiction, and no real people or animals were harmed during the writing. Any similarities in personalities are unintended, although I'm sure many of the names are real. All the places are genuine, as are the street names, although they are not always where they're supposed to be.

The early settlers on Whidbey were creative in naming streets and roads. Here are just a few:

Little Dirt Road, Dirt Road, Milky Way, Brainers Road, Moondance Lane, Smugglers Cove Road, Fox Spit Road, Volcano Road, Useless Bay Avenue, Deer Foot Lane.

Made in the USA
Columbia, SC
28 January 2022

54890440R00150